ACCIDENTAL

ACCIDENTAL

ALEX RICHARDS

BLOOMSBURY

NEW YORK   LONDON   OXFORD   NEW DELHI   SYDNEY

BLOOMSBURY YA
Bloomsbury Publishing Inc., part of Bloomsbury Publishing Plc
1385 Broadway, New York, NY 10018

BLOOMSBURY and the Diana logo are trademarks of Bloomsbury Publishing Plc

First published in the United States of America in July 2020
by Bloomsbury YA

Bloomsbury books may be purchased for business or promotional use. For information on bulk
purchases please contact Macmillan Corporate and Premium Sales Department at
specialmarkets@macmillan.com

Library of Congress Cataloging-in-Publication Data
Names: Richards, Alex, author.
Title: Accidental / by Alex Richards.
Description: New York : Bloomsbury Children's Books, 2020.
Summary: Sixteen-year-old Jo must decide whether to trust her estranged father
or the grandparents who raised her but hid the truth about the way
her mother died when Jo was only two.
Identifiers: LCCN 2019048182 (print) | LCCN 2019048183 (e-book)
ISBN 978-1-5476-0358-9 (hardcover) • ISBN 978-1-5476-0359-6 (e-book)
Subjects: CYAC: Secrets—Fiction. | Fathers and daughters—Fiction. | Grandparents—Fiction.
Classification: LCC PZ7.R3783 Acc 2020 (print) | LCC PZ7.R3783 (e-book) | DDC [Fic]—dc23
LC record available at https://lccn.loc.gov/2019048182
LC e-book record available at https://lccn.loc.gov/2019048183

Book design by John Candell
Typeset by Westchester Publishing Services
Printed and bound in the U.S.A. by Berryville Graphics Inc., Berryville, Virginia
2 4 6 8 10 9 7 5 3 1

All papers used by Bloomsbury Publishing Plc are natural, recyclable products made from wood
grown in well-managed forests. The manufacturing processes conform to the environmental
regulations of the country of origin.

To find out more about our authors and books visit www.bloomsbury.com
and sign up for our newsletters.

For Trixie, my editor in chief

ACCIDENTAL

1

MY BEST FRIEND WENT to Barbados and all I got was this crappy T-shirt.

I mean, just kidding. Gabby has vials of scotch bonnet pepper sauce for Leah and me too. Which will taste great on scrambled eggs. But honestly? It's not quite the same as jetting off to some fabulous Caribbean island with a Jamaican sailing-pro dad and bohemian-artist mom. All *I* did over Christmas break was sit at home with my grandparents, picking my ass. Not literally. Leah's family stayed in Santa Fe too, so we not-literally picked our asses together. But still.

"Don't you look refreshed," I say, shoving irritation and hot sauce into my school bag. "How was Barbados?"

"Yes, how *was* Barbados?" Leah glares meaningfully at Gabby, then shoots me an eye roll. "She wouldn't say a word after she picked me up, insisting we get to your house first. And now, I am *dying*. I'm telling you, *I might literally explode*."

"Gabby," I gasp. "Leah's life is at stake here—come on already! Did you cure cancer? Surf? Hook up?"

"No, yes, and *yes*." A mysterious grin lingers on Gabby's glossed lips. Her skin has deepened to an even richer dark brown, and she looks all kinds of tropically euphoric. I, on the other hand, could pass for Elsa of Arendelle.

We pile into her jeep, and Gabby tosses me her phone, all cued up to a montage of highlights from her trip. Leah and I ooh and aah, commenting on the sexy surfer guy from New Year's Eve; the crystal-clear beaches where she snorkeled and swam with tortoises. The fish balls, the starfish, the starry nights.

Eye roll.

Okay, loving eye roll.

"What about the T-shirts?" she asks, hard braking at a red light. "Cute, right?"

Buttery-yellow cotton, geometric-trident pattern. Leah squeals and I nod, because it *is* going to be cute, once I run a cheese grater over it for that distressed look and cut the bottom hem.

The light turns green, and I punch Gabby's arm.

"Ow—someone's in a hurry to get to school." She snorts a laugh and turns right on Peralta. "So, tell me everything. What did I miss over break?"

"Nothing," Leah mumbles, unscrewing her hot sauce. She brings it up to her nose, and her whole face sours. "Less than nothing."

"Don't forget about Grandpa," I remind her. "He finally

stopped using his cane after the hip replacement surgery. So, I mean, that was pretty big."

"Jo, that is *huge*. Why didn't you lead with that hot gossip, and why aren't there videos of your gramps on all my feeds, dancing the Pachanga?"

I laugh. "Nobody puts Grandpa in the corner."

Even though she's crammed in the back seat, Leah manages a half-decent *Dirty Dancing* move. She's been perfecting it since seventh grade, when her mom insisted the movie was a rite of passage. The hip gyrations have Gabby and me doubled over laughing, joking about Grandpa's newly minted hip and the idea of Gran getting frisky with her ol' man (okay, ew).

Making fun of them is a kind of therapy for me, though. That sounds bad. What I mean is, most adopted kids live with like, regular-aged adoptive parents. Not me, though. My *dead mom's* parents are raising me. And, I mean, they're sweet and all. It just makes me feel like a foreign exchange student sometimes.

We reach the school parking lot, and our laughter withers into a dull hum. Because—hooray—the first day of second semester. For a minute, we fall into our usual before-school routine. Gabby with her NARS Blush, Leah on lips. I smudge some eyeliner around my upper and lower lids, slipping chunky rings over my fingers, a crisscrossed cuff around my upper ear, blond hair twisted into Minnie Mouse knots. I make sure my ancient Sex Pistols sweatshirt falls casually off one shoulder, and *then* I'm ready.

One day, in a galaxy far, far away, I am going to have a colorful peacock-feather tattoo coming up my back and curving over the top of my shoulder. But, yeah—no. Not *now*. My grandmother would go ballistic if I did *any*thing to defile the body our Lord 'n' Savior bestowed upon me. Hence the mounds of jewelry in my backpack and a temporary tattoo addiction.

Leah and I ditch Gabby at her favorite class—political science—and go find a couple of seats next to each other in US history. The classroom has a dull, stale-cheese smell from being unoccupied for the past week and a half, and if it weren't thirty degrees out, I'd be begging Mr. Garner to crack a window.

"Look what the vampire bat dragged in."

I glance up from my backpack, lips souring at the sight of symmetrically blessed Tim Ellison in his hunter-green polo and pressed jeans. "And look what the janitor forgot to throw out," I purr.

His glare narrows. "Nice eyeliner, freak."

"Thanks. Your dad lent it to me."

"Freak," he mutters again, bangs flopping over his eyes as he stomps confidently to the front row where he can more effectively brownnose.

Poor Tim. Since seventh grade, he's thought calling me a freak is a put-down, when merely interacting with his stuck-up, asinine self has already lowered my day from a ten to a six. I turn to Leah and say, loud enough for Tim to hear me, "Maybe I should get a lip ring—what do you think?"

Leah's eyebrows hike up, followed by an unsavory nostril flare.

"What? I said I'm *thinking* about it."

The eyebrow remains hesitant. "How about this. You get a lip ring and *I'll* get a crucifix tramp stamp."

I chuckle, picturing the reaction of her rabbi dad. "I'm talking about *someday*. Like when I'm living in SoHo, running my own boutique. I could cover it up with one of those sick-people masks when I go home for Christmas."

"*Well*," she says. "In *that* case."

The whole room goes quiet as our slightly Hagrid-looking AP history teacher stands from his desk and immediately starts rattling names off his roll-call ledger. *Nice to see you too, Mr. Garner.* I do my little Johanna Carlson finger-twiddle when he gets to my name, then basically zone out until the door swings open around the *V* names and cold air tickles my cheeks. All eighteen of us look up. I mean, you are *not* supposed to be late to *any* class *ever* at our magnificent institution for academic excellence, because God forbid Yale wait-lists you for getting *one* tardy. Anyway, everybody's eager to see which lazy dumbass is going to get written up, but then—RED ALERT. A boy appears. A *new boy*. Even with the door wide open, with the wind rustling our papers and goose bumping our arms, heat blasts my cheeks. I swear to God, my heart wobbles.

"Yes?" Mr. Garner snaps. But then his face brightens, palms smacking together as he squeezes around the side of his desk. "You must be our new transfer student!"

"Yeah. Hey." He shakes Mr. Garner's hand. "Milo Schmidt."

That voice. Deep, smooth. Joy Division wrapped in chocolate. Mr. Beautiful shifts his hips as he takes a brand-new textbook from Garner and tucks it under his arm. Brown hair pokes out from under a gray knit cap. An Adam's apple bobs under olive skin as he swallows. I swallow too.

"Take a seat, uh, let's see . . ." Garner pauses to scan the room. "There's one. Beside Johanna."

Leah squawks and kicks my boot. I kick her back and sit up a little straighter, then quickly slouch. Milo Schmidt. Broad shoulders tucked into a wool coat. Milo Schmidt, looking cautious but confident. He walks closer, and I take in the sharp cut of his jaw, a callus on his right thumb. Eyes, stormy blue and wide. He flashes me an amiable grin as he sits, but my stupid lips only twitch in response.

"Well, class. Say hello to Milo Schmidt. Hailing from Las Vegas, right? Milo, meet some of your fellow juniors at Archibald Chavez Academy."

The guys nod 'sup, but in a tense way—new competition. And rightly so, judging by the way most girls wave and bat their lashes. Not me, though. I stare hard at my pen.

"We need to get started. Unless you'd like to say a few words?" Nobody new ever comes to our three-hundred-head-count private prep school, so even Garner knows this is newsworthy. "A brief introduction, perhaps?"

"Nah, I'm good," Milo says casually. "Take the mic, Mr. Garner."

Everyone laughs, even Mr. Garner. Even me, even though my heart is pounding a gazillion beats per second. Garner heads back to his desk, and I keep my eyes glued to my ridiculously interesting pen. Like maybe if I'm lucky, it will levitate.

But who am I kidding? Out of the corner of my eye, I watch Milo wiggle off his coat, put a cracked iPhone on vibrate, and shove it into his messenger bag. At the front of the room, Mr. Garner turns toward the board, and Milo glances my way, jolting me so bad that I actually drop my magical levitating pen.

Smooth.

Before I can blink, he's reaching for it. I hold my breath, spellbound by his shoulder blades, the way his tan fades below the neckline of his T-shirt. He bobs back up with the pen and a *ta-da* flourish.

"Thanks," I whisper.

"Sure." He smiles, then furrows his brow. "Page number?"

I swallow hard. Heat creeps up my cheeks and swirls around my earlobes as I glance at my textbook. "Um, one-nineteen."

"Thanks, Johanna."

I gulp. Because . . . he remembered my name.

• • •

"I mean, he did, right?" I ask, kicking shut my bedroom door after school.

Leah nods and flops onto my bed.

"Well, he checked you out in the quad before sixth period," says Gabby. "I'm positive."

"Ew, don't make him sound like a perv."

"No, it was sweet. Very PG."

"Jo and Milo sitting in a tree!"

"Shut up, Leah."

"K-I-S-S—"

"Shut *up*!"

"—I-N-G!" she spits out with a laugh.

I huff as I nestle into my usual seat behind the sewing machine, pressing my foot on the pedal, picking up where I left off yesterday. Silky blue material slides between my fingers as I guide it gently under the presser foot. Polyester satin, a slippery challenge but worth every cent of my Christmas money. The machine rattles at a frantically familiar pace, the perfect soundtrack while Gabby sifts through my closet and Leah checks her phone. I pause to take out the last few pins and then press the foot gently along to finish the hem. When it's done, I release the fabric, warmed by a simple twinge of pride as I cut the extra threads and then take off my Sex Pistols sweatshirt, slipping the new creation down over my bra.

"Look at you!" Gabby cheers.

"Wow." Leah grins and jumps up to stand beside me, a foot shorter but twice as busty as we survey my reflection in the floor-length mirror. The shirt hangs perfectly, a one-shoulder strap sloping down across my chest, material hugging my torso and falling at my hips. She puts her hands on my waist, spinning me as if I'm a wind-up doll. "What's the inspiration?"

"Debbie Harry."

"Obviously."

"Obviously." I laugh. "Circa 1978. A one-shoulder, sequined top she wore for a photo shoot. Mine's a bit shorter—hers was more of a minidress. But it works, right? I wanted to channel her disco days."

Not that I look like Debbie Harry, except in my dreams. My

cheekbones are sad little slopes compared to her glaciers, but we have the same wiry hair, the same bored stare—a look Gabby says I perfected during my "Rapture" phase in ninth grade. That's "Rapture" as in the song off Blondie's *Autoamerican*, not the Bible-thumping end of times.

"It's killer," Gabby says, still holding a handmade mod dress on its hanger. "Kind of on the sexy side, though. What if Gran says you look like a hoochie?"

"I would give *anything* to hear my grandmother use the word *hoochie*."

She grins. "True. But she's never going to let you out of the house in that. I mean, what would God say? Plus, I can even tell you've got boobs under there. Do your grandparents *know* you have boobs?"

"Boobs!" Leah squeals. "Oh man, you are *stacked*!"

I swallow a grin. "You guys, stop. They'll hear you."

"Will they, Jo? *Will* they?"

"I bet they don't even know you got your period," Leah mutters.

"*Four years ago*," adds Gabby.

"Look—" I clear my throat extra-pointedly and walk over to my style-indexed closet, toward the basic section. "Exhibit A. My compromise."

Gabby's eyebrows crinkle. "That Mother Teresa–looking cardigan?"

I sigh, a little forlorn as the dull, merino wool swallows up my latest masterpiece. "Now how do I look? Mo' Tizzy or what?"

"Do you think people called her that?" Leah muses. "Like, her friends?"

"Who, Mother Teresa? Definitely," Gabby says, shaking her head no.

"Mo' Tizzy was probably her DJ name," I offer. "Spinning beats at the hottest clubs in—"

"Knock, knock?"

Our heads whip toward the door, and I tighten the sweater around my chest before opening it. Gran's standing there in a long white parka and wool beanie, cold air still radiating off her. She notices the sweater, pausing to admire her knitmanship.

"Hello, girls. Y'all have a good first day back? Lots of homework?"

"Tons," I say.

Leah waves. "What about you, Gran? You good?"

"Am I *well*," Gran corrects. "And no, Leah, I am not. Neck's still bothering me. Grandpa says I ought to see Dr. Ortega, but I think the windows need replacing. Muscle spasm from a draft—that's what I say. I'm starting to think he wants to get out of more housework. Lord knows I don't need another child to take care of."

The girls smile at Gran's accent, the honey lilt of it, but my heart snags on her throwaway words. *Another child to take care of.* Because that's what I feel like so much of the time. A burden. Taking in a motherless three-year-old probably wasn't on their bucket list.

"Sorry, Gran. I'll talk to Grandpa about the windows."

"Aw, thanks, sweetheart. He listens to you." She's halfway through a troubled sigh when her eyes pop wide. "I almost forgot! They were having a sale on crabmeat at the store—I thought I'd make gumbo for dinner. It's been ages since I made my mamma's gumbo recipe."

"I'll come help in a little bit."

Gran turns to leave, but then Leah frantically lunges for a stack of mail on the bed. "Wait!" she says. "Don't ask me why I feel the need to check your mailbox every time I'm here." She flicks through, handing over all but one white envelope to my grandmother. "Sorry."

Gran accepts the jumble of bills and catalogs, chuckling at Leah as she heads toward the kitchen. I let the door click shut. "You're weird, Leah."

"What?" She shrugs. "Mail brings me joy. *And* there's something for you, Jo."

"For me?"

I catch the envelope as she tosses it. How dumb to be excited about a letter, but nobody ever writes me. Not except the youth newsletter from church and rare credit card applications. This envelope has my name neatly printed and a smudged postmark from Houston, Texas. It almost looks personal. The girls stare expectantly, so I make a big show of tearing the seal and unfolding the page, handwritten in blue ink. I clear my throat and put on this ridiculous British accent that always cracks them up.

"*Dear Johanna. Hello and happy new year*—ooh, now there's a scintillating intro, huh, guys?—*I don't know how to say this, so I'm just going to come right out and say it.*"

Fake British dies on my tongue as I slowly sink into my desk chair. I read the rest under my breath.

My name is Robert Newton. If that name sounds familiar to you, it's because I'm your dad. Yes, really. I don't know if Kate and Jimmy ever told you much about me. If they did, it probably wasn't exactly glowing—we had a complicated past. The way I see it, too much time has gone by without me reaching out to you, and I'm sorry for that.

"Jo? Are you okay?"

"What does it say?"

Any chance you'd like to meet me? I'm living down in Houston these days, but my new job means I can work remotely. If you give me the go-ahead, I can drive to Santa Fe. It's a lot to take in, I know. But I miss you, Johanna. Is that what you go by? Johanna? I called you Joey as a baby because you had this little stuffed kangaroo that you refused to put down. Do you remember that? Probably not. Anyway, here's my number. Call, text, send a carrier pigeon. Whatever works. I'm here.

—Robert

"Jo, you look like you ate lead paint."

"What did it say?"

"Um . . ." Words gum up in my mouth and make the scarlet walls swim laps around my galloping heart.

"Is it bad?" Leah asks. "Did somebody die? Oh my God, are you pregnant?"

"Leah, on what planet would Jo be getting a random letter saying she's pregnant?"

"It could be from the doctor."

"Doctor *who*?"

"Probably not Doctor Who, but—"

"Shut up, both of you!" I yell. Instantly, their lips zip. I toss the letter onto the floor by their feet. "Just. Read it."

Gabby raises an eyebrow and scoops the page into her hands, sitting gingerly beside Leah on the bed. I study their bouncy curls and somber faces, eyes sweeping from left to right as they discover their orphaned best friend has a father.

A *father*. Holy shit.

Gran's never said much about him other than I shouldn't waste my time asking questions about the man who left me—his own three-year-old daughter—right after a freak car accident took my beloved mother. *Leave well enough alone, Johanna. You've got us.* No one's brought him up in I don't even know how long. Not like that's stopped me wondering. Whether he accounts for my sense of humor, my bony knees, the goofy dimple in my right cheek. Despite Gran's urging, I've imagined him showing up at my graduation with flowers, pictured him singing me to sleep at night. My strangely estranged father; a stranger reaching out after *thirteen* years.

"Jo, this is incredible!" Leah whoops.

Gabby hesitates. "Incredible?"

"Yes, *Gabby*. It's a frigging dream come true, okay?" Leah squeezes my fingers. "What's going through your mind right now? You're being really quiet."

I frown at the letter, the simplicity of my father's handwriting, his friendly tone. All my brain can do is throb. Two cymbals, crashing on repeat—FATHER! FATHER! FATHER! I shake my head. "I'm trying to think."

"Okay, but—" Gabby tucks tight corkscrew curls behind her ears. "Your grandparents kept you away from him for a reason. Right?"

My eyes twitch in response. I want to tell her this isn't the SATs with a predetermined right answer, that I feel slapped and naked and clinging to the edge of the universe. But the words don't come out.

Gabby takes my silence as an invitation. "We know nothing about this guy. What if it's a scam? Is your dad's name even Robert Newton?"

"Of course it is," I snap after a few seconds. But my cheeks blaze. I mean, I had to pause. I had to *think* what my own father's *name* was.

Leah stands timidly between us and clears her throat. "Maybe Jo should take some time to think about this on her own. It is ri*dic*ulously intense. We'll give you some space, but we're here when you need us, okay?"

They get as far as the door when she turns back, her brown eyes wide and moist. "God, I can't get over it! This is so special, Jo—and we were here to witness it. This is going to be life chang-ing! But okay. We're leaving. So you can think. Hey, we should grab coffee tomorrow after school. We can chill, maybe talk about it then. Or not. Whatever you want."

I nod, mostly so she'll shut up about giving me space and actually let me have some. I succumb to one of her classic, motherly hugs—a real I-care-about-your-struggles embrace—but for the first time, her arms only act as a straitjacket around me.

"Okay, sunshine." Gabby literally has to pull her off me. "I'm taking you home."

The door clicks shut, and they're gone. It feels weird, sending away my punished children, but I need to be left in peace.

Peace. Like that's a thing anymore.

Gran will want me to set the table soon, but I can't think about cutlery when my whole life just got dumped in a blender. I need a minute. Need to center myself and find a way to stop the room from spinning. In a daze, I stumble toward my antique storage trunk, raising the heavy leather lid. Down at the bottom, below my wigs and yards of fabric scraps and old journals, I find it—a scruffy, one-eyed kangaroo, lumpy from too much love and lack of cotton. With my thumb, I rub the once-brown, now-faded-yellow plastic nose.

"Remember me?" I whisper.

Kenny the Kangaroo seems to smile lopsidedly as I pull him into my chest.

2

MY NAME IS ROBERT NEWTON. I'm your dad. I'm your—

"Hey, friend."

I glance up from the depths of my caramel chai latte and smile at Leah, standing in front of the table I've staked out for us. She smirks a little and pulls a pink beret off her curly black hair. "You're in your own world, huh?"

"Pretty much. Where's Gabby?"

"With the debate team. You were on the group text, but . . ." She trails off, gesturing toward my aura with wiggly fingers. "You seem distracted. Don't waste your time, I'll paraphrase. She's horribly jealous that we're meeting up to discuss your daddy drama without her, but she needs to work on her original oratory or she's never going to get into Stanford, thereby never becoming—"

"A Supreme Court justice," I finish, and I'm not about to argue. Gabby fights harder than any other kid at Chavez—as a young Black woman, she's always had to—so I will never, *ever* give her grief. Even if it does mean missing my daddy drama. "Well, did she at least impart some oratorical wisdom?"

Leah nods. "Something about Pandora's box? She thinks you should skip the reunion and go down a beauty vlog rabbit hole—improve your mermaid eyes. Or take up Roller Derby."

I force a smile. Half disappointed, but also relieved. I mean, if mermaid eyes were going to be her contribution, I'll pass. Leah skitters to the front of Bluebell, this rainbow-toned and relatively new café in town with a fun, pride vibe and about a thousand varieties of tea—hence my new chai obsession—and plops back down at our corner table with a mocha and an almond croissant.

"So." She leans forward on her elbows. "What's the plan?"

I rub my eyes, exhaling till my chest caves in, wondering if insomnia is my new *thing*, or if last night was a one-off. From midnight to five a.m., all I could do was read and reread and re-reread Robert's letter. I memorized the entire thing. Paragraph two, line three: *It's a lot to take in, I know. But I miss you.*

"Oh, sweetie." Leah's whole face twists into a frown. "I can feel the confusion, like, pulsing off you."

"It's just—I've always been curious about him, but am I supposed to come a-runnin' because it's suddenly convenient for him? Know what I mean?"

"Totally."

"But I don't want to ignore it either. This could be my only chance."

"What about your grandparents?" Leah asks tentatively. "Do they have an opinion?"

"Are you kidding?" I scoff. "They *hate* him."

"They said that?"

"No, but I know they do. I'm not telling them."

Leah sighs, chewing her lip. "Try not to let their drama become your drama. He wants to visit *you*, right?"

"I mean, that's what he said."

We sit quietly for a minute, sipping our drinks, listening to Lana Del Rey on the stereo system. Leah won't take her eyes off me, like I'm going to morph into a cell phone and start dialing the guy's number. She lives for this crap—destiny and happy endings. A father-daughter reunion would be better than a double rainbow for her. Maybe make her pity me a little less for being this abandoned sad sack while her life is basically perfect.

She taps my foot under the table. "Think you're gonna call him?"

"I want to," I say, and the lack of hesitation in my voice feels good. "I mean, I really want to. But I don't know."

What-ifs curl my toes tight inside my boots. *What if he doesn't like me? What if he sees me and remembers why he bailed in the first place? What if I don't like him?*

Leah offers a sympathetic sigh. "I get that you have doubts— your grandparents and everything to consider—but be true to yourself. Don't let *them* call the shots."

Even if she's right, I can't help musing. In my mind, there's Gabby, flanked by her cosmopolitan, West Indian parents, visiting MoMA or strolling along the Seine; Leah on these epic hikes, actually *enjoying* family meditation hour. Their parents give them the moon. And then there's me. My "moon" consists of dipping into my grandparents' retirement fund in order to pay for private school. Which almost feels bigger than the moon. Would it crush them if I went through with this?

Shame rattles inside me. "My brain hurts."

"Try focusing on the positives," Leah says. "As my psychic, Dharma, would say—"

"Your psychic?" I groan. "Again?"

"*As my psychic, Dharma, would say,* everything happens for a reason. So it's been a long time—so what? And despite what Gran may or may not think, the guy *is* making an effort. He must have his reasons for staying away. Besides, we all know that if he tries to dick you over, Gabby will hide under his bed with a Freddy Krueger mask and switchblade fingers."

A warm laugh tickles my throat. "I'd pay huge amounts of money to see that."

It feels good to laugh. Hydrating, almost. A reminder that this is not the end of the world. Maybe it's even the beginning. Not of the world, but of *something.* Our giggles fade away, and I'm left sipping lukewarm chai, twisting rings around my fingers. Thinking about DNA and the two strangers that made me. Wondering if I got my love of spicy food from my father, if he could carry a tune better than me, do math better than me. I'm ashamed to admit, I don't even know if my parents were married—was I a Newton before the adoption made me a Carlson?

And if I met him, would Robert tell me about my mother?

Would I learn that she was wise, brave, daring? Did she love sewing? Despise sports? Could she make a cloverleaf tongue as good as mine? I'm ignorant, but not by choice. My grandparents buried her stories along with her body.

An imaginary balance scale teeters within me, weighing down toward my father—or at least the idea of him. Of what he might be able to give me.

With a muddy kind of sigh, I take my chemistry textbook out of my bag and drop it on the table. That's half why we're here—homework waits for no man. Not even Robert Newton.

Robert

Newton

His name bubbles up inside me, a kettle ready to whistle from steam. It hums in time with the coffee grinder, writes itself in cursive along the knotted throw rug beneath our feet.

Too much time has gone by. I'm sorry for that.

It has to count for something.

"*Oh my God,*" Leah whispers. "Don't. Look."

I look. Obviously. Bluebell is empty enough that my eyes go straight to him—Milo Schmidt, standing in the doorway. Gorgeous and freezing and blowing warm air into cupped palms.

Leah and I glue our foreheads together over the center of the table and become telepathic. *Is he here with someone else?* my eyes ask. Leah scopes the room and shakes her head. *Do you think he has a girlfriend?* She shakes her head more emphatically, despite having no actual clue. By the door, Milo pulls a gray cap off his head. Some of his brown hair shoots up, zapped with static electricity. My stomach flips.

"Go talk to him," Leah whispers.

"*You* go talk to him!" I whisper back.

She gives him a fleeting glance. "His boobs aren't big enough."

"So vulgar," I scold. "And I thought you were bi."

"Do you *want* me to charm the pants off him? Because I will."

I giggle and shake my head.

"Then go, already! He's brand-new and doesn't know anybody. Look at him, standing in line looking all lonely. Go ask him if he's as cold as he looks. Because dude looks like an ice pop."

He does look freezing. Adorably glacial. Not that I'm agreeing to anything, but I reapply my burgundy lipstick, the one that makes my skin look angelically fair and brings out the sea green in my eyes. Because, I mean, maybe I'm here on a Serious Introspective Quest, but Milo is barely ten feet away, shivering as he reads the café menu. It's fairly impossible to avoid.

"Casually walk up and get another latte," Leah says. "Yours has food in it."

"No, it—"

But I stop short when she dumps buttery crumbs into my mug. Apparently, yes, my chai has been tainted. I flip her off, feeling my stomach clench as I rise from the table, wishing I'd worn something cuter than a boxy black sweater. It hardly seems to matter, though. Even when I walk right up next to him, Milo's too entranced by the chalkboard menu to notice me.

"Another chai?" the barista asks after a few seconds.

"I'm still deciding," Milo says, right as I go, "Yes, please."

Surprise glitters in his eyes. "Hey, I know you. You're—"

"Chavez," I say, and then die inside. Because, does he think—

"Your name is Chavez?" A smirk catches on his lips. "You look way more like a Johanna."

My cheeks burn. "Yeah, I'm Jo. And you're Milo. From history."

"Milo from History," he muses. "Good band name."

I grin and look at my toes for a second too long, because I can feel his eyes on me and it's making my cheeks so red, I think they may incinerate. When I do look up, he's grinning too, struggling to read the menu.

"What are you choosing between?"

"Bagel and a scone," he says. "Thoughts?"

"Bagel. Definitely. I don't trust a pastry that can be either sweet *or* savory. Too big of a mindfuck."

"Ah, but bagels can be savory or sweet too, right? I mean, somebody explain strawberry cream cheese to me."

"Yeah, or pumpkin spice."

"That's just sick."

The barista rolls her eyes at us, but I can't stop smiling, my heart pounding beneath my sweater. This close, Milo smells of lemongrass and nutmeg. A sexy, human version of the chai latte I'm currently being handed. I pass the girl a five-dollar bill, and Milo orders an Americano and a bagel—cinnamon raisin.

"Cinnamon raisin?" I sneer. "Traitor."

"Hey, my mom's a pastry chef," he says, raising his palms. "I've got a sweet tooth. That's actually why we moved here."

"You moved to Santa Fe because of your sweet tooth?" I marvel. "I thought gambling was the worrisome addiction in Vegas. But, wow."

His chin juts up to the ceiling as he laughs. "Actually, no. The sweet tooth is serious but not criminal. My mom's job, I meant. She's a pastry chef at that new French bakery on Water Street."

"That's cool. What's her stance on scones?"

"I'll have to ask her."

"How about your dad?"

"He's ambivalent on scones."

"Okay." I giggle. "But I meant, *what does he do*? Another pastry chef?"

Milo grabs his coffee off the counter, wincing as he brings it to his rosy lips. "My dad's still in Vegas. Closing on our old house and packing up. But let's get back to the genetics of scone hatred—how do *your* parents feel about savory versus sweet?"

"Oh." My smile crashes. "They, uh, don't."

One of Milo's eyebrows creeps up, and I clear my throat.

"I live with my grandparents. They're retired. Buttermilk biscuit people," I say, but my breath catches. Because, for the first time in my life, maybe disregarding my parents is a lie. Or a half truth, at least.

"You okay?"

"Yeah. Sorry, I—it's complicated."

He nods gravely. "Like scones."

I solidly chuckle. "You know, I think we've just broken a world record for longest scone conversation in human history."

"How about, next time I see you, I promise to have an arsenal of scintillating conversation topics in my back pocket. Are we relegated to baked goods?"

"Sky's the limit."

"Okay, cool."

On cue, my insides turn into a mosh pit of warm gummy bears because, *next time*. He's already planning future encounters. I watch him grab a lid and a cardboard sleeve for his cup. "Hey, I gotta go. But it was really nice talking to you, Jo."

"You too, Milo from history."

He pauses for a second, smiling at me. Like, smiling at my soul, almost. Then he pulls his wool cap back down over his ears and heads for the door. The frustrated barista clears her throat with a look that says, *bitch, would you focus?* and hands me my change, which I promptly put right back in her tip jar. It takes everything in me not to dance as I turn back to the table where Leah is full-on gawking.

"And that's how it's *done!*" she whoops. "Boo-yah! That was honestly one of the most adorable, rom-com-iest moments I've ever witnessed. I wanted to get my phone out and take pictures! We could have done that football thing after—where they go over each individual play on screen with a special pen?"

"You want to critique my flirting moves?"

She shrugs, like, *yeah, and?*

I roll my eyes and resume smiling. "He's really easy to talk to."

"Easy to look at too," she murmurs. "Tight little butt on him."

"Mind out of the gutter."

"Yes, sir."

Despite the lack of photos and stylus to help make her points, Leah wastes no time dissecting every second of my interaction with Milo, breaking down our body language and the way he laughed at my jokes. It's nice. Hearing that I might actually have a shot with this beautiful new stranger. But, even more than that, I like what the past ten minutes has done to me. Bolstered me. As if I, Johanna Carlson, can be one confident, cool-ass bitch. Maybe even a badass. A sudden siren of energy blares through me, and, on a whim, I grab my phone from my jacket pocket.

"Ooh!" Leah shrieks. "Are you texting him?"

"Yes," I say, then shake my head. "I mean, no. Not Milo. My father."

"Holy shit."

"Yeah."

I type a few versions of: *Let's meet for coffee*, and my thumbs freeze. Breath stalls in my chest. Leah grips my arm for moral support, and then—holy shit—I press Send.

She gasps.

I gasp.

And then I turn off my phone before it can explode in my hands.

3

"AMEN."

Gran opens her eyes, releasing my hand in order to scoop turkey casserole onto our plates. Grandpa slices a loaf of crusty bread while I fill our water glasses. He thanks her for the food, I thank him for the bread, she thanks me for setting the table. Cardboard silence follows. I blow steam off my fork and think about the mouth-scalding enchiladas Leah's probably eating right now. The whole Fromowitz clan, roaring with laughter at her dad's goofy jokes, the five of them cuddling up on the couch for family movie nights. Or Gabby's family, frying up dumplings and playing strategy board games till midnight. The meals I share with my grandparents are more like bran flakes—dull and soggy after about a minute.

See, here's how it is: Ever since our first playdate in kindergarten, Leah's parents have described me as Little Miss Polite. Even Gabby says her manners are only that good when she's with her grandparents in Kingston. Which kind of sums it up. It's as if I'm on vacation visiting my grandparents. For my whole life.

"Fixed that leak under the bathroom sink today," Grandpa says after a while.

"Oh, wonderful," Gran says, but there's a familiar hesitation in her voice. "Light bulb off the back porch started flickering yesterday. Did you notice?"

He sighs and shakes his head. "I'll get to it tomorrow."

"Yummy casserole," I say, guiding a wilted leek around my plate. "Thanks."

A quick smile curtsies on her lips. "You're welcome, sweetie. In fact, it's a recipe from that cookbook you gave me for Christmas. I ought to be thanking *you*."

I bat butterfly lashes in response, and both of them chuckle. The conversation veers toward the fundraiser Gran's chairing at the Baptist church, and then Grandpa says something about sandpaper, his benchmark for awesome since retirement. I watch him breathe laboriously through wide nostrils, the way he nods as Gran reels off a list of tomorrow's chores.

Across the table, he winks at me, sensing my epic boredom. I wink back. Nothing ever changes around here but the housework. Not our lifeless calamine-pink walls, not Grandpa's bird feeders or Gran's needlepoints of former presidents. Not the ratio of protein to carbs on our plates. Nutcrackers and kachina dolls line the mantel above our fireplace, but no photographs. Nothing to remember my mother or honor the daughter they lost. If they think about her at all, they don't do it out loud or in any measurable way. I mean, God forbid I get to see Mom's face framed on our walls. God forbid they tell me what kind of person she was or if I'm like her. God forbid.

"Johanna?" Wrinkles jut out like cracked glass from the corners of Gran's eyes as she squints. "Everything all right?"

My gaze follows hers all the way to my hands, clenched into fists on the table, my breath tight and shallow in my chest. A wave of adrenaline bursts through me, and I want to scream that I miss her. Mom thoughts always come fast and unpredictable and sting every time, but more and more, I realize I'm forgetting her, and it scares me.

Only . . . now.

Now there's Robert Newton. I try to imagine what would happen if I told Gran that he's found me, after all these years. In my mind, I explain the letter and how it filled me with a hope I never expected. I want to tell her that I know she means well, shielding me from him, but I can't go on like this, being forbidden from even thinking about my parents because *he* makes her mad and *she* makes her sad. I'm sixteen, and I have a right to find out for myself. I *deserve* to know.

Before I can stop it, a tiny sliver of truth slips out. "I'm forgetting her."

Have forgotten her already.

Grandpa smiles. His hearing aid is a piece of crap. But Gran's body goes rigid. A few times she blinks—Morse code? An apology? Rage? She opens her mouth, and I think, *This is it! The moment she finally opens up!* But something invisible pulls her back.

"God rest her soul," she says softly. After another few seconds, she reaches for the pitcher. "More water?"

Oh.

My balloon heart deflates. I'm such an idiot. Of course she'd chicken out, same as every other time—me scurrying after her like some desperate kitchen mouse, begging for crumbs she'll never drop. Only, *now*. Suddenly everything's dusty rose and shimmering. Robert can give me more than crumbs.

So I say, "Yes, please," like a good granddaughter.

I flash a plastic smile and hold out my glass, then turn back to my plate, succumbing to my thoughts. With each warm, salty bite, I swallow Robert Newton's name and imagine the color of his hair, the tone of his voice. Picture him cradling me as a baby, cooing over me and pinching my cheeks. The two of them together, loving me side by side.

"I'm planning to fix the rocking chair this weekend. You up for helping a doddering old man?"

"What?" I blink twice at Grandpa. "Oh. Sure, I guess. Can I be excused?"

"Take Magic out, will you?"

All three of us look down at the dog, curly and beige and panting on the rug by my feet. Poor Magic, with his halitosis and his bad hip. He was a gift from my grandparents just before I turned three. Right after we moved to Santa Fe, right after Mom's car accident. Magic was my consolation prize. *Your mom is dead, but look, a poodle!* Yeah—no. Mostly, he's a smelly reminder of the human life he replaced. Still, sometimes a smelly reminder is better than nothing.

In the hallway, Magic nudges his wet nose against my thigh as I pull on my boots. He whimpers with anticipation as I zip my coat, twirl my scarf. We head out into the starry night, and I welcome the crisp air into my lungs. Let it recalibrate my psyche.

The two of us walk along the quiet sidewalk and a calmness settles over me, overpowering my grandmother's silence. That's all it takes—the balance scale inside me tips all the way over, clanking heavily in my father's favor. Toward my future. Toward us.

Instantly, I yank my phone out of my pocket, waiting impatiently for the power to flicker back on. And then I see it: a text.

He. Wrote. Back.

Johanna! I'm so glad you replied! I can drive to Santa Fe by this weekend. Does Sunday work? Tell me when and where and I'll be there. I can't wait to see you.

OhmyGodohmyGodohmyGod. I click Reply.

I'll meet you at Bluebell Café on Galisteo Street. Sunday at 10 a.m.

Holy crap. I'm actually going to meet my father.

4

SUNDAY MORNING CAN'T COME fast enough, and when it does, I have a closet fit. Sewing is the only way I feel like *me* sometimes, but right now, there's a little too much *me* to choose from. Miniskirts and cutout jumpsuits, pleated shorts, mod dresses. Plus, regular old jeans and T-shirts. I'm sorry, but there is a lot riding on this outfit.

In the end, I slither into my favorite flared skirt and this wooly, gray sweater with sparrows embroidered on one shoulder. In the mirror, I can't help lengthening my neck and tilting my head, mimicking my mother's senior portrait from high school. It's the only picture I have of her—maybe the only one in the whole house. Gran gave it to me after I begged her on my eighth birthday, after some bitch in third grade made fun of me for not having parents. The picture came with no anecdotes, no context, just a melancholy observation that my eyes were bright green like hers. I glance at the photo now, centered on my wall between Debbie Harry's headshot and a CBGB poster for a '74 Ramones show, and I wonder if Robert will recognize me right away. If it'll be like seeing a ghost.

"Knock, knock?"

Shit. Super fast, I fling my bathrobe around my shoulders and dive under the covers, propping my head languidly against the pillow. This is the plan. A three-part strategy Gabby and Leah helped me devise. Step 1: Fake sick in order to miss church. Step 2: Meet my estranged father for a presumably super awkward and stressful coffee date. Step 3: Slip back into bed before the olds return. Easy-peasy. I hope.

"Your forehead *is* a bit warm," Gran says, sitting on the edge of my bed in a pale-pink dress and matching blazer. It's her favorite ensemble, though not super flattering. I guess God doesn't care about stuff like that.

"I'm sorry, Gran."

"Oh, hush." She gently kisses my forehead, grimacing as she pulls back. "I'm not sure about leaving you. There's a meeting about the fundraiser after services, but . . . Jimmy, maybe you ought to go without me. I'll stay and—"

"No!" I try not to scream. "I just took some cough medicine, I'll probably be asleep soon. You go. Pastor Thompson is expecting you."

"You sure, darlin'?"

"I need to rest."

Grandpa stands in the doorway, tucking a blue collared shirt into his belted slacks and straightening his tie. He pouts a little, then chuckles. "Must have been all that *hard labor* you did yesterday."

"Ha-ha, Grandpa."

He means the rocking chair. The one I said I'd help repair and then basically sat around texting Gabby while he sanded and refinished it. I'm sorry, but it's a rocking chair. It's not like Parsons School of Design cares if I can use wood glue. Or, shit, what if they *do*?

I cough again, for effect. Guilt stirs in my chest over the way I'm lying to them—*what* I'm lying about—but not enough to stop me. Not even when Gran squeezes my hand.

"We'll be home by lunchtime," she says. "There's homemade chicken soup on the stovetop in case you find your appetite sooner."

"Thanks," I croak. Okay, croaking is overkill. "Tell Pastor Thompson I'm sorry."

"Of course, dear. And call Grandpa's cell phone if you need anything. I forgot to charge the battery on mine."

"I will. I promise."

Finally—*finally*—they leave. As soon as they've pulled out of the driveway, I make a beeline for it. The fastest route to the café is down Agua Fria, but I'm feeling kind of sleuthy, so instead, I weave through side streets—a covert, Camry-driving ninja—until I end up on a long, wide street lined with touristy cowboy shops and cozy New Mexican restaurants. I find a metered spot on the road outside the café's cobalt-blue awning and dig around for loose change with trembling hands. This is it. Time to meet my biological father. Half my DNA. The only willing link to my mother, my past, maybe my future.

No pressure.

I push through the door, combing my hair with charcoal-painted fingernails, and doubt swallows me. My eyes sweep. Every guy is on a laptop, but which one of them could be a dad-who-isn't-really-a-dad-but-kind-of-is-a-dad? The tattooed one? The guy laughing into his webcam?

And then . . . there he is.

No question. It just *is* Robert. Rising from a table in the center of the room, surrounded by three empty sugar packets and one coffee—which either means he loves sugar, or he's been here a while. He smiles tentatively as he pulls a baseball cap off chin-length, wavy, blond hair. My knees lock. Unfamiliar heat tightens behind my ribs.

"Johanna?"

I swallow. "Yeah."

"Hi."

"Hi."

A goatee stretches across his chin as he grins, lips closed, brow furrowed. Warm but hesitant. It strikes me that he doesn't look the same as most dads. Not buttoned up or balding or pot-bellied. Dads don't wear bomber jackets or cool jeans, and yet this guy's are skinny and distressed. We're both pale. Similar hair, sort of a peachy, golden blond, but his is bushier, disheveled in a kind of rock-star way. One eyebrow is pierced. *Dads do not have piercings!*

"I'm so glad you came."

I nod, inching toward the table.

Experimental jazz thumps wildly through the speakers, and we stand there. Eyes fixed and petrified. Not a standoff, exactly, but not *comfortable*.

"Can I get you something?" he asks.

"Oh. I can get it."

"No. Let me. Please."

I tell him I'll have a chai latte, and he speeds off, relieved to have an objective, maybe. I take a seat and think about his voice, the record player warmth of it. Somehow, I'd imagined him sounding older. Gravellier.

"I've never had chai," he says, resting the mug in front of me. "Is it good?"

"Yeah, I like it."

"So." He coughs.

"So."

This silence could win awards for its awkwardness. A walking-on-graves kind of quiet. All around us, conversations spread their wings and take flight, but not ours. Robert and I only sit, swallowing air and shifting on rickety wooden chairs. He looks young. Not, like, *young* young, but the grown-ups I spend the most time with are seventy, so, yeah, young. No gray in his hair, no sagging skin. I put him somewhere in the forty zone, which is probably right. Mom was about twenty-five when she died.

Robert bites into a cheddar-and-chive scone, wiping crumbs away as they land on his cable-knit sweater. "Thanks for coming," he says again.

I nod. Again.

"Do you want to go first?" he asks. "Or should I?"

"Oh, um, what?"

"You know, tell me about yourself? Or—"

"You. Definitely you," I sputter, right as he's biting into his scone again.

He chuckles, chewing faster. "Sorry. Um, let's see. I live in Houston. But I already told you that in the letter, didn't I? Originally, I'm from Fresno. That's where you were born—California. My parents, too. They're both passed now, unfortunately. What else? I went to CSU Fresno to study computer science. Actually, I'm in IT now. A systems manager. Y'know, hardware upgrades, maintenance. That sort of thing. It's cool because I can work remotely. Hence the impromptu trip to Santa Fe."

He's talking like everything is normal, but I'm not sure my smile has the same vibe.

"I bet IT sounds boring to you, huh?"

"What?" I squirm. "I mean, I don't know."

"I've always been super into computers."

"Cool."

He launches into this long programming story, and sweat dampens my palms, my heart thumping. I mean, this is my father. My own *dad* sitting across from me. How am I supposed to have any chill right now?

"How about you? Do you like computers?"

"Uh, what?" I gulp. "Yeah, I guess. I mean, I have a laptop. But I don't, like, *do* stuff with it."

"Right. No, totally." He sips his coffee, and we veer toward silence again. "Um, but, yeah. Coding's pretty fun. I could teach you sometime. See how you like it."

A shriek wells up inside me. *My dad wants to teach me coding?!* But I swallow it back down with hot tea.

"How about you?" he asks. "What kind of stuff are you into?"

"Me?"

"Yeah."

"Oh. I don't know."

"Come on." He grins playfully.

"I'm really not—"

"You must have hobbies, or—"

"I said, '*I don't know,*' " I grunt. A couple of seconds go by. "Sorry. But this is a *lot* for me. And you're acting like we're taking Buzzfeed quizzes."

He nods, letting out a tight exhale. "I'm trying too hard, aren't I? I just figured, you're a teenager. I thought you'd want to start off casual. Hang for a while."

"Hang?" My jaw drops. "How can you expect me to *hang* when I haven't heard one single word from you in thirteen fucking years?"

Yeah, I f-bombed. My cheeks full-on *roast* as several eyes whip over to me, probably wondering if they should intervene. *Blink twice if you're trapped in a hostile situation.* These are definitely weird circumstances, but not *abduction* weird. I flash the table next to us a spring-break smile and look back at Robert.

"I have a lot to explain," he admits. "I know that. And, believe me, I've wanted to reach out to you for a long time."

"Then why haven't you?"

"It's complicated."

I squint at him.

"I realize that sounds like an excuse, but—"

"You're right. It does."

"You have every right to hate me, but I really, *really* hope you won't. You have no idea how sorry—I mean, I owe you a whole world of apologies. But I'm having a hard time getting past the fact that I'm sitting across from my *teenage* daughter. In my mind, you're still two years old, you know?" He pauses, eyes and expectations bobbing up. "I hoped we could make up for lost time. Get to know each other? You must be into all kinds of cool stuff, same as Mandy. God, it's wild how much you remind me of your mom."

Your mom.

A punch to the gut. I have to look away to catch my breath. Hearing her name centers me, though. Injects me with a ripple of calm. "You really think so?"

"That you're like Mandy?" he says. "Abso*lute*ly. That can't be a surprise, though. You must see the resemblance in pictures. I bet your house is full of 'em. Mandy was like the second coming for your grandparents."

I shiver.

"What?"

"Nothing." I hesitate and bite my lip. "Actually, that's not how it is at my house. With pictures and stuff. We don't even talk about her."

"Seriously?" Robert seems stunned at first, then he shrugs.

"I guess that shouldn't surprise me. Her death was devastating for all of us."

My whole body fills with this weird mixture of sadness and relief. "Thanks for saying that. I mean, not about them being devastated. But you wouldn't know it by looking at them. Whenever I try to talk about her, they get so quiet. Sometimes I think they want to pretend the car accident never happened and my mom didn't exist."

Robert's face pales. "The car accident."

I look away to rub my nose, swallowing a teary, tingly ache. When I look back, he's frowning, squinting into his coffee. "You miss her too?"

It takes him a second to respond, to get past the shock of being asked. "Oh, God," he says. "I mean, not a day goes by . . ."

His words fade away, and I get this urge to squeeze his shoulder. Which I, of course, ignore. But it makes me want to punish him a little less. Open up more. Be humans together. "Do you think—I mean, I was hoping you'd tell me a little bit about her."

"About Mandy?" He blinks a few times, shoulders releasing. "God, where do I start? She was immensely cool. Funny, smart, beautiful. And I'm not kidding, you look exactly like her. Your hair, your smile. Even little things—the way you're chewing your lip, and those sparkly, curious eyes. That was *so* Mandy. She was this lightning bolt of a person. I can tell you are too."

"I'm not," I say. "I'm not a lightning bolt of anything."

The music changes from experimental jazz to sleepy indie, and Robert reaches into his backpack, resting a small manila envelope on the table.

"What's that?"

"Old photos. Go ahead, take a look."

At first, my fingers hesitate. What do you do when someone offers you the key to the city? But I take a deep breath and empty the envelope, cradling the half-inch stack of printed photographs and old-school Polaroids. The pang in my heart creates an earthquake through my entire body. Picture after picture of Mom with her tongue out, hair teased, pouty faces, and wild grins. Robert beside her, young and skinny, his arm around her waist. For the first time, the man across from me seems old. Spun through the washing machine too many times. In the photos, his hair is buzzed, his face clean-shaven. My mom, though. All you really notice is the way she lights up the frame. As if anyone in her vicinity was instantly happier, prettier, smelled perfume-ier, just by sheer proximity.

I look at the pictures forever, until tears well up in my eyes.

"Sorry," he says. "I didn't mean to upset you."

"No, you didn't. These are—I love them."

He smiles.

"Do you mind if I make copies?"

"What? No, those are for you. I want you to have them."

My heart bursts at the thought. A chance to remember her.

An alarm buzzes on my phone, and we both jump.

"Crap, I gotta go."

"Already?"

"I have to be home before my grandparents get back from church."

Robert scrambles to his feet as I do. "Can we do this again? I can stay in town a bit longer."

I hesitate. Thirteen years without me, and now he seems desperate.

"What do you say?" he asks, voice inching up.

Yes, no. No, yes. I shift my hips. I could pretend I'm not interested, but I obviously am, or I wouldn't have come. "How about Wednesday?" I decide. "After school."

He grins. "I'll be here."

A few uncomfortable seconds pass. I mean, we're standing so close. Less than a foot apart. Normal relatives might hug, but that's not us. Not even close. In the end, I sort of dork-wave and duck around him, rushing out onto the street, head and heart spinning, mind exploding. As soon as I'm buckled up, I text Gabby and Leah.

Me: I did it!!!
Leah: What did he say?
Gabby: Where has he been?
Me: He didn't say exactly.

There's a pause, long enough to make my heart lurch.

Me: He brought a bunch of pictures of my mom. Oh, and he called her Mandy. Can you believe her nickname was MANDY?!

Leah: So cute. 😺 😸 Is he nice?

Me: He was nervous. But nice, yeah.

Gabby: But he srsly didn't apologize or ANYTHING?!?!

Me: He DID. He apologized a lot. Just without going into any details.

Gabby: 😐

Leah: Are you going to see him again?

I hesitate.

Me: Yes.

Leah: Are you excited?!

Yes, I type, then erase it and write *maybe*, then erase that too. Words can't compare to the colossal feelings tugging me in every direction. The epic wonder of coming face to face with my actual *dad* after all this time. Eventually, I type in a couple of screaming-face emojis and put away my phone.

That about sums it up.

5

BUT I CAN'T STOP thinking about the photos.

After Gran's checked on me and funneled chicken soup down my throat, I pull the photos out of my bag. Mom in a hospital gown, cradling a bald, red-faced baby wrapped in pink. Tired but glowing as she holds my swaddled body close to her chest. I stare at it, taking in the curve of her lips, the basil hue of her eyes. I wish I could feel myself there, warm and safe in her arms.

There's a cute one of her and Robert, grinning for an off-kilter selfie in the back of a truck. And another one of Mom, posing in front of a café sign for Amanda's Kitchen.

Amanda. Mandy. Mom.

I pore over this better-than-Christmas snapshot goldmine, her smile overpowering me. Glass half-full and rosy cheeks. Sunshine and laughter. Details appear like lightning bugs. A crooked tooth. Killer bangs. I've always pictured her with long, straight hair, but here it's shorter and more feathered, framed with a thick hem of fringe. Bangs look good on her, and I wonder if they'd work for me too. Debbie Harry obviously rocked bangs.

I wonder if my mom was into Blondie. God, I hope so.

"I miss you," I whisper.

Wish I'd known you.

In a sentimental whir, I grab my phone and snap a picture of my favorite picture. It's of the two of us—her blond hair and bangs framing her face, her chin resting on the top of my head, the both of us wearing giant sunglasses. I'm looking up at her, grinning.

I decide to post the photo with #meandmom and #imissyou. After, I hide the photos in the pages of a notebook and stand in front of the mirror, examining my reflection and touching my cheeks, picturing her face as I count our similarities. The texture of our hair, dreaminess in our eyes, a sparse constellation of freckles.

For the first time in my life, it's like a piece of my heart's not broken.

An untamed urge electrifies me, and I start digging through my sewing box, looking for my sharpest rhinestone-crusted scissors. I line them up along my forehead, holding my breath as I cut straight across my hair in one bold motion. Ten inches of blond pirouette to the ground. For a split second, I completely freak out. But then I look in the mirror, squealing at the sleek shelf I've created, piano keys falling above my eyebrows. I snip-snip-snip until it's perfect, evening it out, creating layers around my face. The resemblance is uncanny.

When I'm done, my stomach rumbles from the smell of Gran's famous cornmeal-crusted chicken. I put on my slippers, gravitating toward the sound of pots and pans clanging in the kitchen.

"Smells amazing, Gran."

"Oh good, you're up," she says, facing the cupboards. She's changed out of her church clothes and into a loose floral sweater and khakis, more comfortable for trimming green beans. "I was just about to—"

She swivels toward me with a cutting board and lets out the tiniest gasp. But, despite my silently chanting *Mandy* over and over again, I can't read her face. Confusion? Surprise? Any kind of shock unscrambles, replaced by a friendly Southern smile. "Want to help with dinner?"

I nod slowly, fingers scrunching my hair. "Okay, but what do you think?"

"Well—"

The kitchen timer decides *that's* the perfect moment to ding. Frantically, Gran reaches for a potholder as if the potatoes might explode, unless they come off the stove immediately. I roll up my sleeves to help her, draining water from the pot because of her bad wrist. Steam moistens my face.

"Will you make the potato salad?" she asks, handing me a green porcelain bowl. "It's always so good when you do it."

My heart falls. "Sure."

Following a recipe I know by heart, I combine mayonnaise with a tablespoon of mustard, celery salt, and a dash of vinegar, then scrape in chopped celery and onions. I want to say something else, but the moment's gone. Potatoes have stolen my thunder. I wiggle my nose, partly to stop my bangs from tickling my eyes, partly to know they're still there. That her silence hasn't obliterated them.

When the potato salad's done, I grab our Sunday china with the pink azaleas and start setting the table. Grandpa's in the living room, reclining on a leather lounger, TV blaring a football game. I wonder if Robert likes to cook and help out in the kitchen or if he's old-fashioned like Grandpa. I wonder if it got under Mom's skin the way it gets under mine.

Gran calls us to dinner, and the TV zaps off. As soon as Grandpa walks into the dining room, it's as if he's transfixed by the sight of me.

"Do you like it?" I ask. "I cut it myself."

"Wouldya look at that." He smiles weakly, eyes darting across the table. "Katie?"

But Gran's lips are stuck in a delicate line. "Hands," she says, and the three of us have no choice but to take our seats and lower our heads. "For what we are about to receive, may the Lord make us truly thankful. Amen."

"Amen," says Grandpa.

"Amen," I say, deflating all over again.

The chicken is warm and smells of butter and summertime, a welcome distraction from the dreariness of winter. I choose a crispy golden drumstick, along with a spoonful of potato salad and boiled green beans. Grandpa pours out three glasses of water. I pass him the salt. Gran asks for the pepper. Forks tap against floral bone china. But I can only squeeze the drumstick between my fingers. My favorite meal, ruined because of this absurd hairstyle-induced elephant in the room.

"Still don't have your appetite?" Gran asks, eyeing my plate.

I slouch in response.

"Is this about your hair?" She puts down her fork. "Well, I'll be honest, I'm not sure why you did it. Have we reached the point where you don't need to ask permission anymore? I don't recall having had *that* conversation."

"Jesus, they're only bangs."

"Watch it," Grandpa warns. He shoots a *work-with-me-kiddo* look.

I tuck my hair behind my ears, some of the layers drifting back, dusting my cheeks. "I wanted to look like her," I say softly. "I barely know how to, since there's no photos up. But I do look like her, don't I? That's why you're being all weird?"

"Of course you look like her," Grandpa says carefully. "But it's easier not having photos up."

"Easier how? For who?" I press. "It's not fair that we pretend she didn't exist."

"Not *fair*?" Gran says, pulverizing the word. "You're right, Johanna. It isn't fair. None of this is *fair*. But this is my home, and I'll grieve how I choose. And if that means not having Amanda's picture plastered all over these walls, then so be it. The least you can do is—"

"Katie," Grandpa interjects, soft but stern.

She blinks as if she's coming out of a trance and reaches for her fork. The bite she manages is small and obligatory.

It's her home. It's mine too, but that doesn't matter. I'm a guest here, and I shouldn't have pushed. I clear my throat. "Sorry," I tell her, rib cage sinking toward my spine. "I didn't mean to."

"I know." She smiles politely. "Now, eat before your supper gets cold. The potato salad's nice, by the way. Your best yet."

My eyes dart toward Grandpa, but his gaze is somewhere else. Somewhere that doesn't exist. We finish our meal stuck in a silence so thick, you could lay bricks with it. Nobody feels much like the apple pie Gran baked for dessert, but I clear the plates and put the kettle on for tea while they watch the evening news.

After I take Magic out for his evening walk, after I've kissed them good night and changed into my PJs, there's a soft knock on my bedroom door and Grandpa nudges it open. Ever since puberty, he's treated my bedroom like a minefield—God forbid he trip over a bra or something—so he lingers tentatively in the doorway.

"You finish your homework?"

"Yeah."

"That's my girl."

His eyes drift over to the framed photo of my mother. He wears the hurt all over him. An ink-stain kind of pain that will never go away, no matter how many times he scrubs it.

"JoJo, your hair looks nice," he says. "You're the spitting image of Amanda. Gran just wasn't expecting it, is all. But it's lovely. Really lovely."

I don't want to smile, but I can't help it. All the way down to my toes and back up to my cheeks. "Thanks."

"G'night, JoJo."

"Good night, Grandpa."

6

"WHAT'S UP WITH YOUR hair?"

I shut my locker door and glance over my shoulder—and then down a few inches—at mousy Annette Martinez, student council president extraordinaire. There's a pout on her pale face, lips souring as she glares at me from behind a clipboard. I swear, she probably cradles that thing in her arms while she sleeps at night.

"And hello to you too, Annette."

"Isn't that look a bit *young* for a junior?" she asks.

I smile back, not about to be mocked by some overachieving Goody Two-shoes with a J. Crew addiction—which, to be fair, defines about 80 percent of our school, my friends included. I fluff my dazzling new 'do and decide to cut Annette some slack. She's the first female president (at least, since I've been here), not to mention the first ever Latinx president at our white-ass private school, and I feel like gals gotta stick together. Even if Annette is way too intense.

"I wanted a change." I shrug. "Sorry you're not impressed."

She raises an eyebrow.

"Is there anything *else* you wanted to talk about, or may I be excused?"

"Oh yeah." Her face softens, and she raises the clipboard. "I need signatures for my petition. I want Chavez Academy to make school uniforms mandatory."

I crinkle my nose, instantly appalled but also totally getting it, coming from Annette in her navy-blue Jackie cardigan and khaki chinos. Yeah, school uniforms would be right up her alley. Better yet, mandatory pantsuits for all.

I refocus my attention on her clipboard, saddened but not swayed by the paltry handful of signatures. "Sorry, but no can do. My entire existence is based around my wardrobe. See this pencil skirt I'm wearing? Sewed it with my own two hands."

"And that's the problem," she says, clipboard rattling in her fist. "Fashion shouldn't be more important than education. We're here to learn, not judge one another's clothes and show off."

"I'm not trying to show off! I just like expressing myself. Putting me in a uniform would be like putting a swan in a straitjacket."

Her head tilts. "You're a swan now?"

"Blow me, Annette." Gabby swoops in with Leah beside her. The two of them glance at the petition. "School uniforms? Please. Do I make you eat oatmeal every day? Is this fucking Hogwarts?"

Annette lifts her chin with gusto. The debate team has prepared them both well for this moment. "What about socioeconomic peer pressure?" she counters. Her eyes dip down Gabby's designer jeans to her feet, swathed in gleaming white Gucci sneakers. "Girls like me show up every day, mortified that we'll never compare to girls like you."

For a second, Gabby falters. "I get it, Annette. And I'm lucky I have it so good, but that doesn't give you the right to turn us into sheep. Make us look the same, and soon we'll start thinking the same. I, for one, am proud of my individuality."

Considering Gabby is one of the only Black kids at Chavez, there's really not much Annette can do to argue against *that* line of reasoning. But she tries anyway.

"You—more than anyone—ought to see the bigger picture, Gabby."

Gabby bristles. "Because I'm Black."

"Because we're *both* minorities," Annette says. "All that matters is college—you know that. And you're telling me, you think the Ivies care if you're wearing Prada to calculus?"

"I know what matters, *Annette*. And the *Ivies* care that I'm a well-rounded individual with myriad interests who works her ass off. Don't you dare play that card with me."

"But—"

"Um, you guys?" Leah squeaks, waving skinny arms between the two of them. "This energy is starting to clog. Annette, you've made some really good points. Unfortunately, I'm allergic to uniform material."

"Sorry," I add, trying to sound genuine. Because I see Annette's point. I just really like clothes.

An eye-roll battle ensues, which Gabby crushes, leaving the rest of us dizzy with minor headaches. Even as we're walking away, Annette's frustration lingers in the air. It's not that all her ideas are bad. I signed the Don't Dissect Frogs petition and the one about better recycling on campus. It's like she's afraid that if she's not the most aggressive president ever, they're going to revoke her scholarship. Which sucks, but I'm just trying to make it through high school like everyone else.

The student lounge is filling up when we push through the doors, but we snag our usual corner spot, arranging our lunches on the smooth oak table. Chavez sells pretty decent food—*you can't ace tests if you're hungry!*—but today I brought some of Gran's fried chicken. Atonement through leftovers.

"So, they were mad about your hair?" Gabby asks, dunking a straw into her Diet Coke. "I don't get it."

"Gran basically screamed at me for going behind her back and trying to keep Mom's memory alive. Like it's *my* fault."

"Your grandparents never want to talk about her. Seeing you like that must've been a shock," Leah says. Which only deepens the guilt hole in the pit of my stomach.

"Yeah, maybe. But it was still weird. They refuse to give me any shred of *anything*. I thought maybe the haircut would get the conversation flowing. Maybe they'd finally open up, but, nothing."

"That sucks."

"Sorry, sweetie."

I shrug, popping a morsel of chicken into my mouth. Chewing occupies the silence for a minute, and I look around the student lounge, eyes landing on Milo a few tables over, his knees tucked up into his chest. He looks up from a copy of *Just Kids*, and his eyes brighten as they land on me. I mean, my dream boy is reading a Patti Smith memoir—*are you serious right now?!*

I bite my lip, enjoying this tiny, private moment. The way the room goes all warm and still as the faintest twitch of a smile passes over his lips. I blush and offer a twitch of a smile back. One of his eyebrows goes up a little, like he's ESPing me a question, but then Gabby swats my shoulder and I jolt, glaring back at her.

"What?"

"I'm trying to give you a compliment."

"Oh. Uh, thanks?"

"I said, you look like Debbie Harry."

"Oh!" I brighten. "Thanks!"

"But almost futuristic," adds Leah. "Like a cyborg porn star or something."

"Did you just call me a *cyborg porn star*?"

"What even is that?" asks Gabby.

"It's a porn star with, like, mechanical boobs. I don't know." I smirk. "Mechanical Boobs would make a great band name."

"Leah, are you saying Jo's new *bangs* make her *boobs* look *mechanical*?"

"Hey, at least she looks like she *has* boobs. I told you they're growing."

"Shut up about my boobs," I whimper as quietly as possible,

firing a baby carrot across the table. "And I do *not* look like a cyborg."

"Whatever you say, RoboBabe."

We finish our lunches, and Leah puts on her coat, zipping it in anticipation of walking across the quad to fifth period. Five seconds later, her psychic abilities manifest as the monotone school bell hums through the PA. I wrap my scarf three times around my neck, subtly looking back to where Milo had been sitting. My heart sinks a little when I see his empty seat.

7

ROBERT HAS TO RESCHEDULE our Wednesday coffee date because of some really important conference call that can't be rescheduled. Which sucks. But I put on sneakers and clip Magic to his leash, heading down the block to distract myself. The air is crisp but not freezing, and Magic seems peppier than usual, jerking me left down Hopi Road and then onto Rosina as he sniffs after a jackrabbit. It's nice to see his mood like this— alert and playful and making me full-on run to keep up. The thought of him eventually going up to the dog park in the sky makes me feel that much further from my mom. As if I could *get* any further away. Even with all those new pictures from Robert. Even with my bangs. The dumb bangs that I thought would magically somehow—

"Jo?"

It takes all my strength to stop Magic in order to look behind me. "Milo?"

He slams the door to a pickup truck and joins me on the sidewalk. "What are you doing here?"

Sweating, I think dismally. I can feel it, cold and sticky and dripping down the back of my neck. Ew. The absolute suckery of looking like shit in front of gorgeous, flutter-inducing Milo with the stormy eyes and the dimples and—well, all of it.

"I'm taking Magic out for a walk. Magic, meet Milo. Milo, Magic."

Milo extends his hand and—I swear to God, I love my dog—Magic actually takes Milo's hand. Even my dog wants in on bonding with this hottie. I can't help laughing, and neither can Milo.

"He's not usually this friendly. You're obviously a dog person."

"Hamster," Milo says. "In second grade. It didn't end well."

"Oof. Sorry."

"It's okay. Snowball's in a better place now."

"You live around here?" we both say. At the same time.

I blush, which probably doesn't matter because my cheeks are already pink from running. I kick the chipped fire hydrant between us, waiting for him to answer first.

"I live in that house across the street. With the chile pepper thing?"

"Ristra," I say, and his eyebrows rise. "The strand of dried red chiles on your front door. They're called ristras."

"My mom calls it 'local flair,'" he says, brimming with an

adorable amount of pride. "She says we have to do as the locals do, if we're going to embrace this move."

"Órale!" I say with a giggle. It basically means *hell yeah* in Spanish. Everyone around here says it. I start to explain, but Magic tugs on the leash and I have to yank him back toward me, shushing him with a treat before this damn dog sabotages my moment. "So, are you? Embracing Santa Fe, or whatever?"

He shrugs, eyes darting toward Magic. "Does he need to keep walking? Because I'm not busy, if you want some company."

"Really?"

A grin lights up his whole face.

We start to walk in no particular direction, and, even though we'd literally been in the middle of a conversation, neither one of us says anything. It feels nice, actually. Okay, my heart is full of lit sparklers, but other than that, it's nice. We walk quickly to keep up with Magic, close enough that our arms brush against each other when the leash jerks. The sidewalk ends, and something flutters through me. A craving to make this walk epic.

"Hey, are you hungry?"

Milo nods without hesitation. "Always. You offering a dog treat?"

"No." I giggle. "But I have something even better in mind." I raise one eyebrow and jerk my head to the right. "Follow me."

Within minutes, we're at this tiny fast-food joint off Cerrillos Road, its signature flame-font spelling out the words Baja Tacos in bright red lettering. A local institution. The place is too small for indoor seating, so Milo leads Magic to one of the little stone tables underneath a banana-yellow umbrella while I go inside to be the expert orderer. The best thing about Baja (besides the food) is that it never takes very long. A few minutes later, I walk out with a tray full of two Sprites, a couple of chicken tacos, and a large Frito pie, which is basically a bag of Fritos brimming with ground beef, green chile sauce, and tons of cheese and diced tomatoes. In other words, heaven.

I hand Milo a fork, and he clinks his Sprite against mine. We both dig in, and for a while we just munch, enjoying the flavors and the crisp afternoon air. I try not to focus too hard on how nice this is. How I don't feel pressured, the way I did with my dad.

"This is amazing," Milo says, mouth full, eyes rolling back in his head. "You come here a lot?"

"Are you asking me if I *come here often?*"

He has to cover his mouth as he laughs.

"Not really," I answer. "In fact, my grandma is probably going to kill me when I go home with no appetite for dinner. But I'm willing to suffer the consequences."

"Do you like living with your grandparents?"

"Basically? It's not like . . ."

"What?"

I force an awkward shrug. *It's not like I have another choice.* That's what I was going to say. A chill rattles my bones, and I pull my knees into my chest, hugging them tightly. The chicken taco on my plate is mostly demolished, and I crumple a napkin on top of it.

"Hey," he says gently, bumping his knee against my foot. "I was supposed to come up with scintillating conversation topics, remember?"

I grin and sit up a little straighter. "That's right! Okay. Hit me."

Milo gulps Sprite through his straw and scrunches his brow. "I'll start easy. Would you rather have superhuman strength or invisibility?"

"Invisibility. You?"

"Yeah, same. Okay, would you rather go back in time or travel into the future?"

"Back in time. Hundred percent." I scrunch my nose, wracking my brain for ideas. "Would you rather have spoons for fingers or a cat butt for a face?"

"A cat butt!?" he yelps. "Wow, you are *really* bad at this! Spoon fingers, I guess." He squeezes the back of his neck with one hand. "What do you like better, reading or writing?"

"Both. And sewing."

"Yeah? That's pretty cool. YouTube or Spotify?"

"Spotify," I say, no hesitation. Well, some hesitation. "Except blender videos. I'm a sucker for those."

"Blender videos? What the hell are those?"

"You know. Like, *will it blend?*"

"No, I do not know."

I dig around on the plate for a non-soggy Frito and grin. "So, this guy, Tom somebody. He puts all kinds of crap in this, like, industrial-strength blender and tries to see if it'll blend. Golf balls, Jar Jar Binks toys, iPhones—"

"He annihilates iPhones?" Milo winces. "God, I think I'm going to be sick."

"No! It's amazing. You should watch one—here, I'll show you."

I start to reach for my phone, but Milo touches my forearm. "Wait," he says softly. "Let's just keep talking. You can show me next time."

I try for a nonchalant nod—because inside I am screaming, *next time?!* from the hills of Austria—but my Frito goes down the wrong way, and I start choking. Full-on, head-between-my-legs gagging. I can feel Milo watching me too, one hand hovering at my back, the other extended in front of my mouth, ready to catch a phlegm ball if necessary. *Dear God, do not let me hack up a phlegm ball.* When he offers me my Sprite, I suck about half of it down before meeting his eyes again.

"Sorry about that."

The cutest crinkle appears on his forehead. "Are you okay?"

"I'm fine. I got something caught in my throat."

"Does that happen a lot when guys ask you out?"

I almost choke again, then manage an unrefined swallow. "Is that what you did?" My cheeks literally roast, but I pinch the gloriously giddy feeling into a tiny ball and tuck it deep inside my heart for later. "Uh, I can honestly say no. No, it does not. But the statistical evidence is limited."

"But it's a yes?" he asks, voice inching up. "To hanging out?"

My grin pretty much answers for me. Milo grins too, nodding slow and victorious. I can't explain the non-awkwardness of it, but, for a few minutes, we stare at each other. Fighting back blushes, having a squinty, flirty showdown. It just . . . *is*. He starts to lean closer, and I swear to God I think he might kiss me, but then evil Magic growls at him.

"Magic!" I shriek. "What is your *prob*lem!"

Kill me now.

I think he might freak out and run away—the dude, not the dog—but Milo only laughs. He reaches down and grabs a chunk of Magic's soft apricot curls and gives him a scritchy-scratch behind the ears.

"That's a good boy," he says, using one of those smoosh-lipped voices people seem hardwired to reserve for babies and puppies. "Lookin' out for your big sis, huh? I respect that."

I laugh and put my hand on top of Magic's head too. Our fingers touch for a second. Long enough to zap me with happy. Again, Milo starts to lean closer. This time it's me who jerks back, my stupid brain screaming, *Save it for your date!* Which is dumb, because, for all intents and purposes, this basically *is* a date. But, whatever. I can't help it. I panic.

"We should probably head back. It's getting dark."

Milo's face falls a little, but he stands, collecting our trash and throwing it in the bin. "Hey, thanks for bringing me here. That green chile was staggeringly good."

"I know, right? Happy to share the local flav."

We hook Magic back to his leash, testing our Would You Rather limits as we walk down the street. Part of me doesn't want him to ask me everything now and then be bored by the time our real date rolls around, but, at the same time, I want this night to go on forever.

We stop on the corner of Rosina Street, and Milo sighs.

"Want a ride home?" he asks. "There's room for Magic in the back."

I shake my head. "We'll be fine. Magic needs to run around a little more."

"I'll see you at school," he says, his breath catching as he hesitates.

My breath catches too. "What?"

"When are we hanging out again?"

It is physically impossible not to soar through the sky before answering. "You tell me."

"How about Saturday?"

"I'm supposed to be sleeping over at Leah's."

Shit. Why did I say that? Like my friends care if I cancel a sleepover for a *hot date*. In fact, they'll probably punch me when they find out.

"No worries, we'll work something out." He smiles, taking his phone out of his pocket. "Can I get your number, at least?"

My cheeks pinch into giddy little knots as I reel off the digits way too fast. He stuffs his phone back in his pocket and pats Magic on the butt. "Good night, Jo. Good night, Magic."

"G'night, Milo."

Milo from history.

8

COFFEE DATE, FINALLY. MINUS the date. Minus the coffee.

"Sorry I'm late," Robert says, rushing over to my corner table with frazzled determination. "We're starting this big project, and it's like everyone wants to use Python, even though Python is awful. I think it would make way more sense to write it in Ruby, because it reads like English, and it's way more expressive. They're being total idiots."

"Wow. Intense," I say, because, um, *whaaaat*?

He smacks his forehead. "God, listen to me."

"It's okay." I shake my head, and my bangs sway a little.

"Your hair!" he says. "Was it like that before?"

"No, I decided to cut it after looking at the—"

"Pictures," he finishes. "Aw, totally. You look exactly like her."

A mild flush turns colossal on my cheeks, burning my earlobes.

Robert clears his throat. "I should grab a coffee. Want anything?"

When I point to the chai I'm currently cradling, he gets in the coffee line, and, for the first time, I let myself look. Really study the slump of his shoulders, slim line of his nose. Because it's *my* nose, really. Fucking identical. We stand the same too—feet turned in, one hand cradling the other elbow. No doubt about it, *this guy is my dad*.

Robert comes back a minute later, slack-jawed. "Man, there was a resemblance before, but now you look *exactly* like her. I can't get over it."

"Really?" I push aside thoughts of our matching noses in order to smile. "Thanks. That's what I was going for."

"Impulsive, same as Mandy." He smirks. "Do you always do stuff like that?"

"What do you mean?"

"Y'know, change your appearance at a moment's notice."

"It's kind of hard to get away with too much, living with my grandparents. They're not super huge fans of spontaneity." I sip my chai, searching for the right words. "I mean, they want what's best for me. To provide for me. Not just food and stuff, but strong values. Giving back to the community. Teaching me how to sew."

"You sew?"

"It started out because Gran wanted me to get into quilting, like her. She makes a thousand quilts a year like some one-woman sweatshop for the church fundraising committee. But I mostly make my own clothes."

"Really?" Robert's eyes widen as he bites into a scone. "Whamt kimd of shmuff moo mou make?"

"All kinds. Here—"

I fish my phone out of my bag, hesitating only slightly as I hand it to him—like, double-checking with my soul if he deserves a free ticket to this part of my personality. But I offset my caution with the eagerness in his smile and remind myself of why he's here—why *I'm* here. It feels right enough that I hand it over, all cued up. A hundred images of gauzy tops, tulle dresses, purses, and gloves. Sometimes it's me modeling. Sometimes Leah or Gabby, who've been playing dress-up with me since kindergarten. I try to explain the epicness of our friendship. That no matter how different we seem, however unrelated our goals, that we have a bond tighter than spandex.

I don't hover or interject as Robert scrolls, but I can see his eyes glowing. Maybe with admiration, maybe pride. Maybe.

"Wait, so you sewed all this?"

I offer a small smile.

"Wow." He makes this explosion gesture as he grins. "Who knew I had such a talented daughter!"

Daughter.

Sirens blare in my head. A flurry of hot snow, sizzling under my skin. I cough and Robert grimaces, handing the phone and our fleeting easygoing moment back to me. I shove it in my bag and will my cheeks to stop burning. *Daughter.* The word seesaws inside me until it sounds blocky and foreign—*dawder, daw-der.*

"I'm also into music," I blurt, out of nowhere. "In addition to sewing. Y'know, since you asked about hobbies."

Robert leans back in his chair. "Yeah? What kind of music?"

"Lunachicks. The occasional Billie Eilish. But older stuff, mostly. Blondie. The Ramones. Television."

With every band I mention, Robert's expression grows more animated, his grin morphing into a chuckle. "Check. Check. Check. You got good taste, kid. I approve."

I grin. As if liking good music is a skill I can take credit for. Not a skill, but maybe a family trait?

"I saw Blondie on tour once. Not, like, heyday Blondie. But Debbie killed it, even though she's getting older."

"You've seen *Debbie Harry*?" I shriek, way too loud. It takes me a second to close my mouth. "That's so cool."

Robert laughs this big, thunderbolt *hah* that echoes around the room. "You know, you kind of look like her."

"Deborah Ann Harry?" I scoff. "Please."

"You do." He nods defiantly, but then his eyes seem to unfocus. "So did Mandy, actually."

The way it hurts him to think about her breaks my heart.

"How'd you guys meet?" I ask, guilty but desperate to keep the conversation about her. "Was it love at first sight or whatever?"

The story shoots out of him like a rocket, this Muppet grin overtaking his lips. Talking about her brings him to life. Makes him look young and fresh, the way she must have seen him.

There'd been a graduation party. Mandy had accidentally spilled a bowl of nacho cheese on his favorite jeans and then gone off to find him something from the lost-and-found in her college dorm. He describes her bubblegum laugh as she convinced him how cool he looked in tight, red running shorts, even though he knew she was lying. The way he'd held her hand. Conversations cascading, from animal rights to lightning bolts and favorite movies. He asks me if I knew she was a strict vegetarian or obsessed with rainstorms.

"No," I murmur, nails digging into my palms.

Surprise dwindles on his face. "You weren't kidding. They didn't tell you anything."

I stare into my empty mug. "My whole life I've wanted to know more about my mom, and now that it's happening—"

"What about your dad?" he asks nervously. "Ever wonder about me?"

"What?" My stomach lurches. "I don't, I mean, you never—"

"It's okay." He smiles and dips his chin. "Don't worry about it."

Awkwardness creeps back between us, a heavy fog seeping into my gut. He says it's okay, but is it? The niggling feeling inside me only grows. Any of my friends would have seen me squirm and asked what was wrong. Anyone who knew me. That's the thing, though. Robert *doesn't* know me.

"You don't get it," I murmur. "Of course I wanted to know you. You're the one who didn't want to know *me*."

"That's not true."

"Isn't it?" I demand. "Then tell me why you left. Or where you've been all this time. Don't I deserve to know?"

"Of course you do."

"Then, come on, already."

Chairs scrape against the floor beside us and a middle-aged couple plops down, so close I can smell hazelnut syrup in the woman's latte. She smiles apologetically for bumping my elbow and then faces her partner, the two of them using outside voices and big hand gestures to discuss an upcoming trip to Peru.

"Not now," Robert says.

He's right. We can't talk with Machu Picchu over there, gesticulating wildly.

"Somewhere quieter," he says, face whitening with each passing second. "My place, this weekend?"

Maybe I should say no—I still barely know him—but it's not like I can invite him over to my house. And I *need* answers. So, after a second, I nod. He types his Airbnb address into my phone, and we both bundle up, heading outside as the sun begins to cast an electric amber glow over the Jemez Mountains. I start to walk to my car, but Robert doesn't budge. At first, I think he's all gaga over the sunset like every other tourist in town, but his eyes are cast down, glassed over.

I pause. "Robert?"

He inhales his way back to reality and looks at me, opening his mouth as if he's going to say something meaningful. But then . . . nothing.

"Is everything okay?" I ask.

Finally, he shakes his head, backing away with a meek smile. "It's not. But it can wait."

9

IT'S NOT. BUT IT CAN WAIT.

I mean, what the hell am I supposed to do with that?

"It's probably my fault," I grumble, reluctantly nibbling the slice of pizza in my hand. We're all in our PJs, sitting in the middle of Leah's too-coral bedroom with a large green chile pie and juice boxes like we're little kids, dissecting my second encounter with Robert.

"*Your* fault?" Gabby sputters. "I'm sorry, but you shouldn't have to feel like shit when he's the one rolling into town acting shady."

"Come on, he's not that shady."

"He's so shady, he's translucent."

"That doesn't even make sense," Leah mutters.

Gabby shrugs, mouthing *shay-dee* again, for emphasis.

I roll my eyes. "Okay, so he's not entirely shade-free. I mean, I wish he would have told me there, at the café."

"Yeah," Gabby says. "Why does he suddenly need to see you *alone*?"

"What do you think he's not telling you?" asks Leah. "Ooh, do you think you have siblings? Holy crap, *a little sister!*" She drops her pizza, clearly envisioning future trips to Disneyland. Just as quickly, her face falls. "Unless she's like my sister. In which case, hard pass. No, I take it back. Rachel gives *great* foot rubs."

"Rachel rubs your stinky feet?" I start laughing, thinking Gabby's going to join in, but her face is aglow with judgment. "What?"

"It's just—why now?" she asks. "After so long. Do you think he needs money?"

"*You're not helping,*" Leah singsongs.

But Gabby huffs. I swear, her temper is like drawing straws— you never know when you're going to get the short one. "What if he's missing a kidney?" she adds. "He probably needs your bone marrow!"

"*He probably needs my bone marrow?* Do you hear yourself right now?"

I drop my pizza back in the box. Appetite, lost.

Gabby pauses for a second then scoots closer, honey-brown eyes wide and apologetic. "I'm sorry. That was harsh. You know I'm only saying this because I love you, and I get that you're curious, but who is this guy? Out of the blue he writes you and expects to pick up where you left off? Isn't that *fucked up*?"

When I don't answer, Gabby keeps going, working to keep her voice even. "He needs to apologize and explain why he left.

As far as I'm concerned, he should be down on his knees, begging for your forgiveness. It's what you deserve."

The room goes quiet. So quiet, we can hear Rachel through the wall, listening to the *Hamilton* soundtrack and laughing into her phone. I chew on my lip, appreciating Gabby's calmness when I bet she probably wants to scream at me for not doing this *her* way. But does she honestly think this has never crossed my mind? Before classes, after homework. Through washing and folding laundry. Even through helping Grandpa take measurements for the windows because, yep, we need new ones. And yet, all day, all I can think about is Robert Newton. One big, fat question mark.

"Are you going to say anything?" Gabby asks after a minute.

I shrug and exhale, puffing out my cheeks. "You're acting like I haven't had these same exact thoughts. Which kind of makes you sound like a know-it-all."

Gabby stiffens. For someone who basically *does* know-it-all, she really hates being called out on it. But, after a second, she nods. "I'm sorry."

And she is. I can tell by the weakness of her smile. I smile back.

"Besides," she adds, grin regaining its twinkle. "I'm not a know-it-all. I'm *right*."

I snort with laughter. "You're such a bitch."

"A bitch is a female dog," she taunts. "And I love dogs."

And just like that, Gabby burrows her way back into my heart. As always.

"Can we change topics?" Leah whimpers. "You guys want to raid the liquor cabinet? Remember last time? With the peach schnapps?"

"I don't think Jo's in the mood for a sexy, drunk photo shoot." I scrunch my nose.

"Okay. What about a movie? There must be a documentary about baby pandas or something. Maybe a rom-com? Dealer's choice, Jo. What do you want?"

"Hold on." Something wicked spikes the corners of Gabby's grin. "I have. The. Perfect. Idea."

• • •

We roll up in front of Milo's house at 10:02 p.m., but I won't get out of the car. Because even though we've texted and flirted, no *actual* date has been scheduled. Showing up feels kind of, I don't know, stalkery?

"It's not stalkery. It's romantic. And gutsy," Leah clarifies. "We all know he only gives that sexy *I'm-James-Dean-reincarnated* pout to you. But if you want to bail, we could always—"

"We are *not* having a sexy photo shoot. Let it go, Leah."

"Once! *Once* we took silly photos in our bras." She snorts with laughter, swatting Gabby's arm. "All I'm saying is, look at what Jo's been through lately. Literally *nothing* exciting ever happens to us, and then she meets her father *and* gets a hot boyfriend all in the same week? I mean, Jo, don't you feel like you won the lottery or something?"

"Okay, first of all, chill. You sound like our old Girl Scout troop leader. Second, he's not my boyfriend. And third, it's not exactly the lottery when your dad's a mysterious stranger. He's actually kind of hard to talk to, whereas Milo—"

"*Ring the doorbell*," Gabby groans.

"What if he's not home?"

"Doesn't he drive that silver truck?"

"And isn't that him, staring at our car through his living room window?"

"Oh, for the love of—" I slither down in the back seat, cupping my palm over my forehead. The girls cackle in stereo. "You guys, shut up. Shut *up!*"

But they don't. Can't. Instead, they start chanting, "*Do* it! *Do* it! *Do* it!"

"Okay, but only if you'll shut the hell up immediately for all eternity."

Gabby locks her lips and hands me an imaginary key. Leah zips hers shut. I zhuzh my hair in the rearview mirror, making sure my eyeliner's not smudged. It is. But in a good way.

"You look hot as balls. Now go get 'em."

With a little *eek*, I jump out of the car and skitter up the path to Milo's small adobe house with the turquoise trim. God, it's freezing. And I'm wearing slippers with my jeans and hoodie because I didn't anticipate actually getting out of the car.

Before I've reached the door, Milo pulls it wide open and stands there, grinning. "So, *you're* the curbside stalker. My mom was getting nervous. New town, new weirdos."

"Oh my God. Shit. I didn't mean—"

"Hold on," he murmurs. "You look like you're freezing."

He tugs the sleeve of my sweatshirt and pulls me into his house, shutting the door softly behind us. There are boxes stacked up in the living room, but the place already has personality. Purple accent wall, a funky driftwood coffee table, a needlepoint in the hallway—which would remind me of Gran except this one says Polite as Fuck. I almost snicker, but then Milo presses his warm palms to my cheeks, and I completely forget what was so funny. The corners of his mouth turn up. *Damn*, he knows how to smile.

"Much better. Your cheeks aren't blue anymore."

"Blue cheeks are all the rage, thank you very much."

He grins. "Oh, I see."

"Your house is nice."

"It's a work in progress. My room's a shithole still, but whatever."

"Aren't boys' bedrooms supposed to be disaster areas? Maybe that's a myth."

"I won't speak for my entire gender, but I know my way around a vacuum cleaner, if you know what I mean."

"I think so?"

"Anyways." He clears his throat. "What're you doing here? I thought you were at a sleepover."

"Oh." I glance through the living room window, toward Gabby's jeep. I can't see their faces in the darkness, but I'm sure they're laughing. "Can't a girl stalk the new guy without getting the third degree? Maybe this is part of the Chavez

Academy Integration Initiative. Harass new students on Saturday night?"

Milo smirks. "And you're head of the committee. What are the odds?"

"A million to one. At least."

"Well, I appreciate your dedication."

"You're welcome." I grin. "Actually, we're mostly out looking for something to do. I'm kind of going through some stuff, and my friends thought this might be a good distraction."

"Oh, yeah?" He squints, scratching micro-stubble on his chin. "Well, your friends were right. I make an impeccable distraction."

I laugh and wiggle my toes, reveling in the airiness of his company. I even do that thing—where you lick your lower lip and then bite it. I've never actually done that before, but I'm pretty sure it's a *thing*, so why not, right? And it works. At least, I think it does. Milo's cheeks go pink, and he cocks his head back a little, grinning down at me with that knowing, inside-joke smile.

"Sweetie, who was outside?"

Over his shoulder appears this stunning, supermodel/tennis champ-looking woman. She's got Milo's stormy blue eyes and wide cheekbones, the same flawless, olive skin.

"Oh, hello," she says, her accent gentle and brooding like a Bond villainess. "I'm the mom."

"Hi, Mrs. Schmidt. Sorry to freak you out."

"You didn't. And call me Anna." She links her arm through her son's, kicking his socked foot with her moccasin. "You going to introduce me?"

"Sorry." Milo coughs. "Mom, this is Jo. The girl I was telling you about."

Okay, okay, okay, wait. First of all, he told his mom about me? And, more importantly, *he told his mom about me?!* My face catches fire. Instinctively, I stand a little taller, eager to seem—I dunno. Taller?

"Ah, yes. The one who took you out for Frito pies. You're even prettier than Milo said."

"*Mom!*"

He definitely groans. But I swear he doesn't seem all that bothered. Whereas I would full-on die if Gran ever pulled that shit with me. It's kind of refreshing, the way he just, y'know, is who he is.

"Mom, seriously. Don't you have Words with Friends or something?"

"Ouch, Son." She clutches her chest and steps back. "It was nice to meet you, Jo. Take this boy out of my house for a while, will you? He's turning into a hermit." She kisses Milo's forehead because she's tall enough to reach it, and then saunters back out of the room, calling, "Don't stay out too late!" over her shoulder, even though it's already 10:20 and my curfew is 10 p.m. sharp.

"Your mom's cool."

"You want to get out of here?"

"Definitely."

Dimples form on his cheeks as he grins.

Yup. An impeccable distraction.

• • •

"Wow, check out how goopy this is."

I hold up a stringy, silklike thread of marshmallow taffy, and Milo nods his approval. His is still chunky, more like marshmallow cement, but it's getting there. We're at Leah's kitchen table but not making too much noise because everyone's asleep—I mean, Leah and Gabby are probably watching movies on her laptop, but at least they didn't make it too obvious. I use an un-sticky finger to switch the music on my phone from Sia to Television, and right away, Milo starts nodding, devouring his taffy so he can pluck the hypnotizing first few chords of "Marquee Moon" on air guitar.

"You know Hendrix inspired them on ax?" he says.

"I didn't, but I can hear it now."

"I love this part."

I watch him strum, the music and his intensity bubbling up, echoing in me. As much as I love my friends, music is one thing we've never really had in common. It's kind of cool to be sharing it with Milo.

"You play guitar, I'm guessing?"

He nods. "Had a band at my old school."

"Called?"

"Clover by Clover. It's a line from *Horton Hears a Who!*"

"By Dr. Seuss!" I cheer. "Man, I used to love that book."

"Me too." He pauses, grinning. "Hey, you want to start a band with me?"

"Can we be called Jo-Jo and the Yo-Yo?"

"Another Horton reference. I like it. So, you in? Me on guitar, you on—"

"Recorder." I cringe. "I know. Super uncool."

He laughs in quick surprise, then points to my phone. "May I?"

I raise an eyebrow and put in my passcode, handing it over. "Here, listen."

After a second, "Marquee Moon" stops playing and something softer comes on. A single guitar, gentle and melodic. It's so familiar, but I can't quite place it. And then—

"Ah!" My lips spread into a grin. "I forgot this song had recorders in it."

"What's the song?" Milo challenges.

"Are you joking? Everybody knows 'Stairway to Heaven.'"

"Jimmy Page is my hero." He picks up his air guitar again, gently strumming.

Without even stressing about it, I watch him. I don't hide behind marshmallows or my blush. The song grows fuller, richer, and my insides gently simmer.

Milo puts down the air guitar after a minute and frowns. "So, you're going through some *stuff*?"

"Yeah, but we don't have to . . ."

"We *don't* have to. But we can. If you want."

Normally, I'd feel nervous being put on the spot like this, but my breath is calm, chest steady. "It's about my dad. He kinda came back into the picture recently. I haven't had any contact with him for a long time, so it's kinda—"

"Weird?"

"Yeah. Kinda weird."

"Weird good?" he asks. "Do you *want* him in the picture?"

I wait for a sign. For my stomach to drop or my brain to scream. But nothing happens. "I think maybe I do."

The words sink in as I say them, resting comfortably in my heart. Milo slides his hand across the table, careful as he laces his fingers through mine.

"I'm glad you told me," he says.

"Me too."

His eyes stay on the crisscross pattern of our fingers. "I'm kind of in the middle of a dad situation too."

My eyebrows twitch. "Yeah?"

"He's not 'packing up' and meeting us out here, like I said. My mom left him."

"I'm so sorry."

"It's okay. I'm just telling you because . . . I don't know."

"I'm glad," I say. "Not about your parents, but I'm glad you told me."

"Me too."

The song changes, and we fall into a comfortable silence. Fingers intertwined. Grins wavering between goofy and sincere. Robert Plant sings about finding a girl with love in her eyes, and I lose myself in Milo's, my thumb dragging along his. The calluses I'd noticed on the first day of school feel hard and smooth.

Milo leans in toward me. I hold my breath, but this time I don't pull away. Right here, in the middle of the Fromowitzes' Spanish-tiled kitchen, sticky-sweet from marshmallow taffy, Milo's lips press into mine. Softer, warmer, more perfect than anything.

10

I DRIVE TO ROBERT'S place after sleeping till noon at Leah's, barely able to function from all the Milo-induced butterflies. Lips still numb, skin buzzing. He left around midnight with more kisses, more promises of *next times.*

"Hey!" Robert says, mistaking my grin as he ushers me through the front door. "Any trouble finding the place?"

I shake my head. "Santa Fe's not that big, and this house is really close to downtown. I was around the corner from here a few weeks ago, actually. On Christmas Eve? They light all the streets in this neighborhood with farolitos—y'know, those little paper-bag lanterns filled with sand and a candle? It's really cool. Sidewalks, walls, rooftops. It's this whole magical little universe."

"Sounds beautiful."

"Mm-hmm."

We stand in the hallway long enough for one of our trade-mark awkward silences before he ushers me into a bright, cozy room with white-painted vigas on the ceiling and a wood-burning fireplace in the corner. I try to remind myself that this isn't my father's living room. That the cheery mango walls and modern furniture belong to the people who rent it out—not Robert. Who knows what the hell Robert's *actual* house is like?

"You want something to drink?"

"No, thanks."

"Food? I might have some—"

"Could we maybe just sit down?"

He gestures toward a fancy gray sofa and then sits across from me on an uncomfortable-looking art deco chair. Outside, piñon branches scratch against a picture window as the wind howls. Snow White in the haunted forest comes to mind, which doesn't ease my mood.

"So," I say, right as he says, "I guess—"

I clear my throat. "You go first."

"I was going to say, the other day you asked me where I've been."

My heart jumps. "Yeah?"

"And I'm going to tell you, I swear. But, first, I was hoping you could tell me something."

"Me?" I squeak. "Like what?"

"Well," he sighs. "It's about something you said. At the café."

My brain turns photographic, flipping back to earlier

Bluebell conversations. Honestly, I said a lot of stuff. Rambled, even. I shake my head, smiling apologetically. "Sorry, what was it exactly?"

"We were talking about your mom. Listen, I know it sounds strange, but I need you to tell me what they told you."

I squint. "What *who* told me?"

"Kate and Jimmy. How did they explain Mandy's death?"

"Her *death*?" I feel the back of my neck prickle. "Sorry, what exactly are we talking about here?"

Robert exhales, pinching the bridge of his nose. "I'm asking—how did they tell you she died?"

"God, I don't know." I mean, seriously. His *tone*. That answer-me-young-lady *dad* voice. It's disorienting. "Why does it matter? I wasn't even three when it happened."

"But—" He sighs again, more pointedly, fingers diving through his hair. "*How* did she die? It's really important that you tell me."

"A car crash. Jesus, why are you asking?"

"*Shit*," he whispers, face souring.

My stomach twists. "You're being *super* weird right now."

"I'm not trying to." He rubs sweaty palms against his thighs and squeezes his kneecaps. "Look. We really—*really*—need to talk. Okay?"

I hesitate. Because, I mean, "Aren't we already talking?"

"I need a second," he says. "I can't *believe* they never told you."

"They did tell me," I insist.

"Right, but—" Again he sighs, wiping saliva from the

corners of his mouth. "It's all so messed up, but I can't explain my side of the story if you don't know hers."

"I'm trying to tell you, I *do* know. I just don't know all the gory highway details."

"No, you *don't* know. There were no *highway details*. Listen to me. You need to hear the truth about Mandy."

"*The truth?*" I say. "Like, what? She was abducted by aliens? I don't know what you *think* you know, but—"

"I'm not trying to scare you. Shit, that's probably why your grandparents lied to you. But that's what they did. They lied."

"Gran and Grandpa? You've got to be kidding me."

"I'm not."

"You honestly think my ancient, Baptist grandparents are capable of some elaborate sabotage? I mean, it's legitimately hilarious."

A nervous giggle bursts out of me, and Robert's face reddens. "Would you stop?" he snarls. "This isn't easy for me."

"*What* isn't? I don't—whatever you *think* you know, it isn't—"

"Jesus, stop being so stubborn and *listen* to what I'm trying to tell you!" he yells. He has to pause and catch his breath before looking back at me. "Johanna, your mom got shot."

My pulse races. I duck back.

Ten seconds go by, and Robert swallows. "Sorry. I shouldn't have yelled. Are you okay?"

I can't answer. Can't even manage to shake my head.

"Do you at least understand what I said?" he asks, eyebrows twisting. "I know your grandparents told you she died in a car accident, but it wasn't like that. It was a shooting."

He waits a beat. Lets it hang in the air again. The words are the same, though. Still bullshit. "Listen to me. You have to know, none of this was your fault."

"*My* fault?" I bristle. Now I'm out of my haze. Head spinning, hands shaking. "This is ridiculous. I don't know who told you she was shot, but it was a *car* accident. A truck crashed into her car—"

"Johanna—"

"Head-on—"

"Jo, stop—"

"And my mother died instantly. *That's* what happened."

"No. It's not."

"But—"

"You're not listening to me," he snaps, and I jolt at the bark of it. "You have to hear what I am saying. *There was a gun in the house.*"

"No, there wasn't."

Why is he doing this to me? *What* is he doing to me?

"One morning, by accident, you found it."

"No," I whimper.

"*That's* what happened. That's the truth."

Over and over again, I shake my head, dizzied by the orange walls pulsing around me. I should stand, but my legs are sandbags, the wooden vigas crashing down on my shoulders. Nothing that happens next makes any sense. Words fly out of Robert's mouth and bob around the room like bats. They're familiar words—dictionary words—but none of them fit together in a way I can understand. It's a story being told to me in a nightmare or some parallel universe, and my vision seems to blacken in response.

The neighbors had heard the gunshot. They'd knocked on the door and run inside. They'd seen Mandy on the floor and found me in the corner of the room. Crying. Soiled. Hiding beside the gun.

Afterward, they'd called 9-1-1. Then Robert, but he couldn't be reached at work. After that, they'd found a number for my grandparents, who were in California visiting. Thank God, because someone needed to come for two-and-a-half-year-old me.

More words describe how Robert arrived home, terrified, only to find me in Gran's arms, police cars everywhere. He'd been arrested, he says, for owning the .22 caliber handgun. He'd been arrested while my mother's body was zipped up in a rubber bag and carted away. Pronounced dead at the scene. Sent to the morgue.

Not sent to the hospital. No attempts to resuscitate.

Just, dead.

"Stop talking," I say, when I can't hear anything apart from the throbbing of my heart inside my ears. "Please, stop."

"I know this must be a huge shock for you."

I rip my eyes from the marble coffee table and glance up at him. It's the first time I've looked at him properly since he started spouting this gibberish. This totally absurd bullshit. Tears stream down his face and into his goatee.

"Are you okay?" he asks, rubbing a trail of snot along the sleeve of his sweater.

"How can you expect me to answer that?"

"I know," he snivels. "I don't know."

It makes me sick to see him cry. Tears can be contagious, but in this case, his blubbering only makes me nauseated. Makes my skin itch and burn like a bad penicillin reaction. I finally manage to stand, legs trembling.

"Where are you going?"

"I'm getting out of here," I say through gritted teeth. "I shouldn't have come."

"I know how crazy this must sound, but you've got to believe me."

"Believe *you*? I don't even know you. You say you're my father, but you've been nowhere for my entire life. Then you appear, acting like you want to be best friends, and you tell me I shot and killed my own mother? What the actual *fuck*?"

"I know. But, please—"

He stands, but I send him back down with a feral glare.

"This ridiculous lie still doesn't explain why you waited so long to find me. Were you in jail all this time? Is that what I'm supposed to believe?"

"That's not—it wasn't the whole time," he stammers. "You're right, though. I was in jail. Things got rough, which is partly what kept me away. But I found God. My pastor helped me a lot, helped me get the job I'm at now. Everything's finally on track for me, but I've always hated myself for leaving you. That's why I really need you to hear me out."

"Why?" I ask. "So you can go into *more* detail?"

My insides scream as I race toward the entryway, yanking

my coat off the hook and slamming the front door so hard, the thud of it rattles my whole body. The air outside feels sharp and crisp, and it shocks some of the life back into me as I stumble across the street.

Every part of me hurts. Physical pain, knowing that my own father could suggest something so cruel. And for what? What does he get out of it, accusing me like that?

Sick and twisted. I feel sick, and he is *so* twisted. All those years spent fantasizing about meeting him, wishing he loved me and that he'd tell me stories about my mother. Now it's all coming true, and—

It takes my shaking hands two tries to fit the key in the car door lock, and another three to jam the key into the ignition. The car screeches out in horror as I peel off down the street. Without thinking, I make a right and then a left and then veer onto a dead end and cut the engine.

Then I sit.

Shaking. Thinking. Weeping. Because I've lost something. Any hope or dream or possibility of having a relationship with my father is dead. Robert Newton is mentally ill. Vindictively, certifiable.

After a while, after I've caught my breath and my blood is no longer lava spilling through my veins, I turn the car back on and start driving. Toward home and the only two people who love and respect me and don't keep secrets from me.

Except . . .

At a red light, I think about my house. The staggering lack of photographs and the way Gran won't talk about her own daughter. Is it more than a car accident's worth of pain? Something more traumatic? More tragic? The light turns green, and I think about Robert and why he let them adopt me. What event could have been so catastrophic as to take him away?

There was a gun in the house.

You were only a baby.

You found it.

11

THE SKY IS LIQUID black and starry when I pull into the driveway. I sit there for a minute with the engine off, coiled around my own confusion. Through the window, I can see Gran at the kitchen sink—scouring pans, squinting out toward the driveway every few seconds. She notices my car and waves, smiling briefly before a dirty pan recaptures her attention. Her face settles back into its usual heavy meditation.

I have to tell them. I mean, it will kill them, but they need to know I've been secretly meeting with Robert, and that he just described the most unthinkable bullshit of all time. They need to tell me that my father is lying. He's a liar, and this is a sick joke.

Magic starts to bark as I walk up the path, and Gran meets me in the front hall, her mule slippers shuffling across the brick floor. She smiles as she dries her hands on a dishtowel.

"How was the sleepover? Pastor Thompson asked after

you—two weeks in a row now you've missed," she says, her sing-song tone masking the accusation. "I promised him you'd be back next Sunday."

"We need to talk. Where's Grandpa?"

She frowns. "Oh. Well, let's see. He's out in the shed, but it's nearly suppertime. Why don't you set the table and then—"

"No," I growl. We both flinch. "I need to talk to you guys right now. It can't wait. Will you get him and meet me in the living room?"

"Is something wrong?"

"No. I don't know. Can you please go get him?"

Gran opens her mouth again, but then forces it shut, annoyance flexing her nostrils. She crosses her arms over her cable-knit sweater, heading for the backyard where Grandpa is probably freezing his ass off, building a bird feeder in the shed.

I run down the hall to my bedroom. Magic trots along after me, all riled up, drunk on the scent of Leah's corgi on my clothes. It's hard to stay calm as I grab the envelope of photographs that's hidden in my bookshelf. Hard to walk into the living room without shaking. Hard not to see a toddler with a gun in her tiny hands.

I mean, I can't see it, but I can't *not* imagine it.

Finally, they come in from the backyard, and Gran scowls. "Sweetheart, what's going on? Did something happen at Leah's?"

I stand in front of the roaring fireplace, heat prickling my back. "You should probably sit."

Alarm flashes in Gran's eyes, but Grandpa urges her beside him on the couch.

"I need to tell you something. Don't be mad, but last week I got a letter in the mail. It was from Robert Newton."

I swear, Gran ages ten years in the span of a second. It takes Grandpa a little longer to remember the name, or at least its significance, but when he does, he glances at Gran. The two of them exchange one of those secret looks that says everything, just not to me.

"I didn't tell you because I knew it would make you mad, but he came to Santa Fe to see me. We've been meeting up, getting to know each other."

"Oh, Johanna, you *haven't*."

"He gave me a bunch of pictures too."

The envelope slides across the coffee table, but neither of them picks it up.

"They're pictures of Mom, and baby pictures of me. He said he wants to make up for lost time. But—" I take a deep breath. "He told me something else too."

"He's lying," Gran snaps.

Which is weird. Because I haven't said it yet.

"What do you mean?" I ask slowly. "Lying about what?"

Fear bleeds into the lines on her face. Grandpa's, too, only with him it's almost resignation, his whole body slackening in unavoidable defeat.

Holy shit. They *know* something.

The thought of it unleashes my heartbeat.

"I was going to tell you guys this completely ludicrous story that Robert said, that I was *sure* was a lie. But he wasn't lying, was he?"

Gran wrings her hands in her lap. "Sweetheart, listen to me. Nothing that man says is to be believed. He's no good and, quite frankly, he's dangerous. You owe him nothing. Absolutely nothing."

"But I haven't even told you yet. You don't even know what he said. He said I—"

"Stop!" Gran screams. And I mean, *scuh-reams*. "Jimmy, say something to her."

"Now, JoJo." Grandpa clears his throat. "You should know, that man's been in and out of prison, doing Lord knows what for over a decade. That sort of man can't be trusted."

"So, you're saying he lied."

Gran's eyes dart sideways. "Yes."

"Does it matter?" adds Grandpa evenly. "The past is past."

"You can't be serious!" I shriek. "Not when he told me I *shot* her."

Gran looks away to cover her mouth.

I shouldn't try her patience, but I stamp my foot anyway. "Well? Aren't you going to say anything?"

"Please, sweetheart." She rises desperately from the couch. "Try to understand—"

"Oh my God," I choke. "This can't be happening."

And then, everything goes into slow motion. The room adopts this lingering pulse; a gradual itch burns my chest. Now that I know it's true, I'm desperate to replay our conversation. Because I wasn't fully listening when I thought Robert had a mental illness. It was a heartless lie until it became the truth, and now it is *everything*.

"Johanna?" Gran whispers.

I look at her, uncontrollable tears spilling over my eyes. "I can't believe you knew and didn't tell me. How could you raise me after what I did?"

"Oh, sweetie." She steps closer and pulls me into a brusque hug. "Listen to me. You didn't do anything wrong. You were a child—a baby."

You were only a baby. There was a gun in the house.

I jerk away from her and she stumbles back, calves banging against the coffee table. I never act like this—all wild and unapologetic—and it shocks us both.

"I can't believe you've been lying to me my whole entire life."

"We were *protecting* you."

"By lying!" I cry. "No wonder you don't hang any pictures of her. I'm surprised you can bear the sight of *me* after I killed your daughter."

By now, I'm bawling, convulsing as I watch my speechless grandparents through sodden eyes. The two of them so frail and foreign. For one desperate second, I wish I could hit Undo and go back to living in ignorance. Or, at least, letting them think I was ignorant. I mean, how are we supposed to face one another after this? After I've shattered the lie they worked so hard to build for all these years.

"We never meant for you to find out," Grandpa says.

I can't bear to look at them. Can't bear to be in this decrepit, airless house, suffering this bullshit conversation.

"I have to get out of here."

"No," Gran begs. "You're too upset. Let's sit and have some supper."

"Supper? Are you kidding me right now? I just found out I'm responsible for my mother's death and you think I want pot roast?"

"Then get some rest," she pleads. "Everything will seem clearer in the morning."

"Nothing will seem clear ever again!" I scream. My voice scratches against my throat, clawing the walls around us. "You lied and let me think I was normal. All this time, I thought— but, God, what an *idiot*! I'm sorry but, *no*. I will *not* forgive you for this, ever."

"Jimmy, stop her!" Gran begs.

He doesn't answer.

As I stalk out of the room, I listen for his footsteps, but Grandpa isn't taking her orders this time. He and I both know there is no stopping me.

• • •

I can't run fast enough. My lungs ache and burn inside my chest, but I push through it. I forget my coat, but it doesn't matter— my skin is on fire and might be forever. I round one more cor- ner, bending over to catch my breath. One hand clutching my heart, the other one wiping away snot with the sleeve of my shirt. Eventually, I look up, blinking in my surroundings. I've run in so many circles, down so many streets, I almost can't believe it when I realized where I've ended up.

Or, I don't know, maybe I can.

Milo's truck sits parked outside his house, and I stumble over to it, hoisting my body into the frosty flatbed rather than knocking on his front door, afraid his mom might answer. Bursts of warm air billow out of me with each jagged sob.

There was a gun in the house. You found it.

I try to imagine myself there, despite having no memory of our home or what I would have been like back then. Blond pigtails, chubby cheeks, a pacifier in my mouth?

You shot her.

Had I been looking for a toy when I found Robert's gun? Did my mother try to stop me?

It was an accident. You were only a baby.

With my eyes shut, I try to picture a real gun, what it would feel like in the hands of a two-year-old. How the thunderous boom must've deafened me.

You're a killer. You picked up a loaded gun and shot your own mother. You're horrible and sinful, and you don't deserve to be alive.

Gunshots ring out in my head, only they don't sound real. Are crime show sound effects real? Or do they sound as fake as TV punches and barroom brawls? I imagine myself crying afterward. Was there a lot of blood? Did my mother see me pull the trigger? Did she die instantly or suffer while I sucked my thumb?

"Jo? What are you doing out here?"

My hot, saturated eyes flutter open. I shake my head, sobbing harder.

Milo jumps up beside me. "What is it? What happened?"

I shake my head again, wiping slippery tears from my cheeks.

"Come inside," he begs.

"No." My voice is hoarse, full of snot and grief and grit.

"You're shivering."

"I don't care."

"What happened?" he says again, warm hands clasping my frozen ones.

I open my mouth, but how do I *say* it? Only tears come tumbling out of me, my heart hammering like an egg being scrambled. Like I can't control anything about myself.

"Hey, hey, hey." He squeezes my hands tighter. "Seriously, let's go inside."

Still I refuse, heaving and convulsing so hard, I wonder if a rib might crack.

There was a gun in the house.

Milo says something else, but I can't hear him or don't try to.

Your grandparents took you away from me. I was arrested. They filed for custody.

A crumpled tissue appears in front of my face and I take it, grateful to clear my head of a thousand pounds of slime.

"Wait here," Milo says.

He hops onto the sidewalk and runs off, reappearing twenty seconds later with a soft, plaid blanket and a whole box of tissues. With a magician's flair, he shakes the blanket out wide and drapes it over my shoulders. I lift my butt, grateful to have something separating me from the ice-cold truck. The warmth relaxes my muscles and eases my tears. Milo kneels beside me, rubbing my shoulders. Wordlessly, I scoot closer, extending one side of the blanket for him.

"Thanks," he says and pulls it tight around us both.

There is nothing romantic about it. The state of my face and my torn-up soul offer nothing to flirt with, but I'm grateful for the extra warmth. For a long time we stay silent, wind whistling gently around us. Every so often, Milo hands me a fresh tissue. A mountain of crumpled white cotton forms at our feet.

"Is it your dad?" he asks after a few minutes.

I hesitate, then nod.

"Shit," he says.

The blanket slides off my shoulder, and he reaches across to gently pull it up. Our eyes connect. The rest of the world stops. It's still so new—Milo and me. I don't want to scare him, but the thought of keeping this bottled up inside me for another second scares me even more. I can't do it. I can't keep this in.

I look into Milo's soft, blue-gray eyes. "Can I tell you something?"

"Of course," he whispers.

"It's something bad. Something really, *really*—"

His lips brush lightly against mine, enough to reassure me. When he pulls away, I tell him everything.

12

WAKING UP ON MONDAY morning is like waking up in a coffin. A dull sandpaper pain coats my skin, but rather than get out of bed to shower or hide behind my sewing machine, I let it soak deeper into my bones. I hold my breath, so I can keep it still within me. I deserve this feeling. Deserve to burn alive in it.

I roll onto my side and picture Robert's stricken face, tasked with telling his own daughter that she shot someone—not just her mother, but his first love. And my dishonest, heartbroken grandparents. I didn't just kill their daughter, I ruined their beautiful fiction too. It's easier to think about Milo. The way he held me and kept me warm for hours. Listened to me cry, shake, shatter. He told me it wasn't my fault, but it was.

Will God have mercy on my soul? Do I deserve His forgiveness? I can hear Pastor Thompson now: *Jesus Christ died for your sins—well, you weren't fucking around with* that *sin, were you, Johanna?* Well. Maybe not quite like that.

My bedroom door creaks open, and I freeze under the covers, afraid to hear my grandmother's voice and too-late apology. The door clicks shut. Two gentle sets of feet tiptoe across the room, mango body mist and Daisy perfume wafting in with them. Leah curls up on one side of me, Gabby on the other. Sweaters warm, skin cold. My trusty Rottweilers don't say anything. Don't need to, after the fifty thousand texts we exchanged till 2 a.m. The way I explained the unexplainable to them. The way they lied and told me everything would be all right. Even though I know it won't.

"Did you sleep?" Leah whispers.

I shake my head and swallow uneasily, my heart blaring in my ears. There's something disquieting about this, despite the spooning and the bear hugs. Yesterday, I knew myself around them—the blend of fibers that made the fabric of *us*. But can we still be that connected? Or are they as horrified by me as I am of myself?

"What are you thinking about?" Gabby asks.

"Milo," I say quickly. "Do you guys think I ruined things with him?"

Leah shakes her head. "No way. He's really into you."

"I can't believe I poured my guts out like that."

"He's your boyfriend," Gabby says. "It's his job."

"Yeah, well, he didn't know I was a cold-blooded killer when he asked me out."

"You're not a cold-blooded—" Leah shivers and squeezes me tighter. "Don't say that."

I stiffen. "Sorry."

"It's okay. But please don't say stuff like that."

Stuff like the truth, she means.

They cradle me for a while longer. Butterfly kissing my cheeks as I manage one jagged breath after another. The smell of bacon permeates the house, reminding me I haven't eaten since yesterday morning. Leah drags my ass to the shower where I brush the grit off my skin, the moss from my teeth. Gabby helps me into a short black pinafore and wool tights. We don't bother with my Mo' Tizzy sweater or any other style-hiding garb because, why should I? My grandparents have been lying to me my whole life. From now on, I'll wear my damn clothes without worrying about their precious Christian sensibilities.

"Mornin', girls," Gran says, layering greasy bacon onto a dry paper towel. "Bacon's ready. I made it crispy, just how you like it!"

The three of us stop dead in our tracks in the kitchen doorway. I glance at Gabby, her mystified shock-horror confirming my own. Because, *como que what?* Is Gran seriously acting like nothing happened? Standing there in her American-flag robe, shoulders hunched, making breakfast and pouring coffee, same as always. The only out-of-the-ordinary thing is how she doesn't comment on my dress being too short or urge me to change. She barely looks at me twice, actually. Just smiles and turns back to the stove, swirling metal tongs in a cast-iron bed of sizzling fat.

"There's time for eggs too," she says. "How do y'all want 'em?"

"Um. Morning, Mrs. Carlson," Leah says tentatively. She laces her fingers through mine and squeezes, eyes darting from the kitchen to the front hall, waiting for the go-ahead to bolt, if necessary.

It takes a second for me to steady myself, queasy from the mound of bacon heaped high on white porcelain. *Mandy was a vegetarian*, Robert told me. *She loved animals.* The words crunch inside me, forming images of my mother, cradling piglets, milking cows, serenading the birds on her window ledge.

"We're not staying for breakfast," I tell her, resolute and repulsed by each sweating slab of maroon pork.

"Sorry, Mrs. Carlson," Gabby adds. "No time."

"Wait." Gran scurries around the counter. "Don't forget your lunch."

She holds up a brown paper bag, smudged with grease. I bet there's a leftover pot roast sandwich inside with Gran's famous caramelized onions. The Sunday roast I walked out on last night when my grandparents had the nerve to tell me they'd hidden the past for my own good. I give the bag one look and my jaw tightens.

"I don't want it," I say, and let the front door slam on my way out.

• • •

Milo's leaning against his silver pickup when we get to school, blowing air into his cupped hands and fidgeting in tight black

jeans and a wool coat. When he notices Gabby's jeep, he seems
to perk up, pushing himself off and walking toward us.

"Dude, he's making a beeline!" Leah shrieks.

"See?" Gabby says. "Told you."

Automatically, I check my makeup—which barely matters,
my under-eyes are gluttonous, gray worms. "God, I look like
ass."

Gabby grabs her bag and starts to unbuckle her seat belt, but
Leah reaches over the driver's seat, pinning her in a headlock.
"Do *not* get out of this car, Gabriella Celeste Sinclair. Jo,
skedaddle. Me and Gabs are . . . flossing. Or having a fight.
Whatever. It doesn't matter."

"Seriously?" Gabby groans, extricating her throat from the
crook of Leah's arm. "Okay, *fine*. But only because it's Jo."

"Thanks." I flash a nervous smile and slide out of the car.

Milo's standing a couple feet away. "Hey," he says, voice so
gentle it's practically on crutches. "How are you?"

"Look, about last night," I say. "I'm really sorry."

"Are you *kidding* me?"

Before I can answer, I scan the half-full parking lot. My
adrenaline boomerangs. People are staring at me—Lucy Bingham, Alice, Oola. *Are* they staring? Or, shit, maybe they're not?
The Kenworth twins walk past, and Iris (the blond-highlights
one) gives me a *look*. I swear, it sends my heart down to my
toenails.

She knows what you did. Milo told her. You're ruined, you're—

"Hey, Jo. Hi, Milo," she says, eyes big as hard-boiled eggs.

"Hey, Iris," I mumble back.

Selene—the edgy twin with the piercings—flashes a border-line lustful grin and gives me the least subtle thumbs-up I've literally ever seen in my life. Then, the two of them scamper up the hill toward the coffee cart. My shoulders drop two full inches. This isn't about my mother, it's about me and the hot new transfer student.

My secret is safe.

I glance at Milo again, and he ducks his head, shoving his hands deep into his pockets. "I wasn't sure you'd show up today."

I shrug. "Me neither."

"How are you, y'know, feeling?"

"Like dog shit smeared on the sidewalk."

"Nice."

"You asked."

A few more kids walk past us, and I have to swallow twice to stop the swampy feeling from bubbling all the way up. *They're not looking at you. They don't know. No one ever has to know what you did.*

"Didn't feel like cashing in a sick day?" he asks. "I'm sure your grandparents would have understood."

"Oh, you mean the backstabbing assholes who lied to me my whole life?" I exhale furiously and lower my voice. "Gran basically pretended like nothing happened. This morning was bacon and business as usual."

"Seriously?"

"Yeah."

"Damn."

Silence creeps up, sucking us in. To fill the void, we walk

across the brittle, wintry grass toward first period, and it's so awkward that my heart starts puttering inside my chest, assuming the worst.

Milo clears his throat. "I'm not sure what to say."

Which is almost a relief.

"It's okay," I say carefully. "Neither am I. In fact, I totally understand if you don't want to see me again. No hard feelings. It was fun, but I'm kind of damaged goods."

Not even a nanosecond passes, and Milo shakes his head, curling his fingers around mine. He raises them to his lips and kisses the back of my hand.

"Not damaged," he whispers. "Just good."

13

ALL WEEK LONG, THE American flag on our front lawn flaps angrily in the wind. Weird how I never used to notice it up there—this huge, durable ad for our patriotism. I wonder if my grandparents owned that flag before or after I shot and killed their daughter. Whether displaying it was a way of buoying their patriotism in a world that no longer made sense.

Or, I don't know. Maybe they just like the colors.

This is the kind of shit I'm thinking about as I drive home from school on Wednesday. Grandpa's Subaru isn't parked in the garage when I get home, and I remember something about a trip to Albuquerque for a post-op hip replacement thing.

Instead of going inside, I hook Magic to his leash and lead him down the street, past Mrs. Strumor's house, past the Zelaznys' and the Greggs'. I look at their homes, so similar to mine—simple stucco frames, not tiny but nothing grand. Same vigas and red brick floors, but what about the decor? The details that make our houses *ours*. Magic drags me farther, sniffing bushes and marking his territory, and I think about the tops of closets. Inside cupboards and underneath beds. Safes and locked drawers. Do any of my neighbors own guns? Multiple guns? Stashed away or on display. Firearms have become such a part of our culture. I've almost grown numb to them, only thinking of guns in the abstract—until now. Now I can practically feel them pulsing around me. The cold click of metal, a stale potpourri of smoke.

"Johanna!"

My head drops out of the clouds and back onto my shoulders at the sound of a familiar, buoyant voice. Across the street I see Mrs. Vargas in her driveway, leaning into the trunk of her car for a bag of groceries. The Vargas family has lived on this street since before us. Super friendly, cup-of-sugar people. Their son, Steve, goes to Chavez, but he's only a freshman. We used to hang out when we were kids, playing the-floor-is-lava and eating Mrs. Vargas's amazing chocolate-chip cookies.

The last thing I want is to talk to her, but I smile and cross the street. "Hi, Mrs. Vargas. Need a hand?"

"No, sweetie, that's all right. How's your semester going?"

"Fine, thanks."

"Oh, good."

Mrs. Vargas has a plump, babyish face. A preschool teacher's face, which is exactly what she is. Kind and patient. I picture the floral sofa in their living room and imagine a semiautomatic wedged between the cushions. A rifle in the broom closet. I wonder what she'd do if she knew about me.

"I wanted to ask you—" She hoists the bag up on her hip. "Did you ever have Ms. Hondo for Latin? Steve says she's real tough."

I nod, tightening my ponytail and swallowing the urge to blurt out that I killed my own mother. That my father did time for it. "Ms. Hondo is the best. I loved her class, but she's definitely a fan of pop quizzes."

Mrs. Vargas shakes her head. "That's exactly what Steve says. He's never been much good at tests."

"Tell him to memorize the vocab every other Thursday. Friday pop quizzes are kind of her jam."

"Oh, that's good to know! Thanks, sweetie."

"Sure," I say. And I don't add that I aimed a .22 caliber handgun at my mother's chest. What even *is* a .22? A style? A size? Is it smaller than a .38, a rifle, an Uzi? I force a smile. "Have a good evening, Mrs. Vargas."

"You too, hon. Say hi to your grandparents."

"Sure thing."

Back in the house, I tiptoe down the hall. Not that it matters. Not that my double-crossing grandparents are even home. The house just makes me feel that way sometimes, like I need to be on my best behavior. Not leave scuff marks. I change into sweats and open my laptop because Mr. Gonzales assigned us an essay on *The Great Gatsby*. Not that I feel much like delving into the failed American Dream. I don't even want to get out my sewing machine to create some kind of fabulous, roaring twenties' ensemble à la Daisy Buchanan. Everything just seems so trivial now.

But Google beckons, glowing from my laptop screen, all blank and inviting. I sink onto my desk chair and ball up my fists before splaying my fingers, typing each letter like I'm picking up individual grains of rice. *A-m-a-n-d-a C-a-r-l-s-o-n.* Why have I never searched this before? When I was a kid, I guess I assumed proof of her car accident wouldn't still be there. Or, I don't know. Maybe I never wanted to make my nightmares worse by reading about it.

Maybe I still don't.

Before I can press Enter, brakes slam in my brain and the fear wins out. Which sucks because I thought I could do this. I slap my laptop shut and hide its smirking aluminum shell in a desk drawer as my heart shivers inside my chest. Seriously, though. How did I manage to fire a gun, and yet I can't carry out a basic internet search? Pathetic.

Hating myself a little, I slink away from my desk and walk into the kitchen, not expecting to see my grandparents unpacking a hundred grocery bags from Trader Joe's.

Gran looks up, pulling out a few boxes of Grandpa's favorite organic crackers. "Oh, you're home. Good. Pizza dough was on sale, so I bought fresh mozzarella and tomato sauce and some of those olives you like as a topping. How was your day?"

"What?" I look around. Like, for a hidden camera or something. "You're not seriously talking about pizza, are you?"

Gran stammers, jaw loose.

"Come on, Gran. The jig is up. You can stop pretending."

Grandpa's knuckles bear down on the counter. "'Scuse you, young lady. Now, I know you're feeling confused, but—"

"I'm not confused," I shriek. "I'm a *murderer*! You want to know how my day was? It was horrible. Tomorrow will be horrible. The rest of my life is going to be horrible, and you don't even care. My dad is the only one who had the decency to—"

"Enough!" Gran slams a bag of carrots so hard on the counter that one comes rolling out, escaping onto the floor. "That man is a criminal! What happened to Amanda was *his* fault, and he never should have burdened you with this. He's a selfish fool and always was. And I'll have none of this my-life's-over nonsense. Grandpa and I chose not to tell you. We made a decision, and we stand by it. The last thing your mother would have wanted was for you to lose sight of your future. Johanna, you have simply *got* to forget everything that man told you."

"You want me to *forget*?"

"It's for your own good."

I cross my arms, too stunned to respond. Does she honestly think people can do that? Forget crucial elements of their lives? Forgetting this would require major surgery. Severed limbs.

The last thing your mother would have wanted.

Looking at Gran now, I realize that's what it comes down to. *My mother.* What their darling Amanda would have wanted. I glare down at our red brick floor, the herringbone weave giving me vertigo. What *would* my mother have wanted for me, back when she'd had wants and needs? A healthy daughter, a happy one? Someone with a 4.0 GPA? The fact that I'll never know absolutely devastates me.

"Well?" Gran says sharply.

For a second, I can't remember the original question. Her

orders, I mean. A demand that I lobotomize everything Robert-related. I stare back and forth at the two of them, so saintly in their expectations when they should be downright groveling. Anger gurgles in the pit of my stomach, but at the same time, a kind of connection is born—imagining my mother standing across from her parents, pitted against them, knowing they would never understand her.

Rather than answer, I spin on my heels, heading for the front hall.

"Where exactly do you think you're going?" Grandpa calls after me.

"Magic needs to be walked."

I mean, he doesn't, but they don't know that.

Gran follows. "I didn't hear an answer, young lady. I forbid you to see him again. Do you hear?"

I hear. Like a fucking bullhorn, I hear the sharp desperation in her voice. And I know what she wants me to say. Telling her yes might be a lie, but haven't I been lied to for thirteen years? Is the truth all that sacred?

I hold my head up high and smile, the way she raised me to. "Sure, Gran. *I. Promise.*"

14

WHICH, OF COURSE, IS a lie.

It takes a few days to work up to it, but when I finally show up on Robert's doorstep after school—unannounced, unexpected—the guy nearly keels over before inviting me in.

"I should have called first."

"No, it's great. This is great." He pulls out a Bluetooth earbud, cradling his laptop in one arm as he glances down at his outfit—a crisp white button-down shirt, blue striped tie . . . and plaid pajama bottoms. He offers a sheepish smile. "Work-from-home attire. In video conferences, they can only see me from the chest up."

"This is bad timing," I say. "You're busy."

"I'm not. Honestly."

He heads down the hall, motioning for me to follow. We stop in a small, white-tiled kitchen, and he opens his laptop on the veined marble island. "Give me two minutes to wrap things up. Flip the switch on that kettle over there, will you?"

I follow his gaze and head toward a row of shiny new appliances, adding water to the stainless kettle before turning it on. Robert's fingers plonk heavily against his keyboard. Am I supposed to stand here? Sit down? Instead, I gravitate toward the fridge, mesmerized by its crayon drawings and family snapshots. An angelic boy and girl beside grinning parents and proud grandparents. *We luv u, Baba + Papa!* one card reads, almost illegibly. This must be Baba and Papa's house. Cozy and small, perfect for snowbirds.

"Sorry about that."

I spin around. Robert has put two mugs on the counter, his computer shut. "You like chamomile?"

"Sure."

We steep our teabags for an agonizing minute, pretending it's rocket science, then head into the living room, taking the same seats as last time.

"How's it going?"

"Fine," I say too quickly.

"School's good?"

"It's great."

"That's good, that's good."

"So, you're still doing the working remotely thing?"

"Yeah, for now."

"Cool."

Seconds, minutes, years pass.

His cheeks hike up as he smiles, and I touch my face, fingers subtly gliding along my chin, wondering if we share the same jawline.

Robert clears his throat. "Have you managed to, uh, process any of this?"

"What? Oh. Not really," I say. "Not even close."

"Yeah. I mean, what I told you was—" He pauses, fingers like fire working out from beside his temples, an explosion sound gurgling through his lips. "But you believe me now, right?"

I nod and try to breathe evenly. Which is harder than it sounds.

Out the window, thick, white snowflakes flutter to the ground like torn paper. Maybe if it snows enough, I can bury myself alive in it. Die of frostbite or hara-kiri by icicle.

"I never wanted to tell you that way," he goes on. "I'm kinda pissed Kate and Jimmy made me, actually. Not exactly the job I wanted."

"I know. My grandparents royally suck."

Robert shrugs. "It's okay."

It's not *that* okay, though, because my heart is still racing. I get up the guts to clear my throat. "You know, there's a lot more stuff you haven't talked about. Like, years unaccounted for."

"It's not that easy to explain."

"Like explaining what I did to my mother *was*?"

"No. I mean, of course not." He sets his tea down, fingers running through his hair as he exhales. "And you deserve to know."

I deserve to know, and yet he still won't talk. The silence makes me think of marshmallows in the microwave, the way Leah and Gabby and I used to cook them as kids. How the marshmallows would bloat and expand, powder crackling on the outside while the inside grew hotter and messier.

"You know I spent time in prison," he says after a minute, voice faded, thick with shame. "It was my gun, and California laws are tough. But, the truth is, I lost it in there. Some people are built for it, but I couldn't see straight after a week. I panicked. I just panicked. And the kind of shit I got into to make it easier . . ."

"What do you mean?" I ask, then quickly flush when it dawns on me. "Drugs?"

All of Robert's features seem to slide down his face as he nods, eyes watery and unfocused. "It was the only way I could survive losing the two of you. Getting high let me off the hook, y'know? The guilt kind of floated away. I never stopped thinking about you, but it was like you turned into a dream. This peaceful fantasy of the three of us. I thought I was doing myself a favor. I thought I'd be able to quit when I got out, but it wasn't like that. I couldn't find work on the outside, couldn't stop using. I was a wreck—in *no* shape to look for you. I'm telling you, you wouldn't have wanted to know me."

His eyes squeeze tight with regret. I don't think I've ever felt more awkward. Utterly and completely lost for words. Are there the right ones out there, to apologize for firing the gun that turned someone into an addict?

I bite my lip. "So, all this time you've been . . ."

"No," he says, chin rising defensively. "It hasn't been easy, but I've taken a really active role in my recovery—rehab, therapy, meetings. Thank God for the church, and my pastor. It's a continuous battle, but it's working. It's how I found you."

He found me.

My insides beam. It's dizzying, almost, the way it feels to be wanted. I tuck my legs up, clinging to this buoyant feeling. Not wanting to talk about darkness anymore.

"Hey, could you maybe tell me some stories?"

Robert raises an eyebrow. "Like what?"

"Like, happy, sparkly Mandy memories. Might be kind of nice right now. If you can think of anything."

"Really?" The doom on his face cracks open, clouds parting into a smile. "I mean, of course. I've got lots of happy memories. In fact—oh, you're going to love this."

He grabs his clunky black laptop, grinning as he pulls up a file and hands me the computer. A video comes to life, a chubby, toothless version of me. I'm sitting in a plastic high chair in a ruffled, pink dress, my hair basically nonexistent. All I do is grin and clap. Gran and Grandpa are there too, looking a million years younger, but I swear to God, wearing the same horrible clothes. They sing "Happy Birthday" along with Robert, his voice rich and booming from behind the camera.

Then she appears. Graceful, poised, beautiful. Belted denim dress, hair long and wavy. She's holding a pink-frosted cake, gliding toward me as she sings. Her voice is karaoke bad, but her smile makes up for it. She places the cake in front of me, and all four of them help blow out the multicolored *1* candle because I'm too busy putting my entire fist in my mouth. Mom can't stop giggling. Even when she dabs icing onto my nose and I cry, she only laughs harder.

"She loved you so much."

"You *have* to say that."

"Come on, look at her!" He pauses the video on Mom's smiling face. "You were it for her. Her soul mate."

The freeze-frame dizzies me, but I see it. Fifteen years later and locked inside Robert's computer, her love for me glistens. I have to put the computer on the coffee table, unsettled by the yo-yo throb of my heart. This is my first time hearing her voice, and it's hypnotizing. Sweet and light as cotton candy. But in a cooler flavor, like dragon fruit.

"Hey, are you okay?"

I force an exhale, releasing this freezer-burn feeling in my chest. "I can't believe that was really her, y'know?"

Robert's lips flatten into a commiserative grin. He gets it. Gets me. The two of us linger on our thoughts for a while, sharing a moment of silence.

I'm not sure how long it should last, but then Robert—low and thoughtful and staring at the ceiling—just starts talking. About the girl who whistled while she washed dishes and got frustrated changing pillowcases. Who loved nineties dance music and fireflies. Funny Mandy, full of wit and one-liners. A good mother, willing to stay up all night and sing to her colicky baby. Superstitious. Fashion-forward. Environmentally conscious. Each story leads to another, and Robert drifts further away from me. From this house, this world. I wonder how often he thinks about her. If it's only me requesting these memories, or if they keep him warm at night too.

The more he says, the harder my nails dig into my palms. It's like she never did anything shitty or dumb or wrong, and all I keep thinking is that I killed a golden unicorn. Because of me, they buried someone who helped old ladies cross the street and volunteered with the ASPCA. A believer of the good in people, defender of the underdog. Someone who could have made a difference. And she never got the chance.

Because of me.

A lull washes over us. Outside, the snow has stopped, leaving a heavy blanket of powder on the piñon branches.

Robert sighs. "There's something else. I feel like I should explain about the gun."

My heart stops. "Oh."

"After you were born, we were hurting for money. Doctor bills, regular bills." He pauses, psyching himself up maybe. "So, I started dealing weed. I swear, I wasn't some kind of drug lord. It was easy money."

"Okay," I say, squirming a little.

"Mandy didn't like having strangers come over to buy weed when there was a baby in the house. My customers were rich college kids, and it wasn't like any of them were going to kidnap you or have some wild trip in the middle of our living room, but it upset Mandy. She wanted to make sure you were protected. That *we* were safe, as a family. So, I bought a gun. *The* gun. She didn't know I did it, but I did.

"Usually, I kept it in the closet, but Mandy found it this one

time, and we fought. She hated knowing it was right there—
that's why I moved it under the bed. Temporarily, so she
wouldn't keep nagging me. I remember, I just shoved it between
some shoe boxes, on my way to work one morning. God, I wish
I could take it back. I was going to move it. *I swear to God*, I was
going to hide it better."

By now, Robert is full-on weeping. Head hung in shame,
barely able to make eye contact. It shreds my heart. So much so
that I reach for his hand.

"Are you okay?" I ask softly.

"I'm supposed to ask you that," he says, forcing a smile. "Are
you okay?"

"Not at all."

"Yeah. Same."

After about a minute's worth of nose-blowing and eye-
dabbing, Robert grabs his computer again, opening one of
those nerdy, computer-expert terminals. I watch him pound the
keys for a few seconds, wondering what he's got in store for me.

"Here," he says, handing me the computer.

"What is this?" I stare at the terminal window on the screen,
no clue what to do next.

Robert smiles a little-boy smile and tells me to press the *S*
and *L* keys. I give him a weird look and tap *S* and *L*, waiting for
a genie to pop out of the screen. Only, it isn't a genie. A little
green choo-choo train, made up of semicolons and quotation
marks, comes chug-chug-chugging along. I giggle, brow furrowed as I look back up at him.

"It's a silly little program I installed when you were about one and a half," he says. "You wanted to play it all the time. You'd run up to me and say, 'Dada, choo-choo!' Snorting with laughter every time the train came across the screen. I know you're too old for it now, but—"

"Can I do it again?"

Robert smiles. "Of course you can. As many times as you want."

15

BACK WHEN GABBY AND Leah and I were in the third grade, we started this club called the Teddy Bear Club. Officially, the TBC was like a fashion club for our stuffed animals. We'd make them these awful little caveman outfits. Actually, Gabby and Leah got bored pretty quick, while I created these over-the-top evening gowns and ruffled skirts and stuff. Mostly, though, the TBC was a chance for us to gorge on junk food and pour our hearts out to one another. None of us had mentioned the Teddy Bear Club in years, but it is exactly what I need on Friday night. The girls are going to do some digging with me, since I was afraid to do it on my own, and since talking to Robert about it got a little intense.

"A *little* intense?" Gabby smirks, leading us into her bedroom after mediocre lasagna with her parents. Her mom's no Michelin-star chef, but dinner at Gabby's is always a million times better than at my house. The way Devon describes sailing the high seas; how Kendra sings while she cooks. They're such free spirits, which, of course, Gabby can't stand. I mean, she obviously loves them, but it's like her tenacious ambition is her way of rebelling. My rebellion usually involves a backstitch.

"Okay, talking to Robert got a *lot* intense," I amend.

"I can't believe your dad was a drug addict. That is *so* hard-core," Leah says. "I mean, for him to just tell you like that— did it make you feel *horrible*?"

"Uh, yeah, Leah. It did. Thanks for the reminder."

Her face sags and congeals.

"It's okay," I say. "You didn't mean anything."

"Well, maybe she should have," Gabby mutters. "I'm sorry, Jo, but he shattered your world and keeps dropping exploding kittens on you. It pisses me off. I should never have let you meet him."

"Oh, like you were going to stop me? You may be bossy as fuck, but you're not the *actual* fucking boss of me."

She huffs, turning to face her computer. "Are we doing this or what?"

"Are you sure you want to?" I ask. "Because—"

"We want to."

"You don't *have* to," I finish quickly.

I can't help it. I need them to know it's optional, but my trusty Rottweilers seem eager as they lure me toward Gabby's desk. We move a stack of law textbooks onto the floor to make room for our butts to sit down.

Gabby cracks her knuckles one by one before opening a new

window. "Let the Teddy-Bear-Club-Shooting-Research-Crossover-Sleepover commence."

"We're not actually calling it that, right?"

"No," Leah promises and reaches over to hit mute on the stereo. Thank God, too, because Justin Bieber is *not* about to play the soundtrack to my criminal unveiling.

"So, it happened in Fresno?" Gabby asks, game face on as her fingers fly across the keyboard. "I'm also going to include words like *toddler, mother, shooting, shot, gun, fatal, fatality*—that's the kind of shit it says in articles like this."

"How do you even *know* that?" Leah marvels, but I'm too busy thinking about *articles like this*. Because children accidentally shooting their parents is a classification. A fucking subgenre.

I hug my arms around my waist to keep my insides from gurgling over. Gabby swats Enter like it's a mosquito, and within seconds, there it is: "Fresno Toddler Fatally Shoots Mother." All this time, her story has been sitting there, waiting for me.

"Are we reading it to ourselves, or . . . ?"

I shake my head. "You do it."

Gabby swallows. Her eyes focus on the screen, and she adopts this decisive newscaster voice. "On Saturday afternoon, a local woman was accidentally shot and killed by her two-and-a-half-year-old daughter, police said. The victim has been identified as twenty-five-year-old Amanda Carlson of Fresno. The sheriff's department announced that the victim was reportedly at home sleeping when the incident took place. The toddler is thought to have woken up from a nap, at which point she found a loaded .22 caliber handgun under the bed and fired a single bullet that struck Carlson in the chest. Police arrived on the scene shortly after a 9-1-1 call placed by a neighbor who heard the gunshot. Carlson was pronounced dead at the scene. Although the fatality was clearly a tragic accident, Fresno police brought the victim's boyfriend, Robert Newton, in for questioning. Newton, also the toddler's father, is the owner of the gun. Authorities said Newton came in voluntarily for questioning but were unable to confirm whether he will be charged for leaving his gun out where the child allegedly picked it up and fired it.

"The victim's neighbor told reporters that Carlson was a beautiful, kind, and devoted mother. 'It's a complete shock. We're all going to miss her so much.'

"The toddler, found crying at the scene and asking for Mommy, has been placed with relatives who declined to comment on the tragic accident."

There's a ringing in my ears when the article ends. Every inch of me spins, sharp and fierce.

The toddler woke up from a nap. Had we been asleep together, big and little spoons in my parents' bed? Blankets over us, picture books at our feet?

The toddler woke up and found . . . and found—

It suddenly occurs to me that I've been clinging to some tiny shred of hope, but there is none. I *was* strong enough to pull the trigger. I *did* aim a gun at her heart. I did it.

"Jesus, how awful," Leah murmurs, her face gently tear-streaked.

They look at me, but I can't bring myself to look back. The two of them with their perfect families—kooky as hell, but still whole and wholesome. Raised by devoted, understanding parents, not abandoned by a junkie dad and forced upon a couple of lying geriatrics.

I pinch the bridge of my nose, squeezing as hard as I can, because I just *can't*, right now. Rather than compare myself to them for the billionth time, I need to focus on *this*. Despite what they both must think of me. Despite what I think of myself.

"Read another one," I demand.

Gabby hesitates.

"The *Fresno Bee* article," I say, pointing at the screen. "Read it."

She clicks it open, but I'm only half-listening, too busy torturing myself. Wondering if my mother woke up before I killed her. If our eyes met. If she begged for her life as I pulled the trigger.

A vision of her flashes neon in my mind. Lifeless, in a sea of red. Skin turning pale. The urge to puke comes on so fast, I nearly don't make it to the bathroom in time. Leah falls off her chair when I push past, my hands clasped tight around my mouth. The door to Gabby's private bathroom slams shut, lasagna erupting out of me as I reach the toilet.

"Sweetie? Are you okay?"

"Give me a *minute*," I bark through the mess.

A few more heaves and splats, and there's nothing left. I stumble to the sink, splashing ice-cold water against my cheeks. Over and over again. Somewhere inside me, I imagine the faint hum of a lullaby, but I can't tell if it's her, if the song is for me. I look back at my dripping-wet reflection. A killer with no memory of it. Without thinking, I slap my face, hard. It stings, but it feels right. What I deserve.

"Jo, come on. You've been in there forever."

"One more second."

I blot my face with a towel and let the door creak open into Gabby's bedroom. The two of them have formed a human shield of best friends staring back at me. Them versus me. It's not the first time I've felt different—because of my upbringing, my weird clothes—but the way they're looking at me now? Pity comes to mind, but something worse too. I swear to God, I see fear in their eyes.

"Jo, are you okay?"

"I should go."

"What?" Leah blocks me and I stumble, shoulders thudding against the wall. "What are you talking about? You can't leave."

I open my mouth and then force it shut.

"What?" Gabby comes closer. "What is it?"

"Nothing," I say. But they won't stop staring at me, hunting their prey. Finally, I throw my hands up. "Admit it. Now that there's proof, you don't want to be friends with me."

"What?" Leah gasps.

Gabby rolls her eyes. "You mean proof that you were a *baby* when your father put you through this?" She tucks her arm underneath mine, guiding me toward the bed. "Yeah, we're fully aware, and we're not going anywhere. Do you want water? Ginger ale?"

I shake my head. Anything that goes down could come back

up, and I don't want to risk barfing on Gabby's Pottery Barn duvet. This floral, girly-ass duvet. I've slept underneath it a thousand times, but it suddenly feels like steel wool on my skin. Being on this bed feels wrong, having friends feels wrong. Everything feels *wrong*.

"When you were in the bathroom, I did some digging," Gabby says delicately. "Do you want to hear the rest?"

Something dirt-covered twinges inside me. The idle giddiness in her voice. A new circus act to follow. I roll away from them, curling onto my side. "Sure, whatever."

"Maybe, like, an abridged version?" Leah suggests.

She tries to cuddle up beside me, but it only makes me think of the newspaper report. Big and little spoons before I wrapped my tiny hands around my father's gun. I make my body stiff and unwelcoming. Maybe it's rude, but so what? I'm doing her a favor, giving her an excuse to perch at the foot of the bed.

Gabby starts to skim, articles exploding like popcorn on her computer screen. "We know Robert was arrested. But did he tell you the charges?"

I stay silent, watching a streetlamp as it flickers outside.

"Criminal storage of a firearm in the first degree," she answers anyway. "Which basically means he fucked up big time leaving that gun out for you to find."

"How long did he, y'know, *do time*?" Leah asks, and I can't help noticing a salacious edge to her voice.

"It says he was sentenced to three years." Gabby shrugs. "Could have been less, though. He could've gotten out in two, maybe even one. It doesn't say."

"Long enough to become a crackhead," I mutter.

It was a joke. Well, it was vaguely supposed to be one, but I'm met with thorny silence. Both of them stare at me, clueless and flustered and achingly sad. Which only manages to double my shame. I'm not only a killer. I've lost my sense of humor too.

Leah shifts uncomfortably at my feet. "Three years," she says. "Jeez, that's—"

She starts nervous-rambling, breaking it down into how many months and weeks and days and how much prison food and how many license plates three years adds up to. My brain spins in another direction, though. Four coffee dates with a convicted felon. Chamomile tea in the home of a criminal, laughing at his jokes. But that isn't the worst part. Not really, not even *close*. Robert went to prison for something *I* did. Maybe it was his gun, but I pulled the trigger. It was my fault. It makes me want to throw up all over again, but I tie my guts in a knot and stare up at the glow-in-the-dark stars we stuck to Gabby's ceiling in fourth grade.

"Holy mother." Gabby's elbows bang on the desk as she leans closer to the screen. "Do you know how many kids shoot people every year? Or themselves? Shit, listen to this:

"A two-year-old in South Carolina shot and killed himself when he found a teal-colored Glock in his grandmother's purse.

"In Albuquerque, a three-year-old grabbed his mom's gun off a mini fridge and shot both his parents. They didn't die, but they got charged with child abuse.

"After a two-year-old accidentally killed himself, the dad reached for the same gun and killed himself too.

"When a five-year-old was looking for Easter candy, he found a gun and killed his seven-year-old brother.

"When a four-year-old and his dad were play wrestling, a gun the dad kept in his waistband went off, shooting both in the head and killing the boy."

A three-year-old, a seven-year-old, a toddler, a baby.

The stories blur together. Accidental deaths, rough and unstoppable. Now, when I squeeze my eyes shut, it isn't my mother's face I see, but all of ours. A dank, windowless room filled with tiny, terrified children, sobbing and devastated. Dead, or surrounded by death.

Did we know the gun was real?

Did it look like a toy?

Was it a hair trigger, or tough to pull?

Afterward, did we realize?

Did we feel guilty?

Are we guilty?

A shudder rolls through me, and Leah scoots closer, not taking no for an answer. "Sweetie, are you okay?"

When I don't answer, Gabby turns off her monitor.

Party's over.

Maybe that's not what they're thinking, but that's how it feels.

If I'd only listened to Gabby—simply followed her advice and ignored Robert's letter—they wouldn't have to be best friends with a freak show right now. *That*, I bet, they really *are* thinking.

I shrink away from them, hugging a pillow to my stomach. In the window's reflection, I can see Gabby mouthing something dramatically with her arms raised. Leah mimes in response, her body shifting beside me. For half a minute, the two of them bicker—because of me, about me, for me.

"I don't know!" I hear Gabby whisper.

My eyelids squeeze shut, and I wish I could disappear completely.

Then Leah says, "Hey," in this odd, scripted way. "Want to go watch TV?"

"Yeah," adds Gabby, equally plastic. "I have a ton of movies downloaded."

I manage a lifeless shrug. "Sure, sounds *great*."

They walk toward the door, stopping when I don't race over to join them.

"Jo?" Gabby says. "Aren't you coming?"

I struggle to swallow. "I'll meet you downstairs."

"Are you sure?"

"Don't wait for me. I'll catch up."

I can see Leah's lopsided smile reflected in the bedroom window. She wants to say more, but Gabby squeezes her hand and they slink out, pulling the door shut behind them. At once, I'm both relieved and livid—abandoned, even if by choice. I grab my phone and start typing.

Me: I finally read the article. Fresno toddler shoots mom . . .

After I hit Send, I jam a tissue against my moist eye sockets. The phone pings back almost immediately.

Robert: Are you okay?
Me: Not really.
Robert: Want me to call you?

I bite my thumbnail.

Robert: Are you alone?
Robert: You shouldn't be alone.
Me: I'm at Gabby's.
Robert: Okay, so I won't call?

I flip the phone around a few times against my stomach, then sigh.

Me: Not tonight. I'm kinda fragile. Pretty sure I'd just cry.

There's a pause, and I start to wonder if the concept of messy emotions scared him off. But then Robert sends a GIF of a young Leonardo DiCaprio, bawling his eyes out. An unexpected snort rumbles out of me.

Me: Are you making fun of me?
Robert: No!
Robert: Sorry. I was trying to commiserate. I thought teenagers loved GIFs.

I send a thinking-face emoji.

Robert: Am I trying too hard?

Keeping in theme, I reply with a GIF of Leo tilting his palm side to side.

Robert: You sure you don't want me to call?
Me: No. I just wanted you to know. Everything you said was true.

I stare out the window. Eyelids heavier than bricks, heart-beat slowing. My phone slips through my fingers as I let my eyes close, jostled open again by another text.

Robert: I think she was asleep.

That wakes me up. I grip the phone tighter, blinking away drowsiness.

Me: You do?
Robert: I really do.
Robert: At least, I really have to.
Me: It's all I can think about.
Robert: I know.

I like that—that he knows. In a way that no one else in my life possibly can.

Robert: You know it wasn't your fault, right?
Me: That's what people keep telling me.

Robert: People can be right.

Me: People can be a lot of things.

Me: Kids can be murderers.

Robert: Don't think like that. As your father, I forbid it.

A second later, he sends a GIF of Oprah scowling.

It gets a tiny smile out of me. Grateful for him to be trying so hard, after he tried so little. I pull the edge of the blanket over my shoulder, burrowing my head back against the pillows. The girls won't miss me. In fact, they deserve a break. A chance to talk behind my back. It's the least I can give them. I yawn again and send my favorite GIF of a baby panda falling asleep.

Robert: Good idea. Get some rest.

Robert: Good night, Joey.

I insert a sleeping-face emoji and delete it. I write Good night, Dad, and delete that too. Is he even waiting for a response? Has he already turned off his phone and gone back to watching TV? Maybe I'm the only one stressing. The thing is, I know what I want to write.

But what if he doesn't write: *I love you too?*

16

"THERE YOU ARE," GRAN huffs. She holds her Bible like an infant, close to her chest. "You said you'd leave Gabby's right after breakfast. Did you get stuck in traffic?"

"No, I—"

"Come on, then. Grandpa and I have been waiting for you."

She takes hold of my elbow, coaxing me away from the large picture windows at the back of the Baptist church. I've been lingering here for the past ten minutes, roasting in a room pumped hot enough to keep eighty-year-olds warm, watching a bird try to peck worms from the frozen-solid earth outside. I bite my thumbnail as Gran whisks me down the aisle. Past the Bennetts, snapping at their five unruly kids, past this chick I recognize from Santa Fe High with her perma-yawn and last night's crumbling mascara. The only people legit *happy* to be here are the oldies, all decked out in their pearls and pressed suits. For them, this is the best day of the week. For *me*, it's the one-week anniversary of my own personal Armageddon, and I can feel it on my skin like poison oak. Maybe church is where I deserve to be. Under God's watchful eye, getting fire-and-brimstoned in my itchy wool dress and Docs.

"Big crowd today," Gran whispers over her shoulder.

Her navy skirt whooshes against her pantyhose as she walks toward the front of the room. In the fourth row, Grandpa sits hunched and dozing, head bobbing up abruptly as Gran parks herself next to him.

"I found her in the back," she tells him. "Daydreaming."

"I was thinking," I mutter. "I'm allowed to *think*."

"There's my girl!" Grandpa leans around Gran and gives my kneecap a pinch. "You find a good parking spot? We got in right next to Pastor Thompson. Second best spot in the lot."

"Nice." I nearly smile but then clench my jaw, resuming my scowl. He lied to me too—he's just harder to hate. "I'm parked by the road."

He nods, not catching my mood shift or at least not challenging it.

After that, the keyboardist takes her seat, and Pastor Thompson, in a boxy, gray suit, makes his way up to the pulpit. He's morphed into a real dough boy in the past few years, but he's still young, still giddy to be sharing his love for the Lord. And camping. Nine out of ten sermons include anecdotes about having the patience to erect a tent or how to find God's bounty in a star-strewn sky.

"Well, good morning!" he calls out to us. "Y'all feel like worshiping the Lord with me today?"

Gentle nods and laughter spin out around the room. Babies cry, kids cough. The choir stands to sing the usual hymns. Pastor Thompson reads Psalm 3. We open our Bibles to Ephesians, which we've been studying since before Christmas—some weird bullshit about God and the Church being in love; how they're devoted like a married couple. I don't know. Chapter six is the last chapter, thank God, and Pastor Thompson brings the microphone to his thin lips as he reads the first few verses.

"'Children, obey your parents in the Lord, for this is right. Honor your father and mother—which is the first commandment with a promise—so that it may go well with you and that you may enjoy long life on earth. Fathers, do not exasperate your children; instead bring them up in the training and instruction of the Lord.'"

A bunch of people start amen-ing. Pastor T segues into a story about scolding his youngest son, Matt, for drawing on the walls with a Sharpie. It's a real #same moment for the moms in the room, but all I can think about is the verse. God's decree that we obey our parents. That if we could just manage to honor them, we might live long, happy lives.

Low down in my throat, a lump takes shape. I swallow, concentrating hard on Pastor Thompson. The guilt he felt for reprimanding Matt, how God entrusted him to raise his kids right, and it's up to both father and son to follow through. The story has a happy ending, full of understanding and recognition.

He pauses to grin at his cherubic little son, fidgeting in the first row. Three years old, feet dangling off the bench as he nestles close to his mommy. Three years old and capable of honoring his parents, not killing them.

Pastor Thompson paces, his volume increasing, mimicking the throb of my heart. My eyes unfocus, and his body becomes a metronome before the cross. Again, I think about Jesus. How He got his money's worth, dying for my sins.

We sing "Christ Is All I Need," and my mouth goes dry and metallic. Sweat moistens my armpits, soaking into my bra. A pulsing-guilt kind of heat, sticky and stuck to my core. I squeeze my eyes shut, but the room only spins faster, heart lurching, breath thin. The more he talks, the more damned I feel. Judged and scorned and—something else, though. For a few unfamiliar seconds, my guilt grows weak, replaced by a nagging rage in the pit of my stomach. I mean, because, God *knew*, right? He saw me grab that gun and didn't stop me from pulling the trigger.

I mean, *what kind of bullshit is that, God?*

"Amen," people say all around me, but I can't. A lightning bolt is too busy crashing into my soul. I gasp for air, pushing my hymnal off my knees and onto the floor.

Gran's eyes jerk over to me. "What are you doing?"

"I'm—it's too hot in here."

She subtly presses the back of her hand to my forehead. "You don't feel warm, honey. Are you dehydrated? And pick that up off the floor."

I tug at the neckline of my dress, desperate for a little help breathing. "I can't. It feels like my skin is on fire. I think I'm going to be sick."

"Johanna!" Gran yells, but it isn't nearly as dramatic as me stumbling out of our pew and running up the aisle. I don't even care when a few kids laugh and almost everyone else gasps. I ram my whole body against the heavy wooden door, hurling myself onto the sidewalk. By the time I realize how cold it is, there's nothing I can do. It's not like I'm going back in. Not with hot tears streaming down my cheeks and bile inching up my throat.

The door creaks again, and Gran hurries out, horror-stricken and holding my coat.

"Sweetie, are you all right? I've never seen you so pale. I wonder if I have any Pepto in here . . ."

She starts rooting through her giant handbag, but I shake my head until she stops.

"Weren't you listening in there?" I ask, still clutching my stomach. "Pastor Thompson was telling us to honor our parents, and I—" I shake my head. "I couldn't sit there, knowing what God let me do to my own mother."

"Oh, you poor, sweet child." Gran pulls my temple to hers, patting the other side of my head. "Grandpa and I never wanted any of this for you. Please try to calm down."

"Oh, am I being too dramatic?" I shriek, pulling away. "What the hell do you expect?"

"*Johanna!*" she gasps.

But I shake my head. "You've known about this for over a decade. You are not allowed to criticize the way I freak out!"

"That's not it. I just don't want you to—"

The door opens again, but it's only Grandpa. He looks back and forth at the two of us and furrows his brow. "Everything all right out here? Things are wrapping up inside."

Gran's face pales. "Maybe we ought to go."

"Yeah." I snort. "Wouldn't want to cause another scene." I stare hard at her, eyes ablaze. "That's literally all you care about, isn't it?"

"No, of course not," she says, heartbroken. "You're the most important thing in the world to me."

The church doors swing wide, and people start pouring out, full of compliments and gossip, on their way to fancy brunches or maybe a dozen assorted from Dunkin'. Every single one of them looks at me—wide-eyed and uncertain after my outburst.

"Everything all right?" asks a white-haired woman in dangly, turquoise earrings. She offers Gran a sympathetic smile, eyes flicking over to me.

"Oh, we're fine, Belinda. Poor Johanna's got the flu. Don't get too close!"

Belinda nods. "It's going around. Y'all're in my prayers."

"That's kind of you. Thanks."

Once she's out of earshot, Grandpa pats his belly. "Who wants lunch?"

"Better not." I glare at Gran. "With my *flu* and everything."

"Jim, no one's in the mood to eat," Gran says, an eye roll in her voice. "Let's go home."

"I'm not going home," I say.

She frowns. "What?"

"I'm not, like, *running away*. I need to cool off for a while. I'll go to the library or something."

"Come on home with us," Grandpa says.

But Gran presses his arm back down as he's reaching for me. "Let her go."

He looks down at her. Double-checking those words came out of *her* mouth. They did, though, and all three of us are too stunned to speak.

So, instead, I go. Without saying goodbye, without telling them when I'll be home. I simply spin around and stalk across the parking lot toward my car, the whole time trying not to think too hard about the fact that Gran so willingly let me go. The fact that maybe I'm not worth fighting for anymore.

• • •

I drive straight to Milo's house (because fuck the library), and this wildly pungent chemical smell hits me as soon as he opens the front door.

"Jesus, what is that?" I ask, shielding my nose. "Are you fumigating?"

Milo laughs and leans in for a quick kiss. "Intense, right? Mom wanted her bedroom painted gold, and I'm pretty sure there's, like, a million more VOCs in the metallic paint. You want to come in, or . . ."

"Or. Definitely *or*. It stinks like dead C-3POs in there. Can we take a walk? Hit up Baja Tacos or something?"

He nods. "Sounds good."

Milo grabs his coat and yells goodbye over his shoulder. I crack a grin when Anna's warm, spy-novel voice wafts out from her bedroom. She's probably ten seconds from drifting into a golden coma. We bound out onto the sidewalk, sucking in lung-fuls of glorious piñon-scented air. It's not until we get to the corner that I realize neither one of us is talking.

"Everything okay?" I ask.

He nods and puts an arm around my shoulder—which makes me feel legit girlfriend-y, grateful that at least *one* part of my world isn't crumbling—but there's something off too. A heavi-ness in his steps.

"Are you *sure* you're okay?"

"Yeah, sorry. It's my dad." He lets out this pained exhale. "He called this morning. In addition to throwing in these passive-aggressive jabs about how I'm a traitor for moving here, he's not-so-passive-aggressively refusing to pay for my creative writ-ing program in Berkeley this summer. I beat out over a hundred people for a spot there, and he's just like, *nope.*"

"He can't do that!" I yelp, swallowing my feelings about the idea of Milo spending a whole summer in California. "What does your mom say?"

"She's already paying my Chavez tuition. Even with finan-cial aid, that shit ain't cheap." He shrugs. "What am I supposed to do? He broke up our family, and now he won't support my future unless I move back in with him? I don't even think he really wants me there. He's just being a selfish, vindictive—"

"Asshole?" I supply.

"Exactly."

"I'm so sorry."

"My mom's going to help me look at options," he says. "It just sucks."

"I didn't know you wanted to be a writer."

"Musician-slash. I don't always advertise it. Not at a new school, anyway. How do you think guys like Tim Ellison would look at me if I said I write poetry?"

I wince. "Tim would probably call you a very rude word. But only if nobody was looking." I glance sideways toward Milo and smile. "You write poetry, though?"

"Mostly song lyrics."

I blush. "Cool."

We walk a little farther, but I can still feel tension, thick in Milo's arms.

"I wish my dad didn't have to make everything about him," he groans. "Refusing to pay for this program is so stupid. He blames me for choosing Mom's side, so now he wants to suck me into their shitty divorce. It makes my mom so neurotic too. She's like, 'If you want to be with your dad, don't let *me* stop you!' But nobody actually cares what *I* want, they just want to hurt each other, and it sucks."

"It sounds like it sucks."

"It does. It chop-your-finger-off-with-a-mandoline *sucks*."

I raise an eyebrow. "That was oddly specific."

He laughs. "I cut off the tip of my finger with a mandoline once, slicing potatoes. But it grew back, see?"

I squint at the ring finger he's wiggling. "So it did. The human body is a miracle."

"Sorry to vent like that."

"Are you kidding?" I bang my head against his shoulder. "We've been together for a week, and in that time, I've submerged you in a swampland of my drama. Listening to you go off on your parents is the least I can do. Literally, I could not do *less*. So, lay it on me. Scream, cry, write a rage song about your dad's epic assholery. And we are *getting* you into that writing program," I insist. "Talk to your dad again. Tell him how much this means to you. Has he heard your music? Flood his inbox with MP3s and don't take no for an answer. Let him know that if he *ever* wants you to visit, he needs to support your dreams and love you no matter what." I pause to catch my breath, then shrug. "And if that doesn't work, I'll rob a bank. I've always wanted to do that."

"You'd pull a heist for me? Aw." He squeezes my shoulder into him, close enough so he can kiss my forehead. "Now it's your turn—how'd it go, researching at Gabby's?"

My stomach free-falls down onto the sidewalk. I wait for it to settle back in place before answering. "Gross, creepy, and depressing. And then church this morning was super weird, and I kind of had an existential breakdown. Publicly."

"You lost your shit in church?"

I flash a cheesy, guilt-ridden grin.

"Do you want to talk about it?"

"Not really," I say. "All I want to do is drizzle my problems in green chile and pretend my life isn't a complete shitshow for a while."

"And kiss," he says. "Kissing would help both our moods, right?"

I grin. "I *suppose* we could give it a try."

I round the corner onto Apache Avenue, but Milo pulls me back, hands firm against my hips. My breath catches, still shocked by the superb newness of it. His Adam's apple bobs as he leans in. And then, it doesn't even feel so much like pretending. When his lips meet mine, warm and sweet, at least part of my world really does stop crumbling.

17

I'M SO SURPRISED TO see Gabby and Leah on my front porch Monday morning that I forget to invite them in. "What are you guys doing here?"

Gabby screws her eyes up, clearly confused. "We pick you up every Monday. Why would today be any different?"

I guess she has a point, but we haven't talked or texted since the Teddy-Bear-Club-Shooting-Research-Crossover-Sleepover, and I thought they might need a break. Like—I don't know—a get-out-of-friendship-free card. But, then, here they frigging are.

"Are you ready?" Leah asks. "Or should we come in?"

"No, don't." I quickly glance over my shoulder toward the kitchen where Gran is humming as she bakes banana bread. We haven't spoken a word since church, somehow managing to silently coexist. I shout a quick goodbye and then push the girls down the porch steps.

Gabby whistles. "What was *that* about?"

"We aren't talking."

"Clearly," she mutters.

"It's so weird that they're mad about all of this *now*," Leah adds. "You shot—I mean, it all happened so long ago."

She thinks I don't see her eyes flick over to Gabby, but this recent nervous tic between the two of them is impossible to miss.

I fiddle with my earrings. "Yup. Weird."

"It's a coping mechanism," Gabby says wisely. "Think about it. They spent all these years trying to shield you, never putting up any pictures, reinforcing that car accident story. You can't blame them for trying to stop the PTSD from kicking in. And then, *bam!* Your dad comes in and blows down their card castle. If there's anybody you should be mad at—"

"Robert?" I pause, fingers curling around the passenger door handle. "After everything that's happened, you think I should be giving *him* the silent treatment?"

"I mean . . ." Gabby shrugs. Like, *if it walks like a duck and quacks like a duck* . . . but instead of actually saying that, she forces a controlled exhale.

We flop silently into Leah's Volvo, and I examine Gabby's face in the rearview mirror. Lips pinched, biting back words. An unfamiliar anxiety rushes through me—shamed by the sullied mention of Robert's name, guilty that Gabby is policing herself. I love her protectiveness, but I hate that she won't budge. So savvy, thinking she knows fucking everything. I swivel toward the back seat so she can unleash this pent-up buffet of concern, but a tall figure outside catches my attention.

"Jo, is that your—"

"Dad," I choke.

Standing there in his navy bomber jacket and ball cap, Robert looks freezing. As if he's been waiting for me for hours. He walks around to my side of the car, making the roll-down-your-window gesture. Instead, I get out and meet him on the sidewalk, ushering him toward Mrs. Zelazny's hedge where Gran won't see us.

"What are you doing here?"

"I wanted to say goodbye."

My heart swerves into my lungs "Wait, you're leaving? But w-when?"

"Now," he says, glancing down at his watch. "There's some all-hands-on-deck stuff going on, and they want me in Houston. You'll be okay, right?"

I nod, ignoring a thickness in the back of my throat, ignoring Leah and Gabby gaping at us through the windshield. They have the radio on, but I can feel their troubled eyes. Judging us, dissecting our body language.

A gust of wind blows, filling me with icy desperation. This goodbye is happening too fast. I'm not ready. I need time to stop or rewind or at least slow down. Robert opens his mouth to say something, but I cut him off, wrapping my arms around him. Our first hug. And now he's leaving.

"Hey, hey, hey," he says, squeezing back. "It'll be okay. I can visit again."

"Really?"

"Sure."

He lets me go and I wobble.

"I'd like that. I feel like we were just starting to . . ."

. . . *connect*, I want him to finish. But Robert only smiles. "I'll miss you, Joey."

"I'll miss you too."

"Sorry for the short notice," he adds, looking down at his watch again as he steps off the curb. "You be good, kiddo."

I watch him jog over to his car and hop in. Watch him try a couple of times to start his rusty Corolla, then drive slowly up the street. He taps the horn gently as he passes, waving through the windshield. I swallow the lump in my throat and wave back. It's stupid to think he'd stick around forever. Houston is his home, not Santa Fe. Of course he has a life to get back to. But I keep staring at the empty road, long after he's turned. Unable to move. Waiting for something that isn't going to happen.

The car door bumps against my thigh as it opens. Leah's leaning across the gear shift with her fingers on the door handle. "Hey," she says.

"Hey." I clear my throat, training my voice not to shake. "Sorry about that. We're going to be late now, aren't we?"

"Don't worry about it," she says softly. "So that was your dad?"

I slide onto the seat and busy myself with the seat belt.

"He's cute."

"Leah, gross," Gabby says.

"Shut up! I only meant he's not dad-looking. He seems nice." She hesitates. "What were you guys talking about?"

"Huh?" I swallow, forcing a shrug. "Oh, he wanted to say goodbye. He has to head back to Texas. It's fine, though."

"Wait, what?" Gabby sputters.

"It's fine," I say, stronger this time. "He's got a life. He can't abandon it."

"Like he abandoned—"

"Gabby," Leah snaps. She squeezes my knee, but I jerk away before she can mother me too much or make me cry.

"I said, *it's fine*. He's going to come back. Now, will you drive already?"

Gabby clears her throat but says nothing.

A melancholy smile hangs off Leah's lips. "Away we go."

• • •

It's not until Milo stops me after first period that I cry. Soon as I rest my cheek against his chest, just—*boom*. Faucet.

"My dad left," I say, salty tears soaking into his soft, black sweatshirt.

"What do you mean, he left?"

"He went back to Texas. For work."

"Seriously?"

He rubs my back, and I let myself drown in the weight of it all. It helps that kids are streaming up and down the hallway, giving me sideways glances—helps me stop blubbering, I mean. I sniffle, my eyes locking with Milo's.

"I'm so sorry," he whispers.

"I don't know why I'm freaking out. It's not like I'll never see him again. He's my dad," I say, the word still funny on my tongue. "He came all this way to find me. I know he wants to be a part of my life. He'll probably call me tonight. At least, I want him to. Do you think he will?"

"Me?" Milo blinks. "I've never even met the guy."

"Yeah, but, you think he'll keep in touch, right?"

"You know I can't answer that."

"Sure," I say. "Okay."

He walks me the rest of the way to second period with his arm tight around me. Which feels nice, but it doesn't erase my disappointment. Maybe he *can't* answer, but I wish he'd at least try.

• • •

At lunch, I sit listlessly between Milo and Leah, listening to Gabby ramble about a recent A in English, and how she's now considering liberal arts colleges for creative writing, rather than law (yeah, right). I feign best-friend enthusiasm, occasionally looking idly down at my butternut squash soup. Stupid soup and my new vegetarianism while the rest of them eat steak quesadillas and chicken Caesars. Not that I'm hungry.

"You okay?" Leah asks.

"It's just this nasty soup. It looks thick enough to be a Korean face mask. Whatever. It's fine."

"Maybe you should get 'It's fine' tattooed on your forehead," Gabby mutters.

My eyes snap over to her. "What's that supposed to mean?"

"In the car?" she says, pitching her voice way up. *"It's fine, it's fine. Oh, don't worry about me, it's fine that my father just up and left me. Again.*"

Her words have spikes attached, but I dodge them. "Maybe it *is* fine."

"That's all you're going to say? How can you pretend this isn't killing you?"

"Jesus, what do you want from me, Gabby?"

"*Anything!*"

"You guys," Leah starts to say.

I slam my wet spoon down on the table. "Did you ever stop to think that maybe I'm keeping my mouth shut for *you*?" I whisper, anger in my voice. "I see the way you guys look at me. All terrified, like I'm some kind of monster. Which I am, so . . ."

"That isn't true," Leah insists, tears welling up in her eyes.

"This is hard for us too," Gabby says. "How do you think *we* feel? Trying to protect you when you'd rather text your dad all night or save your breakdowns for your precious boyfriend."

Milo rolls his eyes. "Cut her some slack, Gabby."

"Excuse me?" she snaps, glistening with adrenaline. "Who do you think you are, showing up, looking like James Dean, stealing my best friend away during the most batshit event of her life? I saw the way she cried on your shoulder outside Garner's class this morning. *Oh, Milo! Make it better!*"

A flush washes over me. I used to love it when she got like this. All vigilant and lawyer-y. Now, it only burns. "Do *not* bring him into this."

"I'm her boyfriend," Milo says. "Not her puppeteer."

"Yeah, well, I'm sure you're a great kisser and all, but I have been Jo's best friend since kindergarten, and I know her better than you ever will."

"You have *no* idea what I'm going through!" I spit back. "Shit, *I* barely know what I'm going through. You're just mad because I'm not letting you dictate my decisions. It always has to be about *you*."

"Oh, bullshit," she says. "I'm asking you to be honest about what happened this morning. Your dad is a dick. Leah, back me up here."

Leah's eyes burst wide as her lips clamp shut.

"I'm sorry you hate my dad," I say, "but *I* don't. And if you want to know the truth, yeah, it really hurt when he left this morning. But I don't need *you* rubbing it in. Why can't you be on my side and see that he's important to me? After what I did, I'm lucky he wants anything to do with me."

"After what *you* did?" Heat rises in Gabby's voice. "Do you *hear* yourself?"

"Yeah, I hear me having to defend my own flesh and blood to my best friend."

"But you're defending a convicted felon!" she whisper-shouts. "A drug dealer who kept a loaded gun in your house. He didn't care about you enough to lock it up, and yet you're acting like he shits gold bricks."

"Gabby, keep your voice down," Leah pleads.

My heart's racing, wishing she'd shut the hell up too, but Gabby's on a roll. Eyes ablaze, head shaking. *She means well, she means well, she means well,* I tell myself over and over, but that doesn't make it better. Doesn't change the fact that heads are starting to turn, gazes landing on us, one by one.

"Look at you!" she shrieks. "Giving that asshole pass after pass, acting as if *you're* to blame. I can't stand it. When are you going to realize that it was your *father's* gun? It is *not* your fault you found it, and it is *not your fault she's dead!*"

Gabby stops shouting and the room spins, taking my guts with it.

Gun

Fault

Dead

"Shit," she whispers. But it's too late.

All the oxygen in the room evaporates as everyone turns to stare. Without looking, I can feel the eyes of the volleyball team, choir, mathletes. Kids can sniff out drama like McDonald's fries, and this is no different. Over by the bulletin board, Annette Martinez has lowered her stapler, abandoning the student government flyers she's posting in order to see what Gabby is frothing about. I've never seen anyone more paralyzed with interest. I pray for silence, but the word *gun* seems to roll through the room like an ocean wave, growing angrier as it laps against each table.

"Wait, what did she say?" someone whispers.

Gabby looks at me, eyes wide with regret. "Jo, I'm so sorry. I'm—"

"You're a bitch," I seethe. "I am never. *Ever.* Talking to you again."

"I didn't mean to," she says. "I got carried away."

"Oh, I think you meant to," I yell, tears welling up in my eyes. "I think you've been waiting for this. Well, congratulations—you officially don't have to be friends with a *murderer* anymore."

The collective gasp of fifty students knocks me off balance. Milo catches me as I stumble back.

"Let's get her out of here," Leah says to him.

They each put a hand on my back—not Gabby, though. She stands comatose while they steer me through the room. Maybe Leah thinks this is a rescue mission, but we're way past that. Our tiny prep school is a petri dish for gossip.

The door bangs against the wall as Milo flings it open. He ushers me outside, shielding me, but the truth has already detonated. Out on the quad, eyes glom onto me. Hushed voices ask one another if they saw my epic fight with Gabby, if anyone knows what it was about or what my mother's name was.

"Amanda," offers this senior, Elise Maxon—a girl from church, which is the only place Gran has ever uttered my mother's name.

Armed with that detail, phones come out, Google spoon-feeding them the information it took me over a decade to build up to. Looks boomerang off me—horror to sympathy and back again. My chest heaves, lockers spinning in my periphery. I can't breathe or see through the tears. I might be dying, I think.

"Come on," Milo says. He squeezes my hand, tugging my arm till it strains in the socket. Over his shoulder, he says to Leah, "I'm going to take her to my house, okay?"

"Yeah, of course," she says, then pauses. "Wait, what about her bag and stuff?"

Milo nods and sprints off toward my locker while Leah takes over the burden of keeping me upright. Cell phones ping and vibrate all around us, information spreading like lice. Leah's motherly instincts take hold, and she wraps her arms around me, whispering that it's going to be okay, that everything's going to be okay. I bury my face in her curls, plugging my ears to drown out the coyote wail of my classmates.

A minute later, Milo's back. It's like a World War II movie, the way Leah hugs me goodbye, weeping as my boyfriend whisks me away, guiding me toward his pickup truck in the parking lot.

The news has already broken out here too.

"Wait, *what*?!" Tim Ellison squawks, pushing himself off the hood of his Lexus. His blue eyes land on me for a split second, and even though he doesn't know yet—doesn't have any of the facts—I can tell his two-dimensional mind is made up as he huddles in with the other lacrosse players.

Milo plants my listless body into his pickup, and the engine roars to life. Even though running away is a Band-Aid, barely even that. We peel out of the parking lot, past all the kids who know, past the ones who don't, past everyone who's about to find out. By the end of the day, every student will have heard my story. Every administrator, teacher, janitor.

By the end of the day, the truth will be everywhere.

18

MILO'S HOUSE DOESN'T SMELL of paint fumes anymore. And his bedroom isn't covered in sports memorabilia and cologne bottles or whatever stereotypical crap boys' bedrooms are supposed to be littered with. No, Milo's room is this vibrant dusk-blue color with the Las Vegas skyline hand-painted in thin, white strokes along one wall. Palm trees, fountains, rows of buildings. I've seen him sketching it in notebook margins at school.

"Thanks for letting me come over," I say. "And for ditching with me."

"Sure." He dumps his backpack on the floor and then pulls his black sweatshirt up over his head. I catch a glimpse of his abs, too distraught to be embarrassed as he starts fiddling with the Bluetooth speaker on his dresser. "But if I get detention, you're going down."

"Such a gentleman."

"Right?" He smirks. "Hey, I would have broken through that shitty gate with my superhuman strength if the security guard hadn't been on a coffee break."

"You have superhuman strength?" I gasp. "How did I not know that?"

He flexes.

We lay on his bed for a while, listening to Lou Reed. Clothes on, shoes off. Fingers laced together between us. I listen to Milo breathe and try to emulate the same gentle movements, even though my brain is exploding-throbbing-dying. Worrying about who knows and what they must think of me. Picturing my life as one of Magic's mangy tennis balls, bouncing to a slow roll and then dropping off a cliff.

"*She shot and killed her mother*," I can hear them all whispering.

And then more and more gasps. "*Are you serious?*"

"*She was only a toddler!*"

"*Who would* do *something like that?*"

"*And her* dad *went to prison for it?*"

"*How does she live with herself?*"

"*Her poor mother.*"

"*Her poor grandparents, having to look at her every single day.*"

I squeeze my eyes shut and then open them with a sharp inhale, noticing a gun-shaped crack above the closet door. Even Milo's ceiling knows what I've done.

He rolls onto his side and puts his hand on my stomach, swirling tiny, gentle circles on top of my shirt. "Did you tell your dad what happened? I saw you texting him in the car."

"Yeah." I exhale, focusing on the feel of his touch, the throb of Lou Reed's "Vicious." "He said he was sorry and sent a GIF of some giant marshmallow hugging a scrawny guy."

"Baymax and Hiro," Milo says sagely. "I cried my eyes out at *Big Hero 6*."

"Softy."

"What else did your dad say? Is he coming back?"

I try not to let the hurt show as I shake my head. "He's got all that work stuff. But he feels awful. He wishes my grand-parents hadn't let it get this far. Me too, Dad. Me frigging too."

Milo sighs.

I sigh.

"Want to know what I heard?" he asks after a while.

I crack one eye open. "Not especially."

"It's good. I swear. This girl came up to me when I was at your locker. She told me how incredibly brave she thinks you are."

"Shut up."

"I'm serious!" His forehead gets the cutest, most defiant wrinkle. "It was Millie Redbone, I think."

"Nobody's name is Millie Redbone. That's, like, a children's book character or a brand of butter."

"It is not!" He laughs. "I was standing at your locker, and this Millie chick came up to me and said to tell you how sorry she is. She couldn't imagine what you must be going through, and she's got your back."

"Mm-hmm. And you got all this by my locker? While I was comatose on the quad? How'd you even know my locker combination?"

"Oh, I smashed it. With a fire extinguisher." He nods. "Yeah. You need a new lock. But, the point is, she's right. Millie Redbone is right."

I laugh. "Okay, you've got to stop referring to this fictitious 'Millie Redbone.'"

I prop myself up on my elbow and press my lips into his, relaxing as his mouth opens. We kiss to "Perfect Day" and some of the humiliation fades away. The reality of three hundred gawking faces becomes a little more diaphanous in my mind. Milo slides his hand along my back, nuzzling my neck. Kissing helps, but it can't take away the rotting pulse in my gut, the slow burn of this forever kind of shame.

The song ends and Milo pulls away, lips rubbing together. "And there was definitely a lot of talk about how beautiful you are."

"Millie Redbone again, huh?"

He laughs. "Not Millie. This one guy—I think he's a transfer. He could *not* stop staring at you. I bet he was undressing you with his eyes."

"The new guy?" I say, giggling and shivering and exploding all at once. "He's pretty hot. And you think he was undressing me with his eyes?"

Milo's face reddens as he smiles faintly.

I kiss him again. Deeper this time, lips on fire, desperate to give him everything. When he pulls away, we're both breathless. His eyes search mine and tell me he loves me—even if neither of us has said it out loud yet. Things are moving at warp speed, but it's also the only thing keeping me grounded. I need this to be my silver lining. With an exhale, I lean back, slow and deliberate as I undo each button on my leopard-print shirt, my eyes steadily on his.

Milo gulps. His mouth opens as if to say, *Are you sure?* or some other generic bullshit guys think they're supposed to say to virgins. But I bug my eyes out, pursing my lips as I give him a death glare.

He takes the hint with a laugh.

"The new guy is going to be *really* jealous," he murmurs and pulls his T-shirt over his head.

19

WHEN I GET HOME, Gran is expertly mashing the potato crust of her shepherd's pie with the tines of a dinner fork. Which seems like an anticlimactic meal after losing my virginity. Not to mention, I've stopped eating meat. But did I forgot to tell her that? Probably. She looks up as she's putting the dish in the oven to brown. We exchange pleasantly guarded smiles, and I don't wonder if I *look different*. I already studied myself in the mirror when I was getting dressed at Milo's, and I look exactly the frigging same. Just with messier hair. Which I have since brushed.

Silverware's already in heaps on the granite counter, so I grab it, along with our everyday plates, and head into the dining room. Fork, plate, knife, spoon. I lay them out like solitaire, slow and distracted. Leah is going to freak when she finds out I spent the afternoon naked, tangled up in Milo's warm flannel sheets.

Fork, plate, knife, spoon.

Shit, though. A pang of sadness dips through me when I realize I thought "Leah," and not "Gabby and Leah." Gabby was the first of the three of us to lose it. Sex on a summer exchange program in Belize. I remember her describing how good it felt, but also how sand got all up in her business from doing it on the beach. Which honestly still makes me laugh.

Fork, plate, knife, spoon.

All the bajillion times we've confided in one another. So many sleepovers, so much marshmallow taffy. I mean, am I *never* going to tell Gabby the way sex with Milo made me feel? I guess it's too hard to explain, anyway. The root of its importance. The way Milo doesn't judge me or withhold information or smother me in sympathy. That's what I get from everyone else—a seven-layer dip of history. Milo only knows me as the person I am now. Someone half-broken and unsure of herself. Both younger and older than my years on Earth. With Milo, I get to be myself. Moaning included.

"You feelin' feverish?" Gran asks, cradling her shepherd's pie between two potholders.

Holy Lord. I am thinking about orgasming. *In front of my grandmother.* "Oh, uh, nothing," I stammer. "Is dinner ready?"

Grandpa makes his way into the dining room, and I flush even harder.

We take our seats, take hands, take a moment to pray. Afterward, Gran grabs the serving spoon and plops this giant, steaming heap of ground beef, peas, and mashed potato onto my plate.

It smells delicious, with a hint of Worcestershire sauce mixed in, but I force myself to stare at it, limp-lipped.

"Something wrong?"

I wince. "Gran, I'm a vegetarian now."

Grandpa laughs heartily. "Since when, JoJo?"

"Since recently," I say, sitting up straighter. "Since I found out *Mom* was a vegetarian too."

The two of them exchange a look over the table, petrifying in their seats.

"Robert told me," I add, as if that wasn't obvious.

"I thought we told you not to see him anymore," Gran says.

"You did, and I haven't," I say, which isn't a total lie. "But before he left, he told me a lot of things about her. Best conversation I've probably ever had in my life."

Gran stares at me for a beat, misery-eyed. Her voice catches as she says, "Yes. Amanda was a vegetarian. She was many things. I can see why you took comfort in Robert's stories. But I honestly think you ought to see the larger picture. You were happy before you knew. We've kept you *safe*. The less you know, the better—the less anyone knows," she adds under her breath.

I blink back at her.

Because, it's almost funny, right? That she would pick today, of all days, to suggest that I—and basically the world—don't already know *everything*? The fact that she still thinks she can hide it is just so tremendously, incorrigibly obtuse. Borderline sweet and naïve, but I don't have it in me to sympathize anymore. Not after today.

I rest my napkin beside my untouched plate and gently push my chair back from the table. As I rise, I am met with zero argument. "You know what," I say, enunciating each word the way they taught me. "Keeping it a secret has worked out perfectly. You're right. The less everyone knows, the better."

Gran opens her mouth to say something, but when she sees me walk out of the room, she doesn't bother.

• • •

In my bedroom, I feel the need to pace for a while. It's barely eight feet across, but enough to get a good stomp-stomp-swivel going. Really, I should be doing homework, but then I remember that I didn't get all my assignments because I left school in a flurry of disgrace at lunchtime. It becomes painfully obvious that Gran and Grandpa aren't going to barge in after me, so I flop on my bed, glaring at the dull, wooden ceiling. I'm almost afraid to look at my phone, but when I do, there are about sixty texts from Gabby. All apologies, acknowledging her short temper and protective streak. I archive them without responding and notice an unfamiliar number sandwiched between a plea from Leah to remember self-care, and a cornucopia of heart emojis from Milo.

The text bubble pops open. Hey, it's Jenny Ireland.

Pause. Our school is not that big, but I can't actually picture her. She must be a freshman. Blond, maybe?

I hope this isn't weird, but I got your number from Leah.

I heard about what happened today. 😨 I think I can
help. I mean, I think my mom can help.

I pull the comforter up to my neck, wriggling down till only
my nose is above the covers. Her mom wants to help me? Does
her mom sell time machines? I turn on my bedside lamp and
keep reading.

My mom's a therapist and she deals with stuff like this.
Traumatic stuff.

I roll my eyes.

I hope I'm not totally freaking you out right now!? I just
wanted to put it out there. I can't imagine what you're
going through. I heard that you only recently found out,
so I'm really sorry you have to be dealing with it so
publicly.
This is Jenny Ireland, btw.
Did I say that already?
My mom says we did Jam-Sing together one summer
when we were kids.
Okay bye!!!!!!!!!!!!!!!

I reread the whole thread again and plug my phone in to
charge. I barely remember that stupid music class, but whatever.
Now a total stranger thinks I need therapy, so that's cool.

I close my eyes, thinking about the idea of getting my brain seen to by a legit pro-shmessional. What they'd say to me. What I'd say to them. At my house, reading the Bible is how you deal with your problems. *Heal me, O Lord, and I shall be healed; save me, and I shall be saved, for you are my praise. Jeremiah 17:14.* That, or you take a walk, or a nap, or a shower. Build a bird feeder, needlepoint a prez. Carlsons don't actually, like, unpack our feelings.

Thanks, I write. Then erase it. *I'll think about it.* Erase. *Butt out?* Nothing feels right. Instead, I open my downloads and throw on an early Blondie album. Debbie Harry belts out a song I've heard a thousand times but, weirdly, it seems more meaningful than it ever has before. She's singing about accidents, and how they don't happen in a perfect world. Which only makes me want to sink deeper under the covers.

What I did to my mother, that was an accident, right?

In a perfect world, it wouldn't have happened?

In the end, I leave them all hanging—Jenny Ireland, Leah, Gabby, Milo. I play the song on repeat until I fall asleep, dreaming of a world without heartbreak. A world where accidents like mine don't exist.

20

YOU KNOW THAT DREAM where you walk into a room and everyone's staring at you? That record-scratch reaction of a nun entering a biker bar. That's me when I walk into AP English on Tuesday. *The Great Gatsby* and the Greater Devastation of Johanna Carlson. Usually, in the dream, you're naked. In reality, I have on this cool obi top I made last spring, paired with plaid joggers and my white high-tops.

"Oh. Uh, good morning, Miss Carlson," says Mr. Gonzales. He clears his throat as he looks up, hands dancing awkwardly across the desk until he decides to grab a pen, busying himself with today's lesson.

I try not to roll my eyes before looking around for an empty seat. It never used to bother me that I don't have friends in English. Key words: *used to.* Now, a roomful of acquaintances is staring at me like I'm in a wet T-shirt contest.

I head for the back row, flopping down beside surfer-haired

Tim Ellison and his bestie, Brandon O'Connor, with the frosted tips. I've always thought they'd make a great boy band—Tim would be the super stuck-up (and annoyingly gorgeous) crowd favorite, while Brandon, with his twenty-four-hour biceps and vacant smile, ticks the meathead box. Aside from the occasional dig, we never say hello or acknowledge one another's existence, but today I realize Brandon's eyes are bugging out at me, his fair skin blanching. He's covering his mouth, whispering something to Tim. They both cringe, and all my skin tightens.

For a split second, I think, *Should I move?* There are other seats, other English classes, other schools in other states. But you know what? No. I'm sitting here, dammit.

"Mr. Gonzales?" Brandon hollers in his deep, boy-band voice. "Hey, Mr. Gonzales?"

"Yes, Mr. O'Connor?"

"Um." He pauses, glancing at Tim, then me, then Tim again. I crinkle my brow, like, *What, asshole?*

Brandon and Tim go quiet, and I realize they're having a *moment*—the telepathic kind Leah and I have too. Finally, Tim gets up, his designer jeans inching between desks toward the front of the classroom.

"Sir?" He pauses to artfully guide blond bangs across his forehead. "Should we be taking some *precautions?*"

Mr. Gonzales laces his fingers on his desk, furrowing his brow.

"Y'know—" Tim casts a nervous glance back at me. "Do something to put peoples' minds at ease. Maybe check her bag or something?"

"Mr. Ellison, what are you talking about?"

"C'mon, Mr. G," Brandon demands. "Check Johanna's bag for a *gun*!"

My heart pukes its way out of my mouth. Nearly.

The air in the classroom turns greenhouse-moist, thick with sweat and strain. I want to roll my eyes—play it off like we all know Tim and Brandon are massive jackasses—but the looks coming back at me are tighter than that. Cagier. A lot of shock, some sympathy. Maybe even guilt, but nobody's big enough to stand up for me, cowardice tugging at their shoulders and chins. And Mr. Gonzales. He says *nothing*. His demeanor sure as hell changes, though. Eyes darting to the back of the room, bulging as they lock onto me. Onto my eyelids and fingernails painted black, lips neon red, an Old School Anarchist pin on my coat. It shouldn't be enough to make him balk, but he does.

Brandon can't seem to handle the silence. He clears his throat meaningfully at Tim, who turns back to Mr. Gonzales and goes, "As our teacher, doesn't it behoove you to protect us? Maybe she doesn't have a gun in her bag, but what if she *does*? Do you really want that on your conscience when she shoots up the whole school?"

"Oh, for God's sake," Selene groans at him.

Selene. Not my teacher. But perky, blond Selene frigging Kenworth. Is this honestly happening?

Mr. Gonzales sighs. "Tim. Please take your seat."

Only, Tim doesn't. He just stares, lips hinting at victory. It reminds me of a scene in that movie *Pretty Woman*. Where the salesgirl asks Vivienne to leave the fancy boutique on Rodeo Drive, and when Viv comes back looking all couture, she goes, "Big mistake. Big. Huge," to the saleswoman before walking away. In this case, big-mistake-huge is probably the fact that Tim's dad is this fancy real estate developer and president of the school board. Ergo, Tim could probably get Mr. Gonzales fired if he wanted to.

"What is it exactly that you want?" Mr. Gonzales asks quietly.

"We want you to take this seriously."

"I don't want to sit next to a *murderer*!" Brandon yells.

Actually *yells*. It's meant for the whole class, but his words go straight through my soul, killing something inside me, making my worthless lips tremble.

We're all caught up in this vortex of silence until Tim shatters it, muttering, "Just check her bag," like everything can go back to normal if we get this over with.

And it really happens. Mr. Gonzales stands up. He caves in, eking out a sigh as he walks slowly toward me. Students squirm all around us. Irked by the injustice, just not moved enough to defend me outright. I'd be a fool to think otherwise. I don't know what I'd do, if the roles were reversed. Before all this, I might have sunk down in my seat too.

"Miss Carlson?"

I grit my teeth, steadying my voice. "Yes?"

"May I please take a quick look in your backpack?"

Selene huffs wildly from the front row.

"Do I have to let you?"

"She's resisting!" Brandon wails. "She's resisting. She's really got a gun. Holy shit. Holy—"

"Brandon, enough," orders Mr. Gonzales. But he swallows. "Johanna? Your bag?"

The way he starts to squirm—the way *so many of them* start to legitimately *fear for their lives*—I can't take it. I yank my backpack up onto my desk and fling the zipper open. But I don't just show him. I dump everything out. Every pen, notebook, tampon, lip gloss. All of it spills out onto the desk and the floor, loose change rolling across the carpet. Everyone gasps.

"That is not what I meant!" Gonzales snaps, bending down to grab the tampons first—because he obviously cares *deeply* about my privacy. "Collect your belongings and go see the Head of School."

"What?!"

"You are being disruptive."

"But—"

"Not up for debate, Miss Carlson."

Selene jumps out of her seat, scurrying over to help. Anger radiates off both of us as we jam all this shit back into my backpack. We don't even make eye contact. Nobody else moves. Except Mr. Gonzales, who walks uncomfortably back to his desk to jot a few words on a pink slip of paper to hand me on my way out.

I want to spit in Brandon's smug face as I'm leaving. Tim's and Mr. Gonzales's too. I want all three of them to apologize for humiliating me. For accusing me. For thinking I'd ever, *ever* do something to hurt the kids at this school.

Instead, I slink quickly through the room, fighting back tears as I let myself out.

• • •

In all my years at Chavez, I have never been sent to the Head of School's office. Dr. Sanders is this pompous old white dude with no hair on his head, and shit-tons coming off his eyebrows. Super old-school rigid, but like, masking it with colorful bow-ties and a smile that says, *I'm your cool, hipster cousin!* Which he is not. This one time, we saw him dribbling greasy fried chicken at a back-to-school picnic, and everyone's secretly called him Colonel Sanders ever since. That fond memory usually makes me laugh, but my hands only tremble when I knock on his frosted-glass door.

"Come in," calls a muffled voice from inside.

Before I twist the knob, I remind myself to try and calm down. That I've done nothing wrong—Tim's the raging dick; Mr. Gonzales is the spineless bootlicker.

"Miss Carlson?" Dr. Sanders says, surprise in his smile. Just as quickly, his eyes grow heavy. I can tell he knows—*about my past*—because he can't quite think of what to say next.

"Mr. Gonzales sent me."

"Oh?"

I swallow hard and pull the note out of my pocket, handing it to Sanders. His eyes widen at the implication of pink, growing even wider as he reads the words Mr. Gonzales has hastily scrawled. Words explaining my lack of obedience, how I disrupted the class with a messy outburst. Nothing about Brandon. No mention of Tim. Sanders puts the note on his desk and gestures toward the seat across from him.

"Want to explain what happened?"

"Tim Ellison and Brandon O'Connor," I mumble. "They thought I had a gun in my bag."

"Oh? *Oh.*" His eyes twitch, darting toward my bag before he looks back up at me. "I see. And this is all in relation to—" He clears his throat. "I heard about your mother's death. I'm so sorry for your loss."

I nod a heartfelt *thanks* for his sluggish condolences. He seems expectant, but on no planet would I want to talk about *that* with *him*, so I point down to the note again. "After Tim blatantly accused me of concealing a weapon, Mr. Gonzales asked to search my backpack. I mean, can he even do that? Isn't it private property? Like, what's the probable cause or whatever?"

Sanders nods evenly. "And did Mr. Gonzales *force* you to remove the contents of your bag?"

"No," I say slowly. "Not exactly. I guess I kind of dumped it out."

"I see. So, you opted to open your bag willingly." He hesitates. "Were you doing anything to . . . raise suspicion?"

"What? No! I was sitting there! Tim's the one who—"

"All right, all right. No need to raise your voice." Sanders lifts his palms with a curt smile. "I think I have a fair idea of what happened, but I'll speak with Mr. Gonzales as well."

"I wasn't doing anything wrong."

"No, no, of course not," he says. "If there's nothing you wish to add—"

"Well, it'd be nice if you didn't let pricks—sorry, *young men*—like Tim get away with stuff like that. It was humiliating. Are they going to get in trouble?"

The question seems to catch him off guard. "Oh. Well, I see no need for this matter to be dragged out. Tim was voicing a concern, and we encourage our students to ask questions. I agree that he could have done so a bit more privately, but it sounds to me as if the whole thing got out of hand. It was a misunderstanding. Tim's a good student. A Harvard legacy."

Harvard. The word clogs my arteries. Tim won't be punished. Not with Harvard sniffing up his ass. Sanders doesn't know I've got my heart set on Parsons, but he wouldn't care. I mean, it's not fucking Harvard, now is it?

"I see. So, I'll just forget this ever happened," I say, swallowing a lion's roar inside my chest. "Go back to business as usual? That sounds easier."

"Wonderful idea." Only an idiot could miss the sarcasm in my voice, but he grips my hand and adds, "Thanks for coming in."

"No, thank *you*, Dr. Sanders."

"And you shouldn't have to go back to class. I'll write you a pass. Why don't you go to the library—take a little break." He flashes a toothy grin, and I swear I can see the angel on his shoulder, applauding his lenience. "And please let me know if there's anything else I can do to help. My door's always open."

"Thanks, Dr. Sanders. I *really* appreciate that."

"Of course," he says.

And he actually hipster cousin *winks* at me as he's shutting the door—that's *always open*—right in my face.

21

"YOU OKAY?" MILO ASKS.

It's Friday afternoon and we're on his bed, all naked and sweaty and kissing, and I'm trying to forget about school and all the dirty looks . . . but. Apparently, it isn't working.

"I'm fine," I lie, forcing a smile. "How 'bout you. What are you thinking about?"

"Me?" He snorts. "Guys don't think after sex. We basically turn into cavemen."

I laugh, but too automatically. Too cardboard.

Milo props himself up against his pillow, gently brushing hair out of my face. "Bet I know what *you're* thinking about."

"Sorry," I groan. "I can't stop remembering everyone whispering behind my back—or in front of it—acting like I'm a bomb in jeans. People seriously think I've been keeping this secret since preschool! Can you believe that?"

"They're bored. Everyone's gonna forget about it soon."

"Not soon enough," I grumble. "Did you see there's a GIF of me?"

Milo scrunches his eyebrows.

"Yeah. I'm a GIF now."

I reach onto the floor, grabbing my phone out of my jeans pocket. My GIF fame comes from a video someone took a couple of days ago in Mr. Gonzales's class. When I got punished for basically being a human being. Well, and dumping my shit everywhere. For three excruciating seconds, there I am, shaking my bag with this maniacal, Bellatrix Lestrange look on my face. I didn't even know my face could do that, but apparently my range is *that good*.

As far as bullying goes, this stupid animation is fairly tame, so I'm almost smiling as I search for it. I scroll past mundane poetry, bypassing selfies and food photography. But then, something entirely different catches my attention, putting my heart on lockdown.

"Oh my God."

I—I honestly can't believe what I'm looking at, so I thrust the phone at Milo for verification. It's a photo. The one of me and my mom. The one I posted a few weeks ago with the hashtags #meandmom and #missyou. The original picture was this beautiful, innocent moment with her chin resting on the top of my head, my hand pinching her cheek as I look up at her, grinning. Now, though—someone has photoshopped it so that instead of pinching her cheek, I'm holding a gun, pointing it at her face. There's even an artful spattering of blood coming out her other temple.

"Holy shit," Milo gasps. "Who posted this?"

He clicks on the profile but it's some anonymous user named FakerX; the rest of the account is blank. It almost makes me gag. *Somebody did this.* I mean, everybody knows, but only one person chose to do *this* with that information. And they didn't even do it right—I shot her in the chest, not the head.

I bury my face in my hands.

"Jo, this is harassment."

"It's the truth, isn't it?" I cry. "FakerX isn't *lying* about what I did."

"This is serious. We need to report this."

"It doesn't matter."

"Yes, it does."

"I killed her, Milo. Wake up!" I pause as a hot, peppermint heat wells up inside my chest. "Maybe some asshole photoshopped this, but it doesn't change the fact that I'm guilty."

"Jo, you're not. Try to calm down."

I shake my head wildly. "Why should I? I killed her. *I killed her.* I deserve to be harassed and ridiculed and sent to the headmaster's office and whatever else, because I killed my own mother." I sit up and my head throbs. I'm practically panting at the realization. "I don't think I can survive this. I hate myself. The only person who ever really loved me is dead, and it's my fault. I did it. Oh God, Milo. What did I do? *What-did-I-do-what-did-I-do?!*"

Milo tries hard to hush me, hold me, but I refuse. My breath is too thin. Too tangled.

Bang. The familiar clap of a gunshot bashes into me. Terror snakes its way down my temples and into my heart. I squeeze my eyes shut to ignore it, but that only makes me want to push harder. Punch myself in the face or something. Cut something. Will physical pain stop the meteor from crashing? If I hit myself hard enough, can I be forgiven?

"Jo?" Milo says, voice cracking. "Are you okay?"

"No," I wail, full-body shuddering. Giant tears plonk down my cheeks and paint his black sheets blacker. "I can't do this."

"It's going to be okay."

He scoops my rigid body toward him, tight into his chest. So close that I can hear his heart beating, each *bu-bum bu-bum bu-bum* turning into a gunshot. One after another.

Bang. Bang. Bang.

I push myself off him and fall onto the floor. Naked. I'm butt naked, but it doesn't matter. A volcanic heat is welling up inside me. Insides blazing. Breath shaking. I'm aching as my eyes dart around the room—for what? My clothes, my sanity, my innocence?

"Jo, what are you doing? Please, lie down."

"No!" I scream.

And scream. And scream. With another gasp of air, I scream again. I want to scream until my ears bleed. To scratch my arms till my skin comes off. My heart pumps so fast, there could be a trampoline inside my chest.

"I think you're having a panic attack," Milo says. "Try not to breathe so fast."

"I can't," I growl. "I really can't."

"Stay here. I'll be right back."

Milo grabs his boxers off the floor and disappears. Dusk closes in on me. I try to focus on the hand-painted Las Vegas skyline on his bedroom walls. Such peaceful, beautiful details, yet all I can think about is that mass shooting at the country music festival—a thousand people screaming, bleeding, begging for their lives while some crazed gunman picked them off, one by one. I can't breathe, I can't breathe, I can't breathe. My lungs won't let me. Invisible gnats flicker in my vision.

"Milo?" I scream into his empty bedroom. Shivering, holding myself. What if I really could scratch off all my skin? I drag my fingernails along my forearms, and then again, harder. Harder and harder and—

"What are you doing?" Milo gasps as he runs back in.

"Trying to make it go away. I'm scared I'm going to feel like this forever."

"You won't. Here, take one of these—" He hands me a little pink pill and some water. "It's a Xanax. It'll help calm you down. Can I touch your wrists?"

The pill tastes bitter against my tongue. I look down, like I forgot I even have wrists. And then I notice my forearms. All red and raw, little specks of blood hovering beneath the surface. I can't bring myself to look at Milo, but I give him my wrists and watch as he presses hard against my pulse with three fingers. One minute goes by. Two . . . three . . .

"I hate this," I whimper. "It's like I'm trapped inside my own body."

"I know," he says softly. "It'll pass."

"No, it won't. I don't think this feeling is ever going to go away."

"It will. I promise."

Another minute goes by. Two . . . three . . .

"That's better," Milo says. He takes a deep breath, in through his nose, out through his mouth. "Try breathing like this."

"I can't breathe," I say, but my voice feels thick.

"There you go. That's better."

I blink up at him, watching his blue-gray eyes stare straight into mine. His lips tremble as he smiles. I smile back. Blink. Eyelids slow. I can feel my heartbeat idling; no longer aflutter outside of my body, but nestled back down inside my chest. Milo releases my wrists and takes my hands to steady me.

"Lie down," I hear him say. Far away. Soft.

Then I'm on the bed, safe, tucked under black flannel sheets.

"Don't leave," I murmur. Far away. Heavy.

"I won't."

• • •

The room is dark when I wake up from a sluggish, dreamless sleep. I sit up too quickly and my head throbs. Skin stiff on my face, dry and crusty from the salt of my tears. Music's playing somewhere, and I roll cautiously off the bed, quickly slipping into my jeans and Sex Pistols sweatshirt before walking toward the door. I open it and begin to hear Elvis Presley. I can't see Milo or his mom, but I can hear their voices. Gentle murmurs, running water. I comb my fingers through my hair and tiptoe toward the kitchen.

Anna's standing beside the sink, still wearing her chef's jacket and Crocs. When she sees me, she smiles, nodding for Milo to look behind him.

He rushes over, pulling my paper-thin body into him. "Are you okay?"

"Headache," I murmur, then smile awkwardly at Anna. "Sorry. I should probably go."

"Don't apologize." She pours herself a glass of wine and smiles a sad sort of grin. "Milo told me what happened. I can't imagine what you must be going through. I'm so incredibly sorry, sweetheart."

"Oh. Um, thanks," I say, blushing.

"If you need *any*thing . . ." She smiles again, then retreats toward her bedroom with her merlot.

I whimper toward the ceiling. "Does your mom think I'm a total train wreck?"

"Of course not," Milo says. "I hope you're not mad that I told her. She can't believe what you've had to go through the past few weeks."

"I can't believe it's already been that long." I shudder, counting back the days. "Up until two weeks ago, I had absolutely no idea I was a murderer."

"You are *not* a murderer."

"Brandon O'Connor thinks so."

"Brandon O'Connor is a piece of shit."

Milo kisses my forehead and hands me a cup of tea containing something called kava that's supposed to help with anxiety, then leads me into the living room. I curl into him on the couch, and this time, his heartbeat doesn't trigger me.

"God, I feel weird," I murmur. "Like, hungover, almost."

"Panic attacks will do that."

"I guess I've never really had one before."

"My dad gets them," he says. "Like full-blown postal. The way you never want to see your own parent. Hence the Xanax. I stole a bottle before we moved. He's got a lifetime supply from his psychiatrist, but seeing the way he gets? When he's in the middle of an episode? It used to scare the living shit out of me. The pills always helped him, and I guess I kind of wanted some for insurance. In case it ever happened to me."

"Or your girlfriend."

"Or my girlfriend."

I pause to sigh. "I'm sorry."

"What are you sorry for?"

"For scaring you."

"You didn't." His biceps flex around me. "Okay, you did. But I get it. I just want you to feel better. I'm glad I knew what was happening."

"*I'm* glad," I say. "Can you imagine if I'd been at home? Grandpa walking in on me hyperventilating? He'd probably make me a sandwich and turn on a football game."

"Mmmm. Sandwiches."

"Shut up!" I snort. "I'm trying to say thank you."

I nestle in closer and tuck my hand up inside his T-shirt. I'll have to make up a lie about having dinner at Leah's, but not now.

Not yet. Elvis is singing "Love Me Tender" from the kitchen, and I let the lyrics pour over me, thinking about this thing with Milo, how it's gentle and tender and a dream fulfilled, just like Elvis says.

The fact that one person can be so lucky. And yet so unfathomably unlucky, all at the same time.

22

"DO YOU THINK I'M going to be the last virgin on Earth?"

"Leah, of course not," I say, but then raise an eyebrow. "How do you classify losing it, if you're bi?"

A frenzied blush sweeps across her cheeks. "I guess I meant in the traditional, hetero sense."

"Wait, what? Are you *not* a lesbian-virgin?" I gasp. "Did you do it and not tell me? *Shut up!*"

"Keep your voice down."

Not that we really need to worry about eavesdroppers. French class ended ten minutes early, so we've got the hallway to ourselves.

"I told you about Robyn from Santa Fe High," she says with a grin.

My jaw hits the floor. "You said you did some 'stuff,' but I didn't know it was, like, all-the-way stuff. Holy shit, Leah!"

She can't respond; she's too busy bumping into walls,

laughing, covering her burning cheeks with both hands while I cheer for her.

I get distracted as we pass the door to Gabby's AP Econ classroom. She's in the front row, face scrunched as she takes notes more copiously than any other student. I feel this little pang of guilt flicker inside me. Mostly because of Gabby, but also because I am probably the only junior at Chavez who isn't in ultra high gear right now, obsessing over college prep. I'm sorry, but how can I, when—

"Any word from Robert?" Leah asks a minute later.

She's way too good at sensing angst.

"He's really busy," I say quickly. "We text, but he's got all this work stuff going on."

She runs her fingers along the wall as we walk. "Hey, so, my parents want to have you over for dinner. Mom's desperate to smother you in hugs. She even lit a candle for you in her shrine."

"Wow." I whistle. "I made the famous Gilda Fromowitz shrine. I'm an even bigger lost cause than I thought."

"Stop it!" she says. "You know that shrine means a lot to her. Remember when my aunt Karen got breast cancer? A candle burned in that shrine every single day until she went into remission. It's an honor, I'm serious."

"I know you are." I nod solemnly and put an arm around her shoulder. "So, how long does your mom have to light candles before I can un-kill my mother?"

My bad joke drains all the blood from Leah's face.

"Sorry. I was trying—"

But I stop. It isn't the joke that has her face the color of vanilla yogurt. We're out of the language lab, stepping onto the quad, and immediately we spot Annette Martinez hovering around my locker, taping something up.

A picture.

The picture.

"What the hell are you doing?!" I shout, shoving her aside to rip the photoshopped monstrosity down. My heart hammers as I glance at it, one thumb covering the fake blood exiting my mother's head. "*You're* the one who posted this bullshit online?"

Annette flinches. "Of course not."

She snatches the paper from me, using it to gesture toward the hundred or so lockers surrounding us. "They were plastered on practically every single one. I've been tearing them down since my study hall ended."

"Really?"

She raises one hand like there's a Bible underneath the other. "I. Swear."

Leah grimaces. "Why should we believe you?"

"Because!" Annette shouts, stomping her loafer against the concrete. "This is vandalism. And bullying!"

The way she's stomping around catches the attention of a few seniors leaving the bathroom. They pause, wide-eyed and snickering, craning their necks to see what Annette's holding.

"Okay, chill," I mumble, my cheeks blistering as I press her arms back down by her sides.

She glares at the seniors till they scatter, then looks back at me, her voice blessedly quieter. "How can *you* tell me to 'chill'? This picture was plastered everywhere."

To prove it, she gestures toward a nearby garbage can. Leah gasps. A hundred crumpled pages—a hundred copies of my mother's brains splattering out of her beautiful blond head—jammed into a dirty plastic bin full of banana peels and snot-soaked tissues. She didn't even take the time to recycle.

My eyes begin to sting. I can't stop myself glancing around the quad. Classes are out now, dozens of kids moving in slow motion, not even pretending not to stare. Did any of them see the printouts? Were they greeted by them, taped to their lockers after sixth period?

"I don't think too many people saw," Annette says psychically. She takes the last photocopy, sandwiching it between the pages of her day planner. "Come on, let's show Dr. Sanders."

"What—now?!"

"Yeah, now." She squints at me. "It's harassment. Don't you want to report it?"

Harassment. Vandalism. Bullying.

Her words become bricks in my stomach.

"She's right, Jo."

I look at Leah, unable to speak.

"Chavez Academy has to set an example about crap like this," Annette pushes. "Zero tolerance."

Her words swat the air around us, but all I can think about are the looks. The ones I'm getting right now, the ones I got yesterday, and the day before that. The fear in Brandon's eyes when he accused me of having a gun. The way Elise from church has started peering into my locker when I have it open between classes. Nearly everyone inching away from me in the hallways.

Should there be a penalty? Or will that only make me look guiltier?

Annette starts to walk toward the admin building, and I grab her arm. "Don't."

"What? Why?"

"I already talked to Sanders. Last week. Something happened with Tim Ellison, and when I told my side of the story, he made it pretty clear that he has Tim's Harvard-bound back."

"Harvard?" Annette goes pale. "He told me his top choice was Brown. There's no *way* they'll accept two students from Chavez into Harvard in one year. Will they?"

"Dude." Leah snaps her fingers in Annette's distraught face. "Focus."

"Sorry." She squints back at me. "Don't you at least want to know who posted it?"

My eyes dart around the quad. "Well, Tim's an obvious choice. Or Brandon, who *also* thinks I've got a gun emporium in my backpack. There's also the stranger who drew a gun next to the words *wash me* in the dust on my bumper. Maybe Elise Maxon, maybe Carrie Schlegel. Literally, in the past week, it's harder to think of who *didn't* post it."

"Hey." We all turn to see Selene Kenworth, a blond braid cascading down her shoulder as she sidles up to us. Folded in her hand is another copy of the picture. "Thought you might want this."

"Well, I don't."

Leah grabs it instead, crumpling it up small. "Thanks, Selene. Is this the only one you saw?"

She nods. "I think so."

"You *think* so?" I growl. Even though Selene has always seemed nice. Even though I should be thanking her. I sigh. "Thank you."

"Sure." She opens her mouth, then clamps it. Opens it again. "Hey, can I tell you something?"

"Will it piss me off?"

"It's my dad." She squints. "He keeps guns in the house."

"What?" I say. "Why are you telling *me*?"

"Y'know, *because*." She rolls her hand in a circle, filling in the blanks.

"And, what? You think I'm going to steal one?"

"No!" Her cheeks go hot pink. "It got me thinking, that's all. Y'know, like, how easy it is to find guns laying around the house." She chews her lip ring with her teeth, spinning it around. "Do you think I should ask my dad if they're locked? Or if any of the guns have bullets in them?"

"Jesus, Selene. I don't know. Probably?"

"Um, you definitely should," Annette chimes in.

"You're right." Selene smiles apologetically. "Thanks. Anyway, I should go. Cute bracelet," she adds—not to me, but to Annette, who blinks as if an alien has just offered to impregnate her. To be fair, no one as popular as Selene has probably ever uttered two words to Annette. Now someone has, and they were *cute bracelet*. She holds up her wrist in response, silver links dangling toward Selene's back as she skips over to a group of future *Vogue* models.

Annette looks back at me, taking a moment to regain her composure. "Are we going to Dr. Sanders's office or not?" she finally asks.

I hesitate. "Not."

Her nostrils flair with disapproval. "*That's* your decision?"

I nod, head ducking a bit.

She turns to leave, but I call after her. "Annette, wait. Thanks—thank you."

We both look at the trash can, my dumpster of shame. Annette looks back at me and exhales in a way I can't quite read, then stomps off toward the library.

"Oh my God," Leah mutters when it's the two of us again. "Are you okay?"

I stare hard at my locker, teeth gnashing together. There's a tiny sliver of tape that Annette didn't manage to remove. I don't pick it off either. "I'm fine."

"Come on," Leah pleads. "Those printouts were awful. You must be feeling—"

"Don't you have calculus?"

Leah pauses, eyes widening. "Are you getting rid of me?" she asks, voice inching up.

I squint back. Because, her *tone*. There's something arched and almost *hopeful* in it. "Do you *want* me to get rid of you?"

"What?"

"This picture, all the extra attention," I say. "I know it can't be easy, having to stick up for me all the time."

"What are you talking about?"

"I'm giving you a way out." Some inner voice tells me to shut up, but my jaw is too tight, heart thumping too heavily. "If you want an excuse to go be normal with Gabby, go ahead. Now's your chance."

Her sweet freckled face sags. It claws at my heartstrings, but I cross my arms. "I don't need you sticking around out of pity."

"I don't, I mean, I'm not. That's not—" She looks up at me, head shaking wildly. "I—I'm doing the best I can. I thought you *wanted* me on your side. Why are you acting like this?"

Her eyes moisten. God, could I be a bigger asshole? Trying to push her away when she's practically all I've got left? Before it's too late, I put an arm around her and squeeze. "Hey, don't cry," I say, barely above a whisper. "I'm sorry."

"It's okay," she sniffles. "I'm sorry too."

"It's not you. I'm a dickhole. Seeing that picture, though? Plastered all over school? It riled me. I don't know how much more I can take. You know?"

"I know," she says softly. "So, we're okay? Because I really have to get to calculus. But I'll skip it if you're mad at me."

"I'm not," I say, and a smile forms a little easier on my lips. "You're a good friend. Thanks."

"So are you," she says. "Talk later? Text me if anything else happens?"

"What *else* do you think is going to happen?"

"Nothing!" she says, shaking her head. "Just be careful!"

I try not to think about how ominous that sounds.

I try not to think about what a weirdo I was to her too. It takes me a full minute to remember which textbook I need before I grab the chunky, purple psychology one from my locker. My head isn't in the game. The looks, the whispers, this disgusting printout. Visions of homeschooling dance in my head, but that would mean more time with Gran and Grandpa, and we're already at a charades-level silence as it is.

The bell rings, but I don't rush off like everybody else. I'm still petrified in front of my locker, unable to take my eyes off the door and the tiny sliver of tape glaring back at me.

• • •

After school, I'm jumpy as fuck, to the point where I literally jump when Mr. Donnelly taps on my shoulder as I'm piling books into my bag.

"Johanna!" he booms in his usual keyed-up voice. "Didn't mean to scare you. Got a sec?"

I catch my breath and turn to face my impeccably dressed and caring counselor—always urging me to try harder and get more involved, living vicariously through my dreams of Parsons School of Design. Yet, I get the feeling this isn't going to be one of our motivational college prep moments.

"I kind of have to be somewhere," I lie.

"Understood. Just a quick check-in. I wanted to see how you're, y'know, *doing*?"

"Fine," I say quickly.

"I should have asked days ago, but I didn't want to push. And Dr. Sanders said you have a good support system in place with your church and your grandparents. But, well, I'm the guidance counselor!" He laughs awkwardly. There's even a little jazz-hands moment.

"Well, I'm fine," I say again, feeling my jaw tighten. Because even though his voice says *heeeey!*, his eyes scream *helllllp!* It's that same look Mr. Gonzales had last week. As if maybe I've been fooling them all this time. Maybe I really *am* capable of—

"Stoicism is an admirable quality," Donnelly goes on, "but I'm interested in what makes us human. What we go through on a daily basis. And I would imagine that having the whole school learn your childhood trauma couldn't have been easy."

"What, that?" I say. "It was *awesome*."

He pauses, lips tugging into a pinched frown. "As much as I'd like to believe you, the truth is, I'm worried."

That look of uptight concern suddenly has me seething, a harsh reality dawning on me. "Are you worried about *me*, or are you worried about what I'm capable of? Y'know: *Does Jo have a locker full of guns?* Let's check, shall we?" I don't wait for a response before flinging my locker door wide, so hard it bangs against the one next to it. We both jolt. "Go ahead and look, if that's what you're thinking."

A blush edges around Mr. Donnelly's ginger beard. He coughs, gently shutting my locker door without so much as a glance inside. "That's not what I'm thinking. Honestly. I'm here to talk."

Talk about what? I want to ask. *How I'm a stain on your precious private school? How you need to find a way to keep it quiet? To shut me up? To kick me out?*

When I don't respond, Donnelly claps his hands together in action. "Why don't you stop by during study hall in the next couple of days? I really am here for you. Scout's honor."

For a second, I almost let myself believe him. That my adorable guidance counselor could take away any of the pain or guilt or humiliation. But then I see them again, out of the corner of my eye. Kids I've known since pre-K, cowering, glaring, distrusting every inch of me. My problems are an ocean, and Mr. Donnelly is barely a grain of sand.

But I smile dutifully. "Sure, Mr. Donnelly. I'll stop by."

Anything to look less like the murderer they all see.

23

LATELY, MY BEDTIME RITUAL has centered around flipping through photos of my mother. I've only had them for a few weeks, but I swear they're already getting tattered and bent along the edges. I don't want to put them in an album, though. I need them close, need to feel them between my fingers. If I look hard enough, stare long enough, sometimes her face is so fresh in my mind that she enters my dreams. I'm nearly there when my phone buzzes.

Robert: Hey kiddo!
Robert: What's cookin'?

I squint at the time on my phone. Midnight. On a Wednesday. While I'm trying to fathom how to respond in a way that doesn't make me sound exhausted, or self-deprecating and loserish, he writes again.

Robert: Have you heard of a book called Girl Code: Going Viral?

I furrow my brow, trying to switch gears.

Me: I don't think so?
Robert: A buddy of mine is recommending it. Says his daughter loved it.

I wait for him to write more, because, what? Nearly midnight and he's texting me book recommendations? Now I can't sleep though, so I grab my laptop off my desk and bring it over to the bed, googling the title. It pops up on the screen, and I start to tug on my lower lip as I read the description. Maybe not totally my cup of tea, maybe a little young, but it could be interesting. I guess.

Me: Looks good!

I mean, it's the correct response, right?

Robert: I'm going to buy you a copy.
Robert: Is that cool, or will Kate and Jimmy go ballistic if they see you're getting mail from me? Don't wanna get u in trouble.
Me: Oh.

I pause.

Me: Just send it from Amazon. I'll say it's for school.
Robert: Right!

Robert: Got it. Will do.
Robert: Good night!

I look at my phone, mystified. *That* was worth a midnight text? Must be a really fucking scintillating book. But I'm here now, in bed with my laptop. I yawn, clicking open some of the bajillion tabs dotting the top of my screen. A few kids in my grade have posted a quiz, which sounds like the perfect amount of mindless for my mood.

1. **What is your favorite childhood memory?**
   a) **Sailing**
   b) **Disney World**
   c) **Shooting Mommy**

My neck stiffens. I sit up straighter.

2. **As a kid, did you prefer playing with:**
   a) **Seashells**
   b) **Dinosaurs**
   c) **Dad's .22**

Heat rushes through my body.

The third question's just sloppy. It's not even a question, just three possible answers:

   a) **Fungicide**
   b) **Insecticide**
   c) **Matricide**

My breath goes ragged. I skim the last few questions and click *C* for every one, and then, there it is. Typed in bold and comic sans: **Murderer.**

"Jesus," I whisper.

I grab my phone to text Leah or maybe Milo, but it's so late. They'd answer, but they'll be groggy and confused, and they don't deserve my midnight meltdown. I think about texting Robert again, but I don't want to drag him into this either. Not when he's off in Texas being so thoughtful, buying me books and stuff.

My hands shake as I scroll through the comments. Lots of LOLs and laughing emojis; just as many vomit-faces and removal requests. The worst, though, are the people who say they are "Johanna-ing" the shit out of this quiz.

Johanna-ing. When did I become a verb?

In a moment of blind rage, I type out an all-caps comment, calling the creator of this quiz a million of the nastiest insults I can summon up. It feels good. It feels glorious and justified . . . but it also feels pointless. I select the whole rant and press Delete.

I stare at the ceiling for a few minutes, heart thwacking my chest, making it impossible to fall asleep. Outside, the wind howls, mocking me. I grab my earbuds and put on Echo & the Bunnymen, hoping some haunting post-punk will absorb the pain. It does. Ish. But I can't resist taking the quiz again. This time I click through with all *A*'s, only to find out I'm destined to be *Moana*. Enough *B*'s and I'm some character from *Jurassic Park*. Then I full-on Johanna it again, just to twist the knife.

Matricide.

Such an ancient-sounding word.

I'm still staring at the quiz results as my laptop screen goes dim and then black, leaving me alone in the dark, with nothing but "The Killing Moon" and my crime running circles in my head.

24

MRS. FROMOWITZ IS DESPERATE for my presence at Shabbat dinner on Friday night.

Leah won't shut up about it, promising various perks. Between her legendary challah bread and a little kosher wine, it sounds significantly better than another silent dinner with my grandparents, so I put on my charcoal gray DVF knockoff and then sneak into the living room, ducking over to Gran's antique oak credenza on my way out. The top display half is all china and tchotchkes, but the lower half has tablecloths and a liquor cabinet. And by *liquor cabinet*, I basically mean one ancient bottle of half-drunk sherry. Gran and Grandpa aren't big drinkers, so they'll never notice it's missing.

"You heading out?" Gran asks as I poke my head into the kitchen.

I nod. The Shabbat card is a low-hanging fruit, but Gran never argues when I tell her that's where I'm going. I think she feels secretly self-conscious for knowing nothing about Judaism. "I'll see you tomorrow."

She offers a weak smile and turns back to the stove.

Yeah, not going to miss another evening of *that*.

Fifteen minutes later, I'm parked outside Leah's ranch-style house, uncorking the bottle and downing a hefty swig of sickly sweet syrup. My whole body shudders. I mean, no wonder this bottle is only half-full. It is truly a disgusting, *disgusting* beverage. I take another sip, bigger this time, to calm my nerves. Night hovers quietly around me, waiting for my next move. Just a few more minutes, a few more sips, and I'll be ready.

I keep thinking about how many times I've been in Leah's house. Hundreds? Thousands? And yet, for once, I feel dread. I exhale, trying to steady myself as I apply some eyeliner to my bleary, bulldozed eyes. Another two gulps and the sherry bottle is accidentally empty, leaving me warm and lightheaded with a sluggishly thumping heart. I wipe my mouth with the back of my hand, searching the car for mints I don't have. Spearmint ChapStick will have to suffice.

I let myself into Leah's house through the open garage door and the kitchen practically vibrates. Garlic in the air; Madonna, the corgi, yipping at my feet. Aretha Franklin's on the stereo at volume a thousand, feeling like a natural woman.

Leah rolls her eyes when she sees me. Rolls them twice when she smells my breath. "Dude, you're late," she whispers. "I saw you park like fifteen minutes ago."

"Sor—" I start to say, but that's as far as I get when a grown version of Leah bounds over to me in black spandex and platform wedges that still only bring her up to my shoulder. Mrs. Fromow-itz is a teacup poodle in the best possible way, jumping up and down as she hugs and kisses me. I have no choice but to do the same, and I don't even mind, thanks to the sherry. She pulls back and licks her thumb, wiping cranberry-colored kisses from my cheeks.

"Jujube, you made it!" Gilda squeals. "Look at you. Are you losing weight?"

"Stop," Leah says, elbowing her way between us with a tissue. She rubs my cheeks harder. "Mom, you made her look like the Little Drummer Boy."

"Nonsense. A little color on those pale cheeks."

"Shabbat Shalom, Johanna!" says Leah's dad. "So glad you could make it."

I smile and wave at Mr. Fromowitz who is balancing a platter of roast chicken in one hand and a lite beer in the other. "Shabbat Shalom, Jeff. Thank you for having me."

"Come," says Leah, grabbing my hand.

The warmth in my chest makes my body sway after her. We get to the dining room, and I swear you've never seen so much furniture. There's their regular dining table, plus a card table, plus I'm pretty sure the ironing board, all underneath long white tablecloths surrounded by every chair ever and a piano bench. The glasses range from colorful stemmed goblets to plastic sippy cups.

Twenty people take their seats—I'm sandwiched between Leah and this older guy who kind of looks like Kylo Ren—and

Gilda reaches across the table for my hand, quickly squeezing it with sad, sympathetic eyes before Jeff gets started singing the prayers.

My body teeters as I mumble along. I've heard these songs before, but really, I'm thinking about Gilda. The way she squeezed me and how my skin still throbs. Not because it hurt, but I don't know why I thought tonight would be different. What's that saying? *Wherever you go, there you are?* Like, there's no escaping *me*.

Now there's a shitty thought.

Jeff says some more blessings while the bread gets passed around, and I down my kosher wine, sneaking a refill even though anybody could be watching.

"Jo!" Leah gasps. Yup, she was watching.

I chug my second glass too, and groan out loud when she refills my cup with grape juice. After that, the whole table goes into Disneyland-mode. Gilda's discussing diaper rash with a fellow pediatrician. Jeff's talking football with his son, Dan, and a few other third-graders. Poor Leah is trapped in a conversation with I don't even *know* who.

"You go to Chavez Academy?" Kylo Ren asks, offering the salad bowl. "My daughter's going to be a freshman next year."

"No way! *How cool is that!*" I whoop, then force my voice down a couple decibels. "I'm a junior. Maybe you've heard of me? I'm *pretty* well known around there."

He offers a curious smile, but I feel Leah yank my elbow. "Are you about to tell him about your mom?" she whispers.

I burp yes.

"How about no? He's my dentist. I really don't think it's any of his business."

"Fine," I say with a wink. "You got it, toots."

Across the table, I notice Rachel, Leah's fourteen-year-old sister. She won't stop staring at me. I've known her since she was a baby—even babysat her—and yet she's looking at me like I'm wearing nipple tassels. Her friend too. Mousier and blonder, but full-on gawking at me.

"What are you looking at?" I slur.

Rachel ducks her head, turning instantly magenta.

The other girl waves. "Hey, I'm Jenny. Remember?"

I squinch my nose, watching her head as it blurs.

"Jenny Ireland?" she adds. "I texted you last week?"

My brain takes one . . . two . . . three seconds to remember. And then I snort, elbowing Leah in the ribs. "She's the one who thinks I need therapy!"

Leah wipes her mouth. "What?"

"Y'know, *therapy*," I stage-whisper.

"Jo." Leah's eyes dart around the table. "Do you want to talk about this later?"

"You seemed pretty willing to talk to her about it at school," I scoff. "I'm obviously a complete whacko, since you spammed my number to this *freshman*, so she could harass me like a 1-800-INJURED lawyer."

The room grows quieter. Only a little at first, conversations drying up like summer rain. Forks still scrape, mouths brimming with Gilda's potato kugel.

"Everything okay?" Jeff asks.

I scrunch my nose. "Maybe I should es-explain," I say, hiccupping. "See, I ki—"

"Jo," Leah pleads. Her eyes go heavy on mine as she shakes her head.

"No," I snap. "I want to tell them that I killed my mom."

Nobody says anything—they don't even breathe. Which is a little disappointing, honestly.

"Maybe you heard about it already," I relent. "At the grocery store or the dentist's office, or—oh, hey, you're a dentist!" I turn to Kylo Ren for a high five, but his white face has gone gray, like he's thinking a self-inflicted root canal might be better than this dinner party. I pat his shoulder. "Don't worry, Kylo. It was a long time ago. I was only two and a half when I shot her dead."

Someone gasps—finally—but I can't tell who because my head won't switch directions that fast. Instead, I look at Gilda, sitting across from me. She's got tears in her eyes, a hand pressed tight against her chest.

"Did you know little kids could shoot guns?" I ask her.

Her lower lip quivers.

"Hey, lemme ask a question. Get a group sinsensus—*consensus.*" I glance around the room, squinting one eye. "How hard do you think I had to pull the trigger to get it to go off? Pretty hard, right? Do you think my body jolted from the force of it? I was wondering about that too. Like, if I bumped into a wall and got a bruise on my back. On TV, you always see people using two hands to shoot a gun—" I raise my arms to demonstrate, one hand on an imaginary gun, the other one steady around my shooting hand. "Did I do it like this? I mean, I couldn't have, right? I wouldn't have known how. So, if I only held it with one hand, how come I didn't dislocate my shoulder? Or go deaf from the noise? Or, why isn't my brain scrambled because of it? That could happen, right?"

Nobody answers. But nobody stops gaping either. Even the third graders are silent, all sagging jaws and gap-toothed wonder.

"Jo, let's go to my room," Leah begs, but I swat her hand away.

"You know what's funny—I just thought of this. People go to the shooting range all the time to work on their aim. But not me! I hit her on the first try. Does that make me lucky?"

"Of course not, sweetie," Gilda says solemnly. "Jujube, honey, let's excuse ourselves. Leah, I'll take her for a minute."

Leah nods, but I shake my head, the room or my body starting to spin. "You're kicking me out? Come on, Gilda. I thought you were cool with me murdering my mom."

The room goes ice cold. Even though my skin is on fire and hot salty tears are tickling my cheeks; even though I'm sandwiched among twenty warm bodies, I can't help shivering. They all know. I mean, I guess maybe they didn't before five minutes ago, but they do now. A hiccup turns sour in my mouth, and Gilda lunges for me, taking me by the waist and maneuvering me down the hall.

Her bedroom is dark, but despite my blurred vision, something flickers in the corner—a row of fireflies, bright and delicate. She flips the light switch, and I realize it's the famous Fromowitz shrine, aglow with votive candles. I gravitate toward it, tripping over clothes and shoes, or maybe just my own feet. Seeing the shrine up close makes me breathless. It's this big wooden box, about the size of a dartboard cabinet. In fact, maybe it once was a dartboard cabinet, with two doors opened wide and inviting. The first thing I notice are the mandala beads in an ice cream shop of colors, hanging from little pegs along the back. Lots of photographs too. A wedding portrait of her and Jeff. Baby pictures of Leah and Rachel and Dan. Other friends and relatives I don't know. In the flickering candlelight, I notice a photo of Leah and me, back in fifth grade, soaked and hugging each other in our bathing suits. It's a great picture.

"I lit a candle for you," Gilda says softly.

"Leah told me." I hiccup. "Why?"

"It's . . . it's sort of like an offering."

I smirk. "What do you get in return?"

"I don't know." She takes a slow, steady breath, squeezing my clammy hands in hers. "All I want is for you to be happy. To get the answers you deserve. Find *meaning* in all this. Maybe find peace."

I squint one eye at her, wagging my finger. "Are you allowed to be such a hippie, Mrs. Fromowitz?"

I should be giggling, but sobs barrel out of me instead.

"Oh, sweetie. Come sit."

She rests me on the edge of her bed, gently rubbing my back. "Do you want to talk about it?"

"You mean, *more* than the shit I blabbed in front of your poor dinner guests?" I gasp and cover my mouth. "Shit! I said shit in front of you."

She smiles faintly. "I'll live. It's good to get these things off your chest, Jujube. An uncluttered mind is a peaceful mind. You'll hurt yourself, keeping it all pent up."

"I know," I say, voice quiet and lost. "But it's like I don't know who I am anymore. I'm angry with myself, sorry for myself. I feel claustrophobic. I'm stuck in my body, my life, this world. And what am I supposed to do? I wish someone would tell me, because I don't know what the hell I'm supposed to do anymore. I'm so scared I won't ever feel okay again."

My words begin to muddle, lost between sobs. Thick, dirty tears, smearing my makeup. Gilda hands me a bottle of water from beside her bed. She smells like rose petals. Being around her reminds me of a fancy English garden. I take a sip and wonder what Mandy smelled like—not just her perfume but the scent of her skin. Did it make me hungry, when I was a nursing baby? Would I know it now?

All the tears rush out of me, cannonballing into my lap. My chest heaves and burns. Gilda rocks me from side to side, humming an old Carole King tune. "'You've got a friend,'" she sings, but I don't want one. I want my mother. I desperately need what I can't have. What I stole from myself.

It's calming, though, listening to her sing. Feeling her arms around me.

Does that make me a traitor?

"We love you, Jujube. So many people love you."

I wipe my nose with my palm, burping up a little bit of wine. Gross.

"I'm guessing this goes beyond a glass of Manischewitz?"

"What?" I ask.

"The wine. You look like you've had a few."

I cringe.

"It's okay, sweetie. You're in a safe place, it's okay to let loose sometimes. Just promise me this isn't going to become a habit. I don't think I have it in me to tell your grandmother I got you drunk."

"Oh my God," I gasp. But then giggle. Gilda does too. "Do *not* tell them. Please."

"I won't," she swears. "Let's get some food in you, huh?"

I wipe a straggler tear from my eye. "I'm too embarrassed."

"Nonsense," says Gilda. "You're with family. You can't embarrass yourself in front of family."

"Even the dentist?"

She snorts. "The look on his face! Sorry. I'm awful."

I sniffle. "It's okay."

She helps me to my feet, and when she opens the door, joyfulness pours in. It's clear that Shabbat dinner has achieved its previous vigor. People are laughing, kids running, Jeff strumming on his guitar. I look over my shoulder before we leave Gilda's darkened bedroom, glancing one last time at the candle whose sole purpose is to burn until I find peace.

25

ON THE BRIGHT SIDE, I doubt I'll ever become an alcoholic.

My brain is doing a war reenactment inside my head when I wake up, not helped by the ten million third graders blasting cartoons and sword fighting throughout the entire house at 7 a.m. I blink a few times, looking over at Leah under the covers beside me. Drool drips from her mouth as she snores. It blows my mind that anyone could sleep through this, but then, I'm an only child. I'm used to silence.

More and more, lately, come to think of it.

I use Leah's deodorant and splash some water on my face, rummaging through her closet for the one sweater of hers that I really love, and then sneak quietly out of her bedroom. Dan and his friends barely blink twice at me as I weave through their meticulous blanket fort. At least I don't have to worry about my Shabbat meltdown making the elementary school circuit.

"You're up early," Gilda says as I'm trying to slink through the kitchen.

Morning light haloes her as she leans against the sink. Her hair's wild, like she slept upside down. She raises her eyebrows, gesturing toward the coffee mug in her hand.

"No thanks. I think I'll let the headache punish me a little longer."

"I guess I won't ask how you're feeling."

"I'm really sorry for ruining your dinner."

"Sweetie, you ruined *nothing*. Are you going to be okay today?"

I nod, then shake my head, then sigh.

"Do something nice for yourself," she suggests. "A pedi, or see a movie. You like shopping. Here—" She reaches for her wallet on the table and pulls out a twenty.

"I can't take that," I say. "I don't even *want* it. I feel like I'm sick of thinking about myself. It's exhausting."

Gilda nods. "I get it. Maybe it's time to find another way to channel your feelings." She pauses, shrugs, sips her coffee. "You're going to be okay, Jujube. I'm not just saying that. You're a strong girl—Jeff and I have always thought so. It may not seem like it now, but you *will* get through this."

"You really think so?" I whisper, tears inching up my throat. "Because I don't know how much longer I can go on feeling this way."

Then I'm sobbing, Gilda rushing around the table for a hug. It lasts forever, and when she pulls away, we're both tearstained.

"You *will* find a way to heal. It takes time."

"I guess so." I let her hug me again, then pull away, opening the door to the garage. "Hey, Gilda?"

"Yeah, honey?"

"Keep that candle burning for me, okay?"

She nods as I shut the door softly behind me.

• • •

Gran and Grandpa aren't home when I get back. She's written a note, explaining a fundraiser meeting, hoping I slept well at Leah's, an arrow pointing toward a saucepan on the stove full of homemade tomato bisque. I heat up a bowl and eat it with saltines, which are about all my stomach can handle, then take a ridiculously hot bubble bath and text with Milo for a while. My face is splotchy from the heat when I get out, but I feel clean. I mean, duh, but I actually feel *cleaner*. Renewed almost, thinking about Gilda's words. That I *will* find a way to heal.

I brush my hair in front of the mirror and picture my mother's face. Eyes round, with lashes for days. Our chins, strong and square. I reach for the photo of the two of us on my nightstand—the original, un-photoshopped one—needing to be reminded of its simplicity. In this picture, there is love. No gun in my hand, no blood darkening her blond hair. It repulses me that someone could have done that. As if I'm not punishing myself enough. They're not just afraid of me, they *hate* me. For something I did before I could blow my own nose.

Thinking about it makes me want to explode. I'm so goddamn fucking fed up with all of it. The sick humiliation of seeing Annette rip down posters of my blood-soaked mother; how I loathe walking with my head held down in shame, sitting idly by while they all click *C* on some ridiculous quiz. I can't take it much longer.

Rather than suffocate in self-pity, I grab my phone, snapping a selfie. I make my face tough and determined, all hot 'n' bullshit-immune like Debbie Harry on the cover of *Parallel Lines*. The first one comes out bad, so I take a few more, posting the best one in my stories with the caption: *Enough* and a few black hearts and muscle emojis. I like the way it makes me feel, but too quickly the power fades. It's too small a taste. I need more. Need to be more, do more. What I said to Gilda was true. I feel trapped by my story. Defined by a gun I was too small to hold and should never have had access to.

A badass selfie isn't enough and never will be.

I have to *do* something. Be proactive. When Annette asked me to go to Sanders's office, I should have said yes. The day I went in, after the English class bullshit, he treated me like I was less than human—less than *Tim*, anyway—but am I?

Now my skin is on fire, bubbling over with rage. The fact that I've let it go on for this long. Two fucking weeks of allowing imbeciles to push me, pull me, bully me. Not anymore, though. Hell, no. This is about me. It is *my* story. Because of my past, I will make sure my future is different.

I throw on some clothes and fling open my laptop.

But then my phone rings.

"Yeah?" I bark.

"Whoa," Leah says. "I was going to be like *yeah, gurl* because

I saw that fierce picture you just posted, but you sound like Gabby after losing a debate competition."

"No, I'm fine," I say. "You saw the picture?"

"Me and everybody else. Did you *see* how many likes you're getting? I didn't know you even had that many followers."

She's right. I click on the image, buoyed by the flurry of likes and hearts, smiley faces and peace signs.

"I want to do something."

"Sure," Leah says. "Movies? Mani-pedi?"

God, she is *so* her mother's daughter.

"No, I want to do something big. Like, why should I sit around picking my ass while people post stupid quizzes? Don't you think it's time I showed everyone I'm not a doormat or a fucking serial killer?"

"Yeah!" Leah whoops.

"I'm tough," I go on. "I'm strong. I should *do* something with that. Like—" I let a giant puff of air through my lips. Heart racing, clacking with the ferocity of my sewing machine. "I don't know. Fight gun violence. Ban guns. Or, what's it called, with the background checks?"

"Umm . . . background checks?"

"Leah, we could do anything—I mean, *I*." My cheeks burn. "Sorry. Obviously, I won't drag you into it."

"What?" she says. "Of course, *we*. I'm behind you one hundred percent."

"Really?" I'm choking up, even though I shouldn't be. Leah's my trusty Rottweiler, and I'm hers. Now and forever. "So, where do we start?"

The two of us get all *Charlie's Angels* after that, googling different ideas, various school projects to prevent gun violence. Petition ideas, rallies, protests. Leah finds this whole website on gun laws in New Mexico. How they're like, the saddest thing ever. Some of the least restrictive gun laws in the whole country. Out of curiosity, I look up California too. Fresno, where I was born. Gun laws in Cali are a *lot* stricter. Probably why Robert got prosecuted.

When I hear Gran call me to dinner, I kind of can't believe it's already that late. I didn't even know they were back home, but I'm buzzing with ideas, drowning in links to print at the library tomorrow. Stuff I can't wait to throw in Donnelly's *I'm-worried-about-you* face. Because, after today, I have a crystal-clear idea in my head. A full-on mental vision board that is going to change everything.

I head toward the dining room, adrenaline sapping out of me as I smell Gran's tuna casserole. Do I eat tuna now? Was mom a what-do-you-call-it—pescatarian? I don't know, but I decide not to complain because I've pushed the limits enough lately.

The table's set. That's supposed to be my job. I was too far down my gun violence rabbit hole, but I still feel guilty. I take my seat, wondering how long we're going to go on like this— silent treatments and avoiding the truth. Can we make it till I graduate next spring? Would it be better if I packed up and moved to Texas with Robert? I take my seat and let the thought crystalize in my mind. Picturing Robert and me sharing his apartment. Me, cooking us breakfast and sewing him collared shirts; him, helping with my homework and signing up for parent-teacher conferences at my new Houston high school. The movie marathons, the late-night chats. He'll call me *kiddo*, and I'll start to feel comfortable saying *Dad*.

It could be perfect.

Silent treatment or not, Gran reaches across the table for my hand. Her fingers feel smooth and warm as they curve around my palm. I take Grandpa's hand too, and our heads lower.

"O Lord," Gran begins softly. "Thank you for the food we are about to receive. Thank you for the family beside us, and the love between us. Amen."

"Amen," Grandpa says, and spoons a mound of casserole onto my plate while I fill our water glasses and Gran offers around the snow peas.

"Amen," I whisper too.

Silence mounts after that. Mushy noodles, steam rising from our plates, the conversation of audible gulping. But her words trip me up with each bite.

The love between us.

Maybe they still care about me after all.

26

"HEY, CAN I COME in?"

I poke my head through Mr. Donnelly's door before school on Monday. He's sitting behind his desk, rocking a ginger man-bun and staring at his phone while devouring a bacon, egg, and cheese.

"Johanna! Of course." He pushes aside his breakfast, licking greasy fingers clean. "Take a seat. I'm glad you finally came in."

"Yeah," I say. "Me too."

He flashes a sad, overstated smile. "How *are* you?" he asks. "I can't imagine what you've been through these last few weeks. But you're handling it? Your grandparents are helping? They seemed so sweet at the open house last fall."

"What? Oh. Yeah, they're awesome," I say with a dismissive wave. "Hey, so, I've been thinking about it, and I'm ready to take action."

I reach into my bag for the printouts—the ones Ms. Daya,

our school librarian, helped me with when I nearly mauled her as she unlocked the library doors at 7:20 a.m. Anyway, I dump the inch-thick stack on Mr. Donnelly's desk with a *smack*.

He glances down and then back up. "What sort of action are we talking about?"

"Gun control!" I explode. "I've read the *entire* internet. There was this one statistic—did you know gun violence is the second-biggest cause of death for kids in America? And that *one hundred people a day* are killed by guns in this country? I mean, that's over four people an hour. Doesn't that blow your mind?"

"It's heartbreaking," he says. But, like, still clearly mystified.

"It's appalling! And I want to do something about it." I tuck my hair behind my ears and lean forward. "I've been feeling so lost lately, and I finally know why—because I'm not *doing* anything. Guns are everywhere, getting into kids' hands. Now that I'm part of the statistics, it's up to me to incite change. I'm ready to fight for social justice. What do you think?"

The immediate *oh-my-God-definitely* reaction I'm anticipating takes the form of Donnelly's slack jaw. "Wow. I know I've been talking to you about more extracurriculars for a while now, but is this—"

"I know! It's absolutely *perfect*."

I grab an article about my mom's death, the one from the *Fresno Bee*, and try not to shake as I push it far away from me, practically into Donnelly's lap.

"Toddlers in this country shoot people on a weekly basis," I say. "*Weekly*. I mean, Mr. D. It happens *all* the time. It could literally be happening right this second. Doesn't it make you sick?

To think that, somewhere, some innocent little girl just shot her own mom? Or dad, or brother, or sister? She's never going to see them again. No more hugs or birthdays. And she's going to have to live with that guilt forever. *I* have to live with that guilt *forever.* It isn't fair. It's fucking tragic!"

"Hey—swear jar."

I roll my eyes, breaking from my impassioned tirade to rummage through my bag for a quarter to put in Mr. Donnelly's "Retirement Fund."

He sighs heavily. "But you're right. It is fucking tragic." He tosses in a quarter of his own. "I feel like I missed a step, though. What do you want to do, exactly?"

"Initiate." My fingers trip through pages, looking for— "Here. This one. There's a local organization that does all kinds of stuff to raise awareness through education and advocacy and stuff, and they do a lot of work with schools."

"Sounds interesting."

"It *is.* And I want to get them to work with Chavez Academy on a mural project where they bring in a professional artist to work with the kids, teaching us how to paint these epic murals to end gun violence. Look—"

I cue up my phone to a video of a mural they did in Española. All these kids working on stencils, painting these sad, weepy children in bright, psychedelic colors, slogans like *We Are The Change* and *End Gun Violence* dancing throughout. I nearly cried watching it over the weekend, and I know it'll punch Mr. Donnelly in the gut too.

When it ends, I shut off my phone. "Well?"

Because this is it. The end of my plea. My insides are bursting, gleaming with determination. I don't just want this. I need it. It *must* happen.

"That was great." Donnelly exhales, brow furrowing. "But I thought you wanted to come in here so we could talk. Y'know, about your childhood? Don't you want to talk about your feelings?"

He cringes. I'm pretty sure we're both embarrassed by the phrase *talk about your feelings*, but he masks it with a chuckle.

"What I *want*," I say carefully, "is to make a change. With this mural project, we could make an actual difference in the community. It would get the whole school involved. The paper could write a piece about it, we'd be raising awareness about serious issues. It could be your magnum opus, Mr. Donnelly. You have to back me up."

An eternity passes. Donnelly sits there, stroking his Wildling beard, exuding contemplation. Meanwhile, I am slowly developing an ulcer.

"Please?" I whisper. "This could be so amazing."

Maybe he believes in the project, or maybe he's swayed by the desperation wafting off me, but finally, his lips curl into a small, compassionate grin. "I'm in."

• • •

Before bed, I call Robert. All I get is his voice mail, but I decide to leave one anyway.

"Hey, Dad—that still sounds so weird. Sorry. I thought about calling you Robert, but then . . .

"Anyway. I got the coding book in the mail today. Thanks.

"So, I have some kind of exciting news. I just proposed this art project at school, and my guidance counselor approved it! It's all about ending gun violence. Obviously that's been on my mind lately, especially after the way people are acting at school.

"Which, I guess, I kind of wondered if you could relate to? Did people treat you weird, after what happened to Mom?

"I mean, how did you deal with missing her and knowing what happened to her? I know she died a really long time ago. Sorry if this sounds random. But I feel like it's happening to me, like, right now.

"I know you're not used to being a dad, but if you have any words of wisdom, I'm all ears. Right now, I barely know how to live with myself. I just feel so guilty. And, I mean, maybe it's ridiculous to think a school mural is going to solve all my problems. But I don't know.

"Did you do anything like that? Community service, or— sorry, that's probably a really rude question for someone who went to actual prison. But like . . . is that how you got over it? Knowing that you did time and paid your dues, or whatever?

"Anyway, I miss you. I wanted to hear your voice.

"I've been thinking about Houston a lot lately too. What's it like out there? Is your apartment big? Texas always makes me think of cowboy hats and barbeque sauce and mechanical bulls. Not that you're into any of that stuff. But you're there, so my brain keeps wandering east. Do you think you'd ever have room for me, at your house? Things are so bad at home. I hate my grandparents. We basically haven't talked in weeks. They want me to get over it, but, like, how?

"I thought maybe I could come out to Texas for a while? Or—hah—forever?

"God, this message is getting really long. And pathetic. I should probably go.

"I love you. Oh fuck, I mean—shit."

I jam my finger against the pound key, heart racing.

A robotic voice chirps into my ear. "To listen to your message, press one. To continue recording, press two. To erase and rerecord your message, press three."

Without thinking too hard, I press three.

"Hey, Robert. It's Johanna, calling to say hi. Give me a shout when you can."

My chest stings as I hang up. I hide my phone and my shame underneath my pillow and curl up against it. Maybe I'm a chicken shit, but it feels like too much. Like, all those questions are too painful to ask someone, even my dad.

I don't know—maybe it isn't the questions I'm afraid of.

27

IT OCCURS TO ME that I haven't uttered a single word to Gabby in fifteen days. Which is probably why I gasp when I see her sitting on my front porch after school on Tuesday. It makes me fresh-bruise tender to see her there, knees tucked up into her chest, head lowered. She looks up when I kill the engine, but her body stays small.

"Did you know she was coming?" I ask, glaring at Leah in the passenger seat.

Leah's puppy-dog eyes get all tentative and hopeful, but she shakes her head.

Still, I don't get out of the car. Leah and I were supposed to be celebrating how we're badass, mural-making activists now. I'm not prepared for a catfight or an apology or whatever this is supposed to be.

"Are you going to get out?"

"Do I have to?"

"Unless you plan on living in your car, yeah."

I groan a little and slam the door behind me, folding my arms as I meet Gabby's eyes. "What are you doing here?"

"Mrs. Vargas dropped off some cookies," she hollers—has to holler, because I won't come any closer than the driveway. She holds up a heart-shaped tin and gives it a gentle rattle. "Oatmeal chocolate chip. She said Steve told her about what happened to you. She wanted to say how sorry she is, and see if there's anything she can do to help. Your neighbor is really nice."

Mrs. Vargas is sorry, I think, rolling my eyes.

Gabby's chest heaves. "I didn't tell her it was my fault that everyone found out in the first place. Or that we aren't friends anymore. I was afraid she might not leave the cookies, and Mrs. Vargas makes *seriously* good cookies."

I bite back a grin. Nothing's holding Leah back, though. She giggles, and I feel a twinge of jealousy. "Well, unless Mrs. Vargas had anything else to say, you can leave the cookies on the porch and go."

"Jo," Leah says.

But Gabby shakes her head. "It's okay."

She makes this big show of placing the tin on my porch swing and backing away from it. "I'll leave," she says softly. "But let me say *one* thing. I know I didn't make you cookies, but I *am* sorry. Painfully, profoundly, *extraordinarily* sorry for what I did." Her face hangs in this pained, first-day-of-sleepaway-camp expression. "If it weren't for me, Mrs. Vargas wouldn't need to be making cookies. Nobody would have found out about your mom, and we'd still be best friends. I screwed up."

"You did."

"The thing is, I can get loud," she says, painstakingly quiet. "I am loud and passionate and protective. I wear my heart on my sleeve, and you love me for it. Well, most of the time. But I was wrong. I was making it about me, and I got defensive. I had no right to judge how you handle things. Or to yell."

It's a decent apology, but it only makes the trees spin circles around me. A moldy reminder of that day in the student lounge. Eyes, teeth, judgment. My skin burns around the edges.

"Thanks."

I brush past her, glancing back only to make sure Leah is behind me—except, that's when I see them. Across the street, my neighbor Steve and a few of his soccer buddies have abandoned their scrimmage and are standing on his lawn, red-faced and breathless and incapable of shutting their dumbfounded mouths as they stare at me. Brakes slam in my guts. Steve has always been a decent guy, but the others look like jocks. Maybe even bullies.

Gabby must notice my skin go pale. She turns around, squaring her shoulders, widening her stance. "What the hell are you looking at?" she yells across the street.

"Gab, it's okay," I say.

But I can feel her heart breaking for me, desperate to make amends. She juts her chin toward Steve's burliest, toughest-looking friend. "Is there a problem?"

The guy shakes his head in fast-forward. All of them balk.

Whether or not they mean it, Gabby's obviously feeling

extra right now, because she bends down and scoops a rock off the ground, squeezing it in her palm. "You sure about that?"

The burly guy pales, his jaw dropping down to the Earth's core.

That's when Gabby freezes. Her eyes flick over to me, mouth widening into a total grimace-face emoji as she remembers to reel in her temper. The rock makes a little *tink* sound as she drops it into the bushes. I flash a tiny smile back at her because, this, right here? This moment feels like everything. Like I'm an idiot for ever doubting her loyalty. We glance back, and the boys are running toward Steve's house, slamming themselves inside. Steve peeks through his living room curtain, and I flash him an apologetic smile. He does the same. Maybe I owe *him* a batch of cookies now.

"Dude!" Leah swats Gabby's arm.

"What—too much?" she says sheepishly, then frowns. "I'll leave, though. I get that you still hate me."

"Wait," I call after her. "Were you really going to stone a freshman for me?"

"I mean, I could have. Remember little league?" She cracks a grin. "But no, of course not. What do you think they're doing right now?"

Leah snorts. "Changing their underwear."

I shriek with laughter and start walking toward the house. "You coming?"

Gabby hesitates. "Yeah?"

"I think you're safer indoors, with no rocks."

The girls follow me into the house, empty except for Magic.

We kick off our shoes and grab some milk to go with Mrs. Vargas's cookies, and it feels right, the three of us settling down on my bedroom floor, stuffing our faces while I fill Gabby in on the mural. How it's going to be all colorful and epic; how Milo's already offered to paint something for it.

"I didn't know you were into activism," Gabby says after a while.

Which is a weird response? Kind of?

"Well, I am."

Something like doubt flickers across her face, quickly masked by a smile. "It sounds awesome."

"Yeah?"

"Yes!" She laughs. "Now, tell me what I can do to help."

"We need to come up with design ideas."

"Why don't I be your campaign manager?" she says with a stink face. "You know I can't draw for shit."

Years' worth of terrible stick figures come to mind, and I snicker. "It doesn't have to be the *Mona Lisa*. Draw something simple. Like a flower. Flowers are easy."

She raises one eyebrow; challenge accepted. Leah tosses her a Bic from my desk drawer, and Gabby flips over one of my gun statistic printouts, guiding ink along the page, slow and unsteady. When she's done, Leah and I lean closer, eyes bulging.

"What the frig is that?" Leah asks.

I squint. "It looks like a penis. With wings."

"What?" Gabby angles it back toward herself, milk coming out of her nose as she laughs. "It's supposed to be a tulip!"

"That is *so* not a tulip."

I snatch the pen from her and add some hairy balls to the stem. Leah puts a cigarette in its mouth and gives it an eye patch. We literally roll on the floor laughing like complete idiots. Completely perfect idiots, back to being *us* again. As if something invisible has clicked in the universe.

"Okay." I wipe my eyes. "I take it back. Definitely do *not* paint flying dick flowers on my school mural to end gun violence."

"Pretty much, never draw again," adds Leah. "Your mom's a professional artist, Gabriella. For *shame*."

Gabby chucks dirty socks from my hamper at the both of us, and we keep on laughing. Long and hard till my stomach burns. The kind of messing around, girly-ass bullshit that used to be our definition of normal. Laughing used to be normal, and it feels as though I haven't done it properly in a lifetime.

"You guys suck," Gabby huffs, hiding a grin.

"Por vida." I grin back.

For life.

28

ROBERT'S ENTIRE EXISTENCE HAS basically morphed into a voice mail, which is completely freaking me out. What does it mean if it takes him more than eight seconds to reply to a text? Why are we incapable of contacting each other at decent, recipient-ready times? I'm such a nervous wreck about it, that when my phone buzzes in the middle of fifth period on Wednesday, I practically scream when I can't answer it on the spot. At least it's art class (of *all* my teachers, Mrs. Keton will kill me the least), but still. It isn't until lunch that I get around to checking my voice mail.

"Hey! Johanna! It's your dad—man, that never gets old. I'm at work. Been pretty busy. Tons of meetings. Got a business trip to New York City coming up. I've never been there. Have you? I know CBGB shut down a long time ago, but I bet they still sell T-shirts on Canal Street. If I have time, I'll buy you a souvenir. Hey, maybe we could go together one day. What do you think? I could take you to the top of the Empire State Building. Bet all our problems would look a lot smaller from up there. Shoot, I need to go. Oh, hey, so, once this trip's over, I'll look at my schedule and see when I can make it back to Santa Fe. I miss it out there. Well, study hard, and talk to you soon. I love you, kiddo. Bye."

The message ends, but I hit Play again, skipping all the way to the end.

"I love you, kiddo. Bye."

"I love you, kiddo."

"I love you."

29

MY GIF REARS ITS ugly head again, and this time it stings a little more. I still look like this demented Frankenstein's monster and Ursula the sea witch hybrid, but now people are adding captions—about me, about the mural idea. About what a spoiled brat I am; that I'm trying to atone for my sin, throw tantrums, fish for attention. Someone thinks I made the whole thing up, and my mom is living in Romania somewhere with her new family.

I mean, Romania. *Seriously?* I wish I could delete the whole world sometimes. Flatten anyone who's had a single thought beyond the truth.

I'm still sitting in my car in the driveway after school, mesmerized by the way they've added lightning bolts over me, how they've made me into a cranky marionette, when Steve Vargas appears at the hood of my car, waving tentatively to get my attention.

I stick my phone in my bag, my exhale turning into a whimper. I hate that there's dread in me. That I'm *this* close to having a real-life GIF meltdown at the thought of my puny freshman neighbor giving me grief right now.

"Hey," he says, when I finally get out of the car.

My voice pinches. "Hey."

Steve gulps, and I don't know why he looks so nervous. Which only makes *me* more nervous.

"Is this about Gabby?" I ask quickly. "Sorry she freaked you and your friends out the other day. Her heart was in the right place."

"Thanks," he says, scratching his buzzed head. "But that isn't why I'm here. I heard you're putting together an anti-gun violence thing? Rachel Fromowitz said it's going to be a mural?"

"Oh." I pull my bag over my shoulders. "It's not totally a thing yet. I'm working on it with Mr. Donnelly, and maybe Mrs. Keton."

Steve nods and bites his lip, following me up onto the porch. He veers over toward the swing, the whole thing creaking as he sits. Steve Vargas's butt has not touched this porch swing in—what—a million years? Two million? This lanky, pimple-faced boy I haven't been friends with in nearly a decade. He cracks his knuckles, glancing over at me. It's unclear what exactly is happening right now, but I cross my arms and sit gingerly beside him. I'm only 10 percent afraid we'll fall.

"My family is really anti-guns," he says, his adorable freshman voice cracking. "My cousin Henry's friend's brother? Well, he got shot by the police."

Who that is, in relation to Steve, takes me a second to figure out. But I cover my confusion with a frown. "Oh, shit. I'm so sorry, I didn't know."

"They live in Albuquerque," he explains. "I only met him once. But it was really, really sad. I think about it sometimes. I've never met anybody else who was, like, a victim of gun violence before. I just wanted to tell you, I guess."

My heart prickles on the word *victim*. Because I'm not one, am I?

We're quiet for a minute. Me and Steve, gently kicking our feet against the floorboards. It isn't as awkward as I would have thought. Kind of calming, almost.

"I've never even seen a gun," I say quietly. "I mean, not that I can remember. It's weird to be associated with something that feels so foreign to me. Sometimes I still can't believe I really did it."

"That's . . ." He gulps. "I'm really sorry."

"Yeah?" It surprises me how nice it is to hear those words. "Thanks."

His face goes pink, the zits on his cheeks flaring up red. "I should go," he says, voice cracking.

"Me too. I'm trying to get some ideas together for this mural."

"I'm glad you're doing it."

"Thanks for saying that."

He gulps again. "Do you think I could help?"

"Oh, um—"

"Not right now. But, like, when you actually start painting?"

I smile. "Yeah, that'd be really cool."

"Okay, awesome. See you around school, I guess."

Before he makes it down a single step, something comes over me and I reach out to him for a hug. In an instant, I'm holding back tears, overwhelmed by this sharp and grateful appreciation for Steve frigging Vargas. This tactile reminder that not *everyone* is against me. It's not till Steve sort of awkwardly puts one gangly arm around my waist—rapidly raising it up to my shoulder, then removing it entirely to pat my arm—that I realize how possibly *awkward* this moment is. I pull back, blushing. Not blushing as fantastically as pimple-faced Steve, but we're both feeling the glow.

I step back. "Sorry."

"It's okay," he says. His voice cracks for the tenth time, and it makes me want to hug him all over again, but I resist.

"Thanks for offering to help," I add. "It's nice to know people are in my corner."

He keeps his lips zipped, maybe afraid his voice will betray him again.

I wave goodbye, grinning as I run into the house. Gran's at the kitchen counter, her glasses pushed down along her nose, surrounded by cookbooks and Post-its and highlighters. She looks up at me, and her eyes twinkle in surprise.

"Is that a smile on your face?"

The smile fades, but I manage a lopsided replacement. "Yeah. I was outside talking to Steve. He's a cool guy, actually."

"Little Steven Vargas?" Gran says. She frowns, but in a thoughtful—*huh, who knew?*—kind of way. "Well, I've always liked Tina and Hector. Doesn't surprise me they raised that boy right."

I wonder if she thinks she raised me right. How big a disappointment I am to her and Grandpa. Beyond the obvious, I mean. I will never be able to undo what I did to their daughter, but they've been raising me for thirteen years, knowing that I killed her. I bet Gran thinks it's my behavior in the past month that's been the true abomination. Though, I suppose, the same could be said for her.

Before leaving the kitchen, I grab an apple from the fruit bowl and peer at her open cookbook—a recipe for some kind of pizza casserole. She's stuck a Post-it note along the edge and written: *REPLACE GROUND BEEF WITH TOFU???*

Now *there's* an appetizing thought.

On my way out of the room, I turn back. "Gran?"

She looks up, bracing herself for whatever I'm about to unleash.

"What about lentils?" I say. "Instead of tofu."

Her face softens again, lips forming a grim smile. "Lentils. Well, now, I hadn't thought of that."

I mean, lentils or tofu—take your pick. It's never going to taste like ground beef, but I let out a soft exhale as I head down the hall to my bedroom.

30

OUR SCHOOL LIBRARY IS a drink-free zone, but that doesn't stop Leah from bringing in to-go cups for all of us from Bluebell. She drags a chair from Annette's table over to where Milo and Gabby and I are sitting, then peers down at my sketchbook.

"Nice. Is it for the mural?"

"Yup."

All week, I've been spending my free time holed up at the library, surrounded by a thousand colored pencils, working on sketches and emblems, researching inspirational quotes and leaders. Every part of me aches, but in a good way.

"Milo's the real artist," I say. "I'm trying to keep up with him."

"Shut up," he says, kissing me. He glances around the table. "I meant that in the most feminist way possible. Jo's really talented. In fact, so talented that I'm out of my league."

"Hardly. I suck."

"You don't suck," Gabby insists. "I've never seen you so focused—on stuff other than sewing, at least."

Milo starts to get up, putting his books into his messenger bag.

"You're leaving?" I pout.

"I'm meeting Hayes."

"Hayes?" I say, feigning jealousy. "Look at you, making friends."

"Your boy's growin' up."

"Oh my *gawd*, you two." Gabby moans, but then grins.

"Nice to see you too, Gabby. Leah, a pleasure, as always." Milo flashes me a *Hey, Girl* smile, bending down to kiss me again. "Call me later?"

I nod, watching him walk away, wondering if I'll ever *not* get shivers looking at that butt and broad shoulders. Hope not. Across the table, Leah starts snapping her fingers at me. My cheeks flush as I look back at her.

"Good girl," she says, tossing me an imaginary treat. "Now. Tell me what you're doing."

"I found an article," I say. "Y'know—by the artist Barb, who helps with the murals? She said researching quotes can be really inspirational, to help get ideas flowing." I lean forward. "Listen to this one: *In a gentle way, you can shake the world.* Isn't that beautiful?"

Leah curls her hands into a heart shape. "Who's it by?"

"Wait," Gabby says. "Let me guess—"

"Excuse me?" From the next table, Annette huffs. Audibly.

"Could you guys keep it down? This is *the library*, and some of us are trying *to study*."

"Uh, we *are* studying," Gabby shoots back.

"Yeah." I giggle, mostly at Gabby and Leah. They giggle too, which only angers the student council beast more. I clear my throat. "Sorry."

Annette nods. "Just please keep it down, okay? Not everyone wants to hear all that bullshit."

"Bullshit?" Gabby sputters.

"Annette, it's *Gandhi*," I gasp, as if he were my first-born son.

"For shame," Leah adds, *tsking* in disappointment.

Annette's eyebrows pinch—torn between peace on earth and a quiet study environment. She motions toward my notebook. "Is that for the mural?"

I nod. "Why? Do you want to help?"

Gabby snickers, but I kick her foot under the table. Unless Leah told her, Gabby doesn't know about the photocopies-on-the-lockers incident—aka, how Annette saved my ass.

"Who is your faculty sponsor, by the way?" Annette asks.

"Mr. Donnelly. Why?"

"Dude," Gabby says. "If you don't want to work on the mural, can we, at least?"

Annette huffs, looking back at the mountain of SAT prep books in front of her.

I stretch my arms, trying to refocus on my work. Mr. Donnelly said we could set up a meeting with the gun violence prevention group next week, and it's really important to me that we are super ready. Show 'em we mean business. Already, I have an entire notebook full of ideas. Hours spent without me berating myself over my mother's death or worrying about where I stand with Robert or if things will ever go back to normal with my grandparents.

A few minutes later, I tap our table with my eraser. "Did you guys see the flyers I put up? Volunteering for the mural committee?"

Leah frowns. "Where'd you put them?"

"On the bulletin board and in the quad. A few people emailed me about it, but I thought there'd be more. I feel like someone is taking them down."

"It wasn't me," Gabby says. Her voice gets all low and dancehall-Jamaican in this incredibly spot-on Shaggy impersonation. I can't *not* roar with laughter.

"Seriously?" Annette shouts. "Shut *up*, Johanna."

"Why don't you leave her alone?"

I look up, surprised to see Selene Kenworth rushing to my rescue with a French dictionary tucked under her arm. She takes Milo's abandoned seat, sitting so close, I can feel her lavender body lotion moisturizing my own skin. "She's been through enough without your crap. Don't you think?"

Annette's face reddens.

I flash Selene an appreciative smile, only slightly wondering when we became I-got-your-back friends; remembering the days of yore when she complimented Annette's jewelry rather than glaring dagger-eyes at her.

I wonder if Annette had the same thought—about the bracelet—because it takes her a good few seconds to snap back to attention, tightening her ponytail for battle.

"Well, *sorry*." She slams her college prep books shut, carting everything two tables farther away from us for some kind of ultimate solitude. "Johanna's problems aren't any more important than anyone else's. Okay? I'm just trying to study. Showing respect for your fellow students shouldn't be too much to ask," she stage-whispers.

The rest of us sigh.

"Whatever," Leah mutters.

"Are you okay?" asks Selene.

"Yeah, fine." I turn to her. "What's *your* problem with Annette?"

She swats the air dismissively. "She's trying to take funding away from the cheerleading squad. Apparently the 'robotics club' needs it. Such bullshit."

It doesn't totally sound like bullshit. And I don't totally get why the word *robotics* deserves air quotes. But I shake my head commiseratively anyway.

"Oh, wow, is that for the mural?" she asks, eyes brightening as they land on my notebook. "*The best weapon is to sit down and talk.* That is totally beautiful. Did you write that?"

"Nope. Nelson Mandela."

"Wow," she says.

"Oooh. *Deep.*"

We glance behind us. Cringe. The douchebag voice belongs to Tim, the whole room reeking of farts as he stumbles out of the boys' bathroom. He walks up to our table with Brandon and the other boy banders collecting like dust bunnies behind him. I feel my pulse spike as he points to my notebook, like, *May I?* before just grabbing it anyway, skimming the pages.

Brandon snorts with laughter. "*Why is it that giving guns is so easy, but giving books is so hard?*" he says in this horrendously offensive, vaguely African accent. "Who the hell is Malala Yousa-whatever?"

"Seriously?" I say. "Brandon, you never cease to amaze."

"What's this for, anyway?" asks Tim. "Your gay-ass mural?"

"Hey!" my entire table barks in unison.

He raises an apologetic palm. "Just saying, I didn't know you cared about gun control."

"Of course I do." My voice grows claws, cheeks burning. "Would you fuck off already? Give me back my notebook."

"Give it back to her, you dick," Gabby growls.

"Come on," adds Selene.

"Okay, okay. Shit, you guys. Take a joke."

Relief settles in my ribs as Tim drops the notebook. I can tell Brandon wants to add something dickish too, but the shitster grin on his doughy cheeks evaporates when Dr. Sanders pushes through the library doors. Fear whitens Tim's skin instantly. He's probably terrified the whole thing has been caught on the library's security camera. I'm sort of enjoying his petrification until Sanders, in his tweed suit and stupid red bowtie, looks directly at me, beelining toward our table.

"Miss Carlson, a quick word?"

"Oh." My shoulders roll back automatically. "Um, sure?"

He smiles an odd, *my-lunch-isn't-sitting-well* smile and walks over to the librarian's desk for more privacy.

What does Colonel Sanders want? Gabby mouths, and Leah goes, *Are you okay?*

I shrug and walk over to him. "Is something wrong?"

"I wanted to let you know—" Sanders clears gravel from his throat, ducking closer to me. "We're having a lockdown drill tomorrow."

I blink. "O-*kay?*"

"We're required to have one per semester."

Over at my table, Tim picks up a Martin Luther King Jr. biography, suddenly enraptured. Everyone's doing the same thing, eyes hovering from behind books, aglow with anticipation. I look back at Sanders, not really sure how to respond because WTF does he want me to say? *Well done for following the rules? Yay, if it'll get me out of my math test?*

"Out of sensitivity," he goes on, "I wanted to let you know that you won't be required to participate."

"I'm sorry, what?"

"I'll give you an excused absence, if you'd like to stay home and avoid any . . . reminders."

My skin goes numb, voice low. "My mother's death was not a *school shooting.*"

"No, no, of course," he says, tugging the bowtie farther from his neck. "But after all that you've been through, I didn't know if the implications of a lockdown drill might have an adverse effect. I only meant it as a courtesy."

Okay, hmmm. My heart sprints, face attempting neutrality

while trying to muster an appropriate response, so I don't end up screaming *fuck you* to the Head of School. But luckily I'm saved by Annette, who stands and clears her throat. Oh, Annette. So prim and poised in her pressed khakis, always sticking up for her fellow man. My insides exhale.

"Dr. Sanders?" she says. "Sorry, but I'm worried about this 'courtesy' you're giving Johanna. Letting her skip school? Doesn't it send a confusing message?"

Dr. Sanders stiffens. "Annette, this is none of your concern. Why don't you—"

But then Tim happens, slamming my MLK book down on the table. Not, like, *this is an outrage* loud, but clearly annoyed. "No disrespect, Dr. Sanders, but I agree with Annette. What you're offering Johanna sounds like an egregious oversight."

Sanders blinks. Half intrigued, half stupefied as he comes to the mind-bending realization that *everyone in the room is riveted by this.* "Tim, I didn't see you there. What's on your mind?"

Tim sweeps his bangs aside. "I'd like to hear what Annette has to say."

For three seconds, Dr. Sanders stands mute. Which is a really short amount of time. But it also says a lot. "Right. Of course. Annette?"

She beams quickly at Tim before refocusing on Sanders. "Well, in the past week, I've spoken to a lot of students at Chavez Academy. And I think we deserve to be heard. I realize you have a great deal of compassion—as do I—but what Johanna is trying to get away with isn't fair to the rest of the student body."

Wait, what?

"Yes, but the lockdown drill—"

"Not the drill," she says. "I'm talking about this mural she's obsessing over. Have you seen the flyers?"

Sanders coughs, looking around for one.

"There were on the bulletin board," I say.

"And *all* over the quad," Tim contributes.

"And the flyers are for a mural?" Sanders asks, trying to keep up.

"Yes. A mural that is borderline graffiti."

"*Graffiti?*" My eyes almost pop out of my head.

Annette nods, not at me but at Sanders. "Not everyone believes that our right to bear arms should be challenged. What about the rest of us? What about *our* rights?"

Brandon claps fiercely and another dozen people join in.

"Who approved this?" Sanders demands.

"Mr. Donnelly," I say. "But I assumed—didn't he—"

"I'm sorry, but I'm not buying it," chimes in Lucy Bingham, this year's Princeton-bound valedictorian. "All of a sudden *Johanna*, of all people, is an activist?"

Gabby gasps. "She *is*."

"Uh, sure." Lucy snorts. "It's obvious she's scrambling. Every other junior has like fifty clubs on their résumé—and what does she have? About two. I checked. I bet a big fancy mural is going to look great on her college applications. Can anyone say *scam?*"

Whispers erupt, and Sanders starts to nod—actually *nod* thoughtfully along with them. My blood boils. Do people honestly think that? That I'd use my own mother's death to get into college? They're not just idiots, they're monsters.

"Okay, I think we're all getting a bit off topic," Sanders eventually says, patting the air to shush the din of conspiracy. "However, I will look into this."

"Thank you for hearing us out, Dr. Sanders." Annette flashes this blue-ribbon grin that has me throwing up in my mouth. "It's really important that everyone's voices are heard."

Sanders smiles presidentially. "You're quite welcome. And I appreciate you bringing this to my attention. Looking out for your constituents once again, Annette."

"That's why I'm student council president," she says.

"Is that why you're an ass-hat too?" Selene mutters.

Giggles flutter around the room as poor Annette's face spikes crimson.

"For the record," I interject, "I am *also* her constituent, and I think the mural is a great idea. For the *school*—not personal gain, which is an absolutely putrid suggestion."

"Yeah." Gabby and Leah, and even Selene, cheer.

"And no offense," I say, "but I don't care about the stupid lockdown drill."

Sanders sniffs sharply.

"What I care about is the mural. I care about gun violence."

"Of course." He glances at his watch. "Thank you for your input. Lots to think about. Kids, I'm running late for a meeting. This is all very interesting, and I will be following up."

He speeds toward the door, and Annette pads after him, onto

the next case on her docket—some other poor constituents that need saving. As soon as they're gone, Gabby grabs my hand and leads me back to our table, past Tim, who gets a high five from Brandon on their way out of the room.

"Are you okay?" Selene asks.

"That was ridiculous," Gabby says. "I hate Annette."

"Let us know if you need help with the mural," says this freckle-faced senior named Elsa, smiling on her way out of the library. "If it happens."

I smile back, gulping when she's out of earshot. "*If* it happens?"

"That was brutal, right?" Leah shakes her head. "Annette's talking out of her ass."

"And Lucy," adds Selene. "I had no idea that was an actual rumor. Did you?"

I shrug. Mortified, mystified. And super paranoid too.

The library starts to clear out, most notably Elise from church, tightening her cardigan around her chest as she walks quickly past me. Elise who told everyone my mom's name; who's been casually scanning my locker for guns ever since. Now she's using her cable-knit sweater as a bulletproof vest.

"Do people really hate the mural?" I ask dismally.

"Of course not," Leah says.

"Then who are Annette's quote-unquote *constituents*?"

"Not me," Selene promises. "But people must be listening to her and, like, talking to her, for once. I bet it's totally going to her head."

"And since when is Colonel Sanders pretending he doesn't

know about the mural? I'm *sure* Donnelly talked to him about it. I mean, didn't he?"

The girls shrug.

Maybe I look as sick as I feel, because Gabby pats my shoulder. "Don't sweat it. Me and my dick flowers are going to paint the shit out of that mural. Okay?"

Leah bursts out laughing. I know some kind of lighthearted reaction is expected of me too, so I give them what little delight I can muster. "Right."

I sink back into my seat, beside a sympathetic Selene, surrounded by all my sketchbooks and biographies and colored pencils. What was I doing before all this? Oh, yeah. I look back at the drawing in my sketchbook—the one Tim and Brandon found so hilarious. A little girl, kneeling beside a broken heart. I try to steady my hand and let the voices in my head slip away. Deep breath in . . . this is about more than crabby Annette and her fascist agenda. Deep breath out . . . she can't bully me, I won't let her.

Steadying my trembling hand, I pick up the lightest blue in the pack and use it to color in the tears on her cheek.

31

THE LIBRARY DRAMA BLOWS over.

Just kidding. It completely doesn't.

Two days later, I'm called into Colonel Chickenhead's office, and when I get there, he and Mr. Donnelly are both standing like FBI agents, rigid suits and even more rigid looks on their pale faces. Donnelly doesn't need to say "bad news" for me to know that it is cataclysmic.

"Oh, God," I gasp. "Is it my grandparents? Are they okay?"

"No. I mean, yes!" Mr. Donnelly sputters, his eyes instantly enormous. "I'm sure they're totally fine. It's nothing like that. Um—" He pauses, shamefaced as he glances at Dr. Sanders.

"Take a seat," Sanders says. "How are you?"

"Fine?" I say, but I'm wracking my brain now. "Is this about the lockdown drill? It didn't upset me, if that's what you're worried about."

He seems blank at first. "Oh. No, not that. Mr. Donnelly

and I would like to have a word with you about this mural project you've proposed."

My heart speeds up. "What do you mean?"

"Unfortunately, you've hit a bump in the road." His unibrow pinches. "There have been several complaints lodged—among both staff and students—and the school board feels it would be best to view both sides of the argument."

"Wait, *teachers* are against this thing?"

My mind goes straight to Mr. Gonzales, burly and insecure and threatened by my girly disobedience. Maybe even Coach Fishkin, who I can totally picture having a cabinet of rifles in his basement.

Sanders won't answer my question, but he says, "There's going to be a hearing."

"A hearing?" My stomach drops to my ankles. "But I've been working on ideas all week. Sketching and researching and picking which wall it should go on and, and—" I squeeze my temples, scrambling frantically for another argument. "We're supposed to meet with the organization next week. I emailed the founder, and she's excited. You already agreed to it, Mr. Donnelly. Tell him!"

"Hey, cool down," Donnelly says. "It's not the end of the world."

"Yes, it is! Dr. Sanders, don't *you* want the mural?"

He smiles evenly. "It sounds like a nice idea, but—"

"A *nice idea*? Are you serious right now?"

"Johanna," Donnelly says in a warning tone. His eyes bug out like, *Slow your roll.*

But I can't. I mean, this is my life I'm fighting for.

"Annette's behind this, isn't she? She's turning everyone against me."

"I think the *staff* know how to make their own decisions." Sanders almost laughs.

"Fine, whatever." I sigh. "But I know she called it graffiti. Why can't everyone see that it is a mural to end *gun* violence."

"It's not as black and white as that," Sanders says, barely managing not to roll his eyes. "For instance, who is going to pay for this? The school has no funds allocated for a mural. And who will oversee it?"

"The organization gets grants to pay for it!" I cry out. "And Mr. Donnelly will oversee it."

Sanders stares at me with a sort of plastic serenity. He waits a beat after I've stopped talking, like, *Are you done whining, young lady?* Then he nods. "Yes. Well. You can explain your side on Monday."

"The hearing is in *three days?*" I gasp. "No. This is—you can't do this. I've put in so much work already."

"Perhaps you should have secured per*mission* before jumping in head-first."

"I did get permission!" I wail. "From Mr. Donnelly!"

"Well, Mr. Donnelly should have followed the proper channels."

Donnelly looks at the ground and clears his throat, super emphatically. He doesn't need to say anything for me to know he means, *I did tell you, you chickenheaded asshole.* The room goes quiet while my insides spew onto the floor. It's like I can feel my heart breaking. If this mural doesn't happen, I'll—

"This is really, really important to me," I say, my throat tight and aching. "I wanted everyone to stand together for gun safety. What about school pride?"

"But it isn't about the school, is it?" Sanders says. "Not everyone believes this mural is the right choice for Chavez Academy."

Despite the tears welling up in my eyes, Dr. Sanders walks brusquely over to the door. "I like your passion, and I encourage you to present that to the school board. Sorry to cut this short, but I have a conference call. See you Monday."

He practically kicks us into the hallway after that.

"I am *so* sorry," Mr. Donnelly says, reeling beside me as we walk through the admin building. "I feel like this is my fault. I *did* tell Dr. Sanders about it, and I thought he said yes. It's usually fine to get one teacher's approval for a school club or organization. I honestly didn't think there'd be an issue. But this is a small school with a lot of *very* big opinions."

"It's bullshit," I say, and hand him a quarter for the jar.

"I know," he says. "But Dr. Sanders is right about your passion—stay fired up. All you have to do is explain what makes this mural so good for the school. Make the board understand that you are *right* about this. Between you and me—you *so* are."

I smile weakly. "It's bad enough that I have to deal with the hate and the shit-talking on a daily basis, and all that crap online. Now they're taking me to court for an art project? It's ridiculous."

"Do you know who posted it?" Donnelly asks, scrunching his nose. "The photo?"

"I have a few guesses. Annette wasn't one of 'em, though." I shake my head. "I really thought she was on my side."

"She's just trying to do what's right."

"*Alt* right," I grumble.

"Hey, she's a good kid."

"If you say so."

We both sigh, commiseratively, listlessly.

I'm numb as we push through the doors and onto the quad. Back into the real world, down hallways filled with enemies. Three hundred private school brats who straight up refuse to let me move on with my life.

"Stay strong," Donnelly says. He pats my sagging shoulder as we part ways.

• • •

"Wait, so, remind me who Annette is?"

I stretch my legs onto Milo's lap, reeling off details about my newfound nemesis as we listen to Iggy Pop on his couch after school. "She's the junior class president, student council president, field hockey captain, math tutor, eco warrior, blah-blah-blah. Once I beat her in a spelling bee—y'think that has anything to do with it?"

"Sounds like I'm 'unna have to go all Tonya Harding on her ass."

"That would rule," I say, pausing from my frothing anger to kiss him. He tastes like baked apples. I'm hungry for more, but my brain is in too much of a fog. Iggy Pop sings about "Lust for Life" keeping us alive, and I can't stop thinking about my own life, picturing the mural as a swirl of paint, my dreams being flushed down the toilet. I settle back against a pillow and look at the stack of index cards laid out around me. Stuff about the First Amendment, reasons why this is such a positive way for us to express ourselves and raise social awareness. Quotes. Statistics. Stuff I can't *believe* I have to explain.

To punish myself, I google Annette Martinez, looking for intel. Surprisingly, she's got a couple of different social media profiles, so I click on one. The page is predictably pitiful. Barely any updates, even fewer likes. Flyers for swim meets, pictures of her in hideous pantsuits outside Model UN meetings, dorking it up on hikes, firing a rifle.

Hold on.

"Milo, she's got a gun."

"What?" He peers up from his own laptop screen to look at mine. "It says she's a member of the Civilian Marksmanship Program."

"What the hell is that?"

"Hold on, I'm looking it up. Okay, it's basically a private corporation that trains people to shoot firearms and air guns, and then they hold competitions and stuff."

"Shooting competitions?"

The photos confirm it. A website full of confident, smiling, mostly white teenagers holding rifles. They make shooting guns look fun. Character-building. Fulfilling. There's even a quote below a picture of a spiky-haired guy in the same giant headphones Annette's wearing, his hands tight around a long thin barrel. They've quoted him explaining how the program taught him life skills like discipline and responsibility, and how he now has greater self-esteem and respect for others. He looks happy. Happier than I am, anyway.

"Gross," I say, tearing my eyes away. "At least now I know what her vendetta is about."

"You think she's anti-mural because she's ammosexual?"

"First of all, do not say *ammosexual*." I shudder. "That's not a thing. But, I mean, yeah. We're kind of looking at the proof."

"Actually, smarty-pants, it *is* a thing. A *word*, in fact. But come on. She's also cuddling a newborn, and holding a trophy for"—he squints—"a swimming competition. Which she got second place in. *Ooh*, maybe she's *aquasexual*."

"Are you making fun of me right now?"

"Of course not. I'm just saying she looks naturally competitive."

"No," I shoot back, "you're saying I'm overreacting. You're belittling my feelings to pretend that what is obviously a *vendetta* is just a *coincidence*." I kick my feet off him and push myself to the other end of the sofa. "I can't believe you're taking her side."

"Taking her—what?" Milo croaks. "All I meant is that she's not necessarily chapter president of the NRA."

"She's holding a gun!"

"She's holding a baby in the next picture!"

Rage boils up inside me while Milo manages to look as

laid-back as an Abercrombie ad. "Are you saying I should drop it? Let her shit all over my mural because she loves babies?"

He snorts and rolls his eyes.

"I'm sharing a legitimate fear, and you're *laughing* at me?" I pause to huff. "You're my boyfriend, Milo. You're supposed to be—"

"Boyfriend-ier?" he supplies. With dimples. "Come on, Jo."

"*You* come on," I yell. "This is really important to me. I've finally found something that's going to help fix me, and she's trying to take it away. It's like you don't even care."

My voice pierces the air, and we both blush. Milo swallows. I assume he'll follow it up with an apology, but he looks quietly back at his laptop.

"What?"

"Nothing." He shrugs, but in the most *something* way.

"Wait, are you mad at me?"

"I didn't think I was, but—" He scratches his head. "What do you want from me? I get that you hate Annette, but that has nothing to do with me. At least, it shouldn't. And why are you acting like your whole life depends on this mural? You don't need to be fixed, Jo. What you went through was horrible, but it was thirteen years ago. Like it or not, it's a part of you."

"Oh, so I guess I better move on, then, huh?" I spit back. "God, you sound like my grandmother. It makes me sick."

Milo doesn't respond. He gently shuts his computer and gets up off the sofa, walking toward the kitchen.

"Where are you going?"

"I'm thirsty."

He rounds the corner, and I bite my lip, trying to predict our future through sound effects. The fridge door opens, slams shut. The tab of a soda can clicks with relief. A fizzy, frustrated exhale. Each new sound adds another goose bump to my arms. I wait as long as I can and then put my laptop beside his, tiptoeing into the kitchen. He's leaning against the sink, smoldering eyes turned to the window.

"I'm sorry," I whisper.

"For what?" he says stiffly.

"I'm not sure?"

He puts his Sprite down and sighs. "Can I say something?"

I hold my breath and nod.

"This is really hard."

I freeze. "Are you breaking up with me?"

"What? No. I'm just saying *this*—what you're going through—is really fucking hard. And I'm scared I can't help you the right way."

I bite my lip, waiting for him to continue.

"You're so fragile," he says softly. "I barely knew you before all of this, but I know it's changed you. This mural has you so manic, and I think it's a great idea, but I don't want you to get your hopes up, if people really are against it. If Sanders is one of them, maybe you need to be realistic. He's got a lot more authority than you—all the fucking authority, come to think of it."

"You want me to give up?"

"No, but he's obviously kind of a dick. Being all dismissive of you."

"And so, that's it." I cross my arms. "You think he's already made up his mind."

"No, that's not . . ." Milo sighs. "Listen to yourself, though. I'm just talking, and you're getting mad. I'm not *trying* to piss you off, but I shouldn't have to be afraid to speak my mind. It's like you want me to be perfect, but I can't. Sometimes I have to just be seventeen."

He stops talking, and I realize his eyes are moist. It scares me a little, to see him so raw and vulnerable. Makes me feel guilty as hell too. Like an idiot for putting him in this position. I catch his eye and offer an appreciative pout. His lips pinch into a sad, resigned kind of smile. I tiptoe across the kitchen and take his hand, kissing his thumb. He exhales and kisses my forehead.

"I'm sorry," I whisper.

"What are you sorry for now?"

"*Now*, I'm sorry for being Demando Girlfriend."

He grins. "You're not Demando Girlfriend."

"I've never had a boyfriend," I say, feeling my cheeks flush. "I'm used to Leah and Gabby. They've always taken my side, no matter what, because we're best friends. Even my grandparents used to always be there for me. But now everything's different. Nobody knows how to act around me because I'm not *me* anymore, and it's weird and horrible and it hurts."

"I know."

"And maybe I *am* kind of obsessed with this mural," I grumble. "But is that so wrong? To throw myself into something that's going to heal me *and* help the world? I hate that Dr. Sanders called it 'nice.' What a banal word. And that people think I'm doing it to impress college admissions. It pisses me off. But I'm sorry I took it out on you."

"Do *not* be sorry," he says. "*I'm* sorry you have so much shit to deal with. And I know I'm not Gabby or Leah or Gran, but you can tell me anything. I want to be there for you—as long as you don't bite my head off for saying the wrong thing."

I nod and rest my head against his chest.

He looks out the kitchen window, toward the driveway where his mom's car won't be parked for at least another hour. "If I tell you how much I hate Annette, can we have make-up sex?"

I punch him in the stomach. "You've already distracted me enough. I'm supposed to be solidifying my arguments for Monday. I should be with Gabby right now, not you. She's the one with the debate-team brain."

"Fine, back to those notecards." He massages my shoulders as he guides me toward the living room. "I didn't mean to get you down. I think you'll be great on Monday. Just be prepared that if Annette is as hardcore driven as you say, she's going to have a solid argument too."

"I know."

"And," he adds, handing me my computer, "if she wins, I'll reconsider the whole tire-iron-to-the-knee thing."

"See?" I grin. "Sometimes you manage to say the *perfect* thing."

32

"A HEARING?" ROBERT SAYS. "Your school sounds like an episode of *Law & Order*."

"Right? Yeah . . ."

Silence buzzes on the line, long enough for Robert to launch into a clumsy retelling of his favorite episode of a show I've never seen. I lean toward the bathroom mirror, dabbing a mascara wand against my lashes, hand shaking so bad I nearly smear it on my eyebrow. The story ends, and he yawns while I reach into the medicine cabinet for the Pepto. Maybe its pinkness will unknot my gridlocked guts; maybe it'll make me as chilled out as my father seems to perpetually be.

"You nervous?" he asks.

"You have *no* idea."

"Don't sweat it. For what it's worth, I'm impressed that you want to make a mural at all. You're so passionate. I don't remember caring about anything besides video games when I was your age. Your generation is so good at making a differ-ence in the world."

"It's not that big a deal," I lie.

"Mandy would have been proud. I'm sorry she can't be here to see you like this."

Blood drains straight out of my face and circles the sink drain.

"You still there?" Robert says. "Did I lose you?"

"No, I—I'm here."

"Everything okay?" he asks, and when I don't answer, he clears his throat. "I'm never sure if I should bring her up or stay quiet."

"You should," I say. "It's hard sometimes, that's all."

Tears well up too fast in my eyes. *Mandy would have been proud.* Would have been. Isn't. Can't *be.* I sit on the closed toilet lid, tucking my knees up into my chest and trying to keep my sobs silent.

"Jo?"

"I'm here."

"Do you want to talk about it?"

"No," I say quickly. "You're being too nice. I don't deserve it."

"What?"

"If it wasn't for me—" My voice breaks. I pull the phone away for a second, burying my face in a hand towel. "The whole reason I'm doing this mural is because of what I did. You think I'm passionate? Until a month ago, all I cared about was mak-ing clothes and hanging with my friends."

"It's okay to be a kid."

"But I'm not *just* a kid," I bark. "I did something terrible, and I have to make up for it. I *have* to make a difference. The world wouldn't need so much fixing if I hadn't, if I hadn't—" I pause, choking on sobs.

"Sorry," I say a minute later. "You don't have to say anything."

He doesn't, but I hear an exhale slither uncomfortably through the phone.

My heart rips to shreds for him, for everything I've put him through. I blot my tears away and clear my throat. "Sorry. I miss her so much, and I don't even know what I'm missing, you know? It's frustrating sometimes."

"She had a great smile," Robert says after a second. "The way it tugged up on the right more than the left? Yours does that too, actually."

I watch my face in the mirror and smile. "I never noticed that before."

"Your voice too. I don't think I realized it till we started talking on the phone and I could really *hear* you, y'know? You sound like her when she was telling jokes. Kinda droll like that. I still fall asleep most nights thinking about her. Guess it's my version of counting sheep." He pauses, laughing self-consciously. "But now I get to think about you too. All our similarities. That little fleck of brown in your eye, same as me. I play this game when I'm falling asleep, where I picture the way you were as a baby and then try to imagine you changing, year by year, till you're the girl you are today. Your nose was really flat when you were tiny, which always freaked me out, no offense. Mandy said it was normal for babies to come out with flat noses, so I imagine it gradually taking shape over the years. I picture your hair getting longer, that sort of thing. It's amazing to think how you're all of a sudden five-foot-eight. Y'know?"

All of a sudden.

Is that really what he thinks?

I squeeze the phone tight in my hand, studying my nose. Thin and pointy, the same as Robert's. All that he's missed in the past thirteen years. How opposite of *sudden* my childhood felt, growing up without parents. My jaw muscles flex. I need to tell him.

"Johanna?" A hand raps heavily against the bathroom door.

Shit. "I'll be right out, Gran. I'm—I have cramps."

Robert chuckles, and my face glows red. I run the tap to muffle my voice, apologizing for the interruption.

"No, it's my bad," he says. "I totally went off on a tangent."

"It's okay."

I grab a tissue and wipe away the mascara drizzling beneath my eyes. A smokier look than intended, but bold too. Perfect for presenting in front of the school board. I reach for the doorknob, then hesitate. "Um, so, have you figured out when you're going to visit again?"

"Oh—"

"Or maybe I could go out there?" I blurt. "Spring break is coming up."

"Aw, man, wouldn't that be great?"

"Yeah." I exhale. "Cool, so . . ."

"Did I tell you they promoted me?"

"Oh. I don't think so?"

"It means more business trips. More face time at the office. I wouldn't want you to come out here and be bored." He pauses, keys rattling in the background. "Hey, was that Kate's voice I heard a minute ago? Do they know you're talking to me?"

When I don't answer, Robert laughs. "Forget I asked. And good luck today. Let me know how it goes?"

"I'll text you."

"Cool beans. And how 'bout I come see the mural when it's finished?"

"*If* it gets approved."

"Like I said, I'll come *when* it's done."

I smile. "Yeah, okay."

When I open the bathroom door, Gran's standing there, taking a clumsy step back. I hang up without saying goodbye and hide the phone behind my back.

"Were you spying on me?"

"Who were you talking to?"

"Gabby."

She nods slowly, eyes gliding up and down my collared shirt and denim pinafore, white knee-highs poking out of my black Docs. I bet we're both remembering the old days when she would have criticized my outfit, wondering where in the world kids-these-days got their fashion ideas.

"Well, aren't you getting an early start today?" she says, almost smiling. "Will you be home for dinner?"

My heart skips a beat. "Why?"

"No reason. You've been out so much lately. Just wondering."

Not like, *I was finally going to explain our thirteen-year lie!* But rather, *I want to know how many potatoes to bake.*

I clear my throat. "Actually, I've been invited to dinner at Gabby's."

Which is true. We'll either be celebrating or sobbing.

I brush past Gran and into the kitchen, grabbing a banana that I am way too queasy to eat. Too queasy because, in fifteen minutes I'll be in the school auditorium, arguing my case in front of the stuffy, judgmental school board.

"Johanna?"

Something in her voice makes me turn back. I watch her mouth slowly open, hands wringing at her waist. Her eyes are so desperate and childlike. I wait another few seconds, watching as her spine begins to curve.

"Have a nice day," she eventually says.

All I can do is stare at her. Stunned and disgusted and crushed for the millionth time. Finally, I break eye contact, shaking my head as I stomp out the door.

33

APATHY OOZES OFF THE board members. There are about ten of them gathered in the auditorium, commandeering most of the front row. The men lounge with legs splayed; the women rigid and lipsticked. All of them guzzling coffees and glaring at their iPhones. None of them make conversation, which only makes them look meaner.

Annette's all set up at her podium on the stage. It's where I'm used to seeing her, actually. Where she always stands to make announcements during pep rallies and town hall meetings. Which kind of gives her the home-court advantage. Which kind of sucks. Her hair is slicked into an RBG bun, papers neatly organized in a color-coded binder in front of her. Shit, why did I tie my hair in knots today? And why don't I have a binder? All I have is crap written on index cards and a couple of printouts. Goddamn Annette. With her posture so good, she almost bends backwards. And I should have known she'd be wearing a douchey outfit. Except, her beige pantsuit makes her look poised. My A-line pinafore may as well be a Halloween costume.

I take my phone out of my pocket as it buzzes.

Gabby: Nerd alert!!! Here are some tips from your debate coach: pause, gesture, pace yourself, breathe, make eye contact. Be confident. Be you. Good luck!

I reply with about a thousand cold-sweat and barfing emojis.

"Look at you!" Mr. Donnelly says, eyes aglow as he pauses at my podium. "How are you? You look *so* confident."

I do not. At fucking all. But I force a weak smile.

Donnelly turns to Annette and straightens his tie. "Very poised, Annette. As always."

See? *Poised.*

"Ready to get started?" he asks.

"Yes, Mr. Donnelly. Thank you, sir."

"Yeah, I guess."

"I'll tell Dr. Sanders."

I swallow, breathing in our enormous auditorium, with its speckled gray walls and ominous vaulted ceiling. How many hours have I spent in here? Assemblies, orientations, rehearsals for *Into the Woods* and *West Side Story* (costume department, *not* acting). All it feels like now is a tiny spaceship that's about to suck me through a black hole.

"How much longer is this going to be?" one guy asks our school secretary, Miss Garcia.

Right away, I can tell it's Tim's fancy-pants real-estate-mogul dad. A gray-haired, gray-suited version of his asshole son. Does Mr. Ellison know that Tim has been making my life suck for weeks? Or that his son is an insensitive piranha? Looking at him now, with his Bluetooth and his Italian-shoed foot tapping angrily against the floor, I'm guessing Tim's a chip off the old block.

"Good morning," says Dr. Sanders, pep in his step as he strolls down the center aisle. "I appreciate you all starting your day a bit early. As you know, we're here to discuss the implementation of a mural on school property. I believe it's been proposed for outside the . . . ?"

"Science building," I murmur. Then force it out again, louder. "The science building."

He points a finger at me and smiles. "Right. The proposed mural would challenge gun violence. As several people have raised concerns about the proposal, it has been brought to the board's attention. Annette Martinez and Johanna Carlson are here to share their viewpoints. Ladies—" He turns to us. "Keep your arguments to five minutes. Miss Garcia has a timer. Afterward, we'll excuse you briefly, to make a decision."

He takes a seat next to Mr. Ellison, and they shake hands like they're golf buddies. I mean, they probably are.

Sweat drips from my armpits down the length of my ribs. My nose itches but I refuse to scratch it, instead flicking through my notecards one last time.

"I'll go first," Annette says quietly. "Okay?"

"Oh. Uh—" I pause. Is it better to go first or last? First or last?! Why didn't Gabby tell me? "Yeah, go for it."

With a quick nod, she turns to the audience. "Hello, everyone. Thank you for meeting with us and for taking this matter seriously," she says, voice as clear and forceful as the politician she's bound to become. "As Dr. Sanders mentioned, we're here about a mural. But it's not *just* a mural. Johanna probably thinks this is a personal attack by me, but it is not. I, and everyone at Chavez, care deeply about what she went through. Shooting her mom like that—it's horrible.

"But now, suddenly she's upset about gun control? The fact is, it was her father's right to protect his family. That's why he had a gun, and there's nothing we can do about it now. Regardless of our constitutional rights and the safety that guns provide, the Second Amendment is not on trial here today."

She pauses to gesture toward me. Me, a raccoon caught rooting through the trash, my heart on perma-pound.

"Johanna would have you believe this mural will raise awareness for a hot-button issue, but that is exactly what it is: controversial. Please, take a moment to think about it. Do we really want people—*tourists*, Santa Fe's main source of economic growth—driving past a mural that associates our prestigious school with brutality and violence?"

She lets that one sink in, and a bunch of the board members go pale.

"Believe me, I support responsible gun ownership like many

of my fellow Americans, but Johanna doesn't want to fight for better gun regulation. She wants to use school property and resources for a personal crusade.

"During my time as president—both of the junior class *and* student council—as well as being soccer captain and swim team captain, I have worked tirelessly to support and further the needs of Chavez Academy students. And what has Johanna done? Absolutely nothing. Her unwillingness to incite change prior to this moment proves she's not a team player. This so-called mural is a ruse."

This time, when she pauses, she locks eyes with each member of the board. Totally killing it with Gabby's debate team advice. And they grin grimly back, eating up her lies like hot fudge on a sundae.

"Ladies and gentlemen of the board," she says, bright and bold and majestic, "I stand before you today, asking you to see this mural for what it really is. A desperate attempt by a dam-aged student whose primary goal is to boost her standing in order to look good on college applications. Don't set the prec-edent that it is *okay* to vandalize school property for personal gain—who knows what kind of floodgates that might open. Thank you for your time."

Mic. Drop.

Nobody applauds, not with their hands, but I swear the board members are beaming at her. Like, case closed. Stick a fork in it. *Who cares what that other dumbass has to say, amirite?*

"Johanna?" Mr. Donnelly says, gulping. "Rebuttal?"

Blood drains from my face. I look down at my notecards, the bullet points blurring together. My insides go up that first steep ramp of a roller coaster as I grip the podium.

"Okay, so, yeah. Hi. I was responsible for my mother's shooting death when I was two and a half years old. It really happened, despite some rumors going around that I made the whole thing up. Because, I mean, who makes something like that up? It was absolutely, no question, the worst thing I've ever been through—and I don't even remember going through it. I only found out last month. Can you imagine, finding out now? In *high school*?"

I pause, waiting for a tidal wave of sympathy, but Sanders must have filled everyone in beforehand. God only knows what *else* he said about me. I look through my stack of printouts and hold up the photoshopped picture for everyone to see.

"It's funny—some might say *ironic*—that Annette would bring up vandalism. Here, I have one of the reactions I got from my fellow classmates. This photo went viral, someone even taped it on all the lockers at school. Remember that, Annette?"

For a millisecond, her face falters, cheeks turning pink.

"Totally disgusting, right? There was no hearing to decide if this jerk could deface school property, was there?"

Dr. Sanders remains somber, lips sealed and drooping.

"Look, I'm not trying to make this whole thing about me, despite what Annette says, but the bullying has been awful. There are all kinds of rumors about me. What kind of person I must be to have done something so horrible, to be 'cashing in' on it now. Believe me, I *know* how horrible it was. I will never, ever, *ever* forget that.

"But why does that mean I can't make lemons out of lemonade? Crap, I mean the other way around." I cringe, hands balling into fists. "I seriously think this mural could be inspirational. The organization has done it at other schools, and it's been really successful. And they find grants to pay for it, so you don't have to worry about digging into your pockets or whatever.

"Annette's worried about tourism, but what about *real* people? Locals are going to drive by and see it from the road too, and maybe it'll make them think about their own guns. Like, *Is my gun loaded? Did I lock the safe?* Or, maybe they'll want to give it to one of those buyback programs. Maybe some dude who's angry enough that he wants to take a rifle to school or a shopping center, maybe that guy will see this beautiful mural promoting gun safety, and realize we should be solving our problems through peace, not hatred and murder."

My insides thunder down the next slope of the roller coaster, heart thumping wildly in my chest. All eyes are on me, and I stare back at each one of them, even though my knees are shaking and my throat is the Sahara. There are still a dozen notecards in my stack, but I turn them facedown, chest shaking as I exhale.

"Maybe Annette was right about this being personal. Don't get me wrong, I want to raise awareness about this tragic epidemic, but she's right that I'm doing it for me too." I pause, shaking my head, looking for words I can't see. "Maybe it sounds stupid, but part of me thinks that if I create this big, beautiful mural, maybe my mom will look down on it from heaven. Does that sound stupid?"

It must, judging by the way they all look at me. Or don't look at me. Can't seem to make eye contact. Oh, God. Am I losing them?

Miss Garcia makes the one-minute gesture, and I nearly puke.

"Look," I say, rushing my words now. "Don't judge me because I haven't been involved enough, or because I tie my hair in knots and sew my own clothes. I'm not the student body president, or Ivy League–bound, but I'm still a human being.

"I'm a kid with a broken heart, who will never hear her mother's droll voice again or see her lopsided smile. She won't come to my graduation or hold her grandkids. But I need to find *some* way to earn her forgiveness. What if this is my only chance? Can you honestly deny me that? I need it to not hurt so much. Please—"

I choke on my words, tears streaming down my cheeks. Crying was not in the notecards, and I honestly didn't know these feelings were going to come out or that they were even inside me.

"Sorry." I sniffle. "Who knows if this mural is going to make tourists freak out or not, but I *do* know there's a right side of history to be on and a wrong side. Accepting gun violence is the wrong frigging side. Sorry, that's all."

Mr. Donnelly rushes up to me with a tissue, his own eyes red-rimmed. He pats my back, then turns to shake Annette's hand. All the board members squirm but remain frustratingly neutral. Tim's dad looks pissed, but I'm pretty sure that's just his face. He whispers something to Colonel Sanders, who nods.

"Thank you, ladies," Sanders says, lips pinched into a grin. "We'll take a few minutes to deliberate."

"Thank you, Dr. Sanders," Annette says, stepping away from her podium.

I grab my notecards, but Sanders raises his palm. "Miss Carlson, would you please leave your arguments at the stand?"

"What?" I flush.

"Leave everything there. We might take a look while we're deliberating."

Annette rushes back to hand Sanders her binder too. Ugh.

My notecards are pathetic and messy in comparison, but I leave them at the podium, hoping the board won't notice the dick flowers drawn in the margins. Miss Garcia motions for us to follow her and then leads us through stage left to the dressing room, leaving the two of us alone, standing silently between a donkey costume and a row of green dresses.

"How do you think it went?" I ask.

"I'm pretty confident," Annette says, chin high. "Even though you cheated."

"What do you mean?"

She pantomimes these spurting, melodramatic sobs.

I roll my eyes. "I didn't mean to, it just happened."

"Whatever."

"What's your problem with me, Annette?"

She laughs. Like she can't be*lieve* I have to *ask*.

"Are you really so pissed that I wouldn't sign your school

uniform petition? Or that my friends and I make noise in the library sometimes?" I wait for an answer, but she crosses her arms. "I mean, what about the printouts? Why would you rip them down if all you really want is to destroy me?"

"You were being bullied," she says sharply. "Anyone would have helped you."

"Not anyone."

"Yeah, well, those posters were disgusting. But it was worse to watch you roll over. I offered to talk to Sanders with you, and you just went, *Uh, duh, nope.*"

I nod, swallowing regret. "I know. That was stupid of me."

"It isn't even about that," she grumbles. "I've dedicated my life to this school. All I do is push for new clubs, more funding. The trip we took to the state capitol last semester? That was my idea. *I* made it happen. *I* am the one who petitioned to have Japanese offered by the Language Department. But does anybody thank me? Is my hard work recognized?"

My eyes dart down as I shrug.

"And guess how many of my proposals get rejected?" she goes on. "The kind of pushback I get from Sanders. How he looks down at me because I'm not rich or white or blessed with a Y chromosome."

"C'mon. No, he doesn't," I say, but it's a shitty lie, and we both know it.

"You have no idea how it feels—to be Latina at this school, fighting twice as hard and still getting shot down." She pauses, cheeks pink. "And then you come along, freaking out about this mural, getting Mr. Donnelly to kiss your feet and do whatever you say."

Now I'm blushing too, heart starting to race. "Wait, so are you jealous? Is that what this is about? You're punishing me?"

"God, not everything is about you!" she wails, lip trembling for the first time. "I'm trying to explain that Sanders has finally started respecting me. Students are asking for my help. For once, people are glad I'm doing my job. It's a nice fucking change."

I nod, taken aback by the *f*-word on her civic-minded lips.

"Y'know, even Tim thanked me?" she adds. "He bought me a cappuccino from the coffee cart the other day."

"Lucky you."

"Don't be sarcastic."

"Sorry, but I thought you hated him. Your Harvard competition?"

"Yeah, well." She scuffs her ballet flat along the floor. "He has his moments."

We both go quiet, and I do what I always do when I'm in the dressing room: organize. I reach for a jumbled box of scarves and start rolling them up, one by one, while Annette stands there biting her thumbnail.

"I'm sorry Colonel Chickenhead doesn't always take you seriously," I finally say. My nickname gets the faintest smile out of her, but she says nothing. "And thanks for setting up that field trip. It was actually fun."

She straightens. "You're welcome."

"Fighting me now, though? So that Tim Ellison will buy you coffee?"

"That's not why I'm doing it."

"Right," I scoff, white silk loose around my fist. "It's graffiti. You're mad that I'm scamming colleges." I shake my head. "I mean, it's one thing to prove yourself to Sanders, but did it ever occur to you that this is my actual *life* you're ruining?"

"I'm sorry it seems personal," she says, "but there really *are* people who don't want a giant anti-gun mural on campus. I'm only trying to be a voice."

"Do you have a gun?" I ask, before I can stop myself. "I know you're in that marksmanship group."

She hesitates. "Yes. My parents keep one locked up. And I'm glad. I don't live in the best part of town. It's nice to feel safe."

I chew my lip. I want to ask her if she really thinks that gun is making her safer. I want to know how she'd feel if a burglar came in and her dad shot him. If *she* was forced to pull that trigger. If she thinks she'd be able to live with herself afterwards. But I don't. Can't. Maybe I already know the answer.

Miss Garcia knocks gently on the door, popping her head back in. "Ready, girls?"

My stomach backflips. Pretty sure I'm never going to be ready. Especially if that group of tight-ass board members voted the way I think they have. Because, for all her underdog posturing, Annette is really fucking good at arguing. Not that I'm going to tell her that.

The whole board is standing there when we walk back in.

Chatting, looking at their phones, ready to deliver the news and then leave. Kill my dreams, real quick, before their morning meetings. The first one to make eye contact is Mr. Ellison, and the guy practically has steam coming out of his hairy ears.

"Miss Martinez, Miss Carlson," Sanders says, standing at the edge of the stage. "Thank you for your time and well-prepared arguments. Although we greatly appreciate what you both had to say, we've decided to follow through with the mural."

"Oh my God!" I shriek. And jump and clap and would do backflips, but A, how do you do a backflip? and B, I am wearing a skirt.

Annette smiles, her chest falling slightly.

"Johanna?" Sanders pulls me aside, handing back my note-cards. "We read the rest of your arguments. Civic participation is something we strive for at Chavez." He looks over his shoulder, then back at me, his voice hushed. "You know, maybe if you'd made some of these points earlier—when you *should* have been securing permission from me in the first place—we could have avoided all this."

"Oh, yeah?" My skin bursts into flames . . . but I stand down. I'm not here to fight or get in trouble. Instead, I plaster a bright, plucky smile onto my face. "So now we can start the mural?"

His jaw muscles flex, but he stands down too. "Whenever you can coordinate with the organization."

"Like, yesterday. They're so ready to help."

"Well, you'll have full support from the school, and week-end access to campus—no cutting class to paint. And the board will have design approval."

"Done," I say, grinning.

A handshake fest feels like the Annette thing to do, so maybe it's my hat tip to her as I race over to the board, palms sweating, thanking them one by one. Even Mr. Ellison, who still looks encircled by pythons.

Annette gathers her things and struts up the aisle, but I catch her before she reaches the door.

"Annette, wait up."

"What, time to gloat?"

"Of course not. I wanted to say, good job—and sorry."

"No, you're not," she says, but she extends her hand to me anyway. "Congratulations."

Then she's gone, ducking into the ladies' room. I don't follow. Instead, I walk outside where it's not just Leah and Gabby and Milo waiting for me, but everyone else who's shown support in the past few weeks.

"Well?" Leah asks, wincing. "Are we happy or sad?"

"We're . . . happy!" I scream. "They said yes!"

A small group surrounds me—high fives from Steve, and Rachel, and her friend Jenny, and the Kenworth twins, and my art class. Leah's arms go strangulation-tight, Gabby and Milo layering over her, adding to my smotherization.

I won. I feel unstoppable. This mural is going to happen. It will be enormous and beautiful and perfect. It will be a brilliant star to grace the darkness.

34

BLOOD. SWEAT. TEARS. THAT'S what goes into the mural, once the design has been approved and all systems are go. February turns to March, and we *work*. Mapping out the structure and flow of the piece, stenciling quotes and mottos and painting them bold and bright and unforgettable.

The looks around campus still give me ulcers. Minor migraines. Nobody straight-up bothers me anymore, but I can feel some of them wanting to. So I stay focused. Dogged. If I show my devotion to the mural, they won't be able to mention the heavy, gray cloud that is drooping over my head. Big plastic smiles help too.

"What do you think?" I ask Barb, the artistic director.

I climb down a ladder propped against the science building's stucco wall and stand next to our short, plump leader, pointing up at the top right section where **G(un)safe** is painted in thick, green letters.

Barb nods as she reweaves her long black braid. "I like the camo green, but what's your end goal? What do you want people to take away when they're seeing it for the first time?"

"I want . . ." I cock my head. "I want to take their breath away?"

She smiles proudly at me. "And does camo green take your breath away?"

I laugh.

"Hey, maybe it does!" She pats my shoulder and slides on a tight leather jacket. "I guess I'll see tomorrow?"

She zooms off on a Harley, and I only have to stare at our stockpile of paints for half a second before reaching for this tub of dramatic, candy-apple red.

"Ooh, good call," Leah says. "That's going to look so dope."

"Diggidy dope."

"Dope-a-rama."

"The Dopeness."

"Okay, stop," Milo says. "You two are embarrassing not only yourselves, but all of humankind."

"Whatever, Dopemeister Schmidt."

I blow him a kiss and shimmy back up the ladder. Vermillion red lands in thick, glossy strokes around the parentheses. Barb was right. She really knows what she's doing, but she never condescends or feeds us answers. After a couple more coats, I climb down again, resting my brush in the paint can. I take a step back and cross my arms, eyes settling on a burst of sunshine in the center of the wall. Dandelion-yellow rays streaming through a tuft of summer-white clouds.

Serene, angelic. Heavenly.

The whole world goes still for a moment, despite the constant churn of acid in my gut. Fists clenched, breath held. I listen for her; try to visualize her as hidden 3-D art, emerging through layers of acrylic.

Mom?

Can you hear me?

Is this what you wanted?

Am I doing it right?

Something.

Anything.

Please . . .

"You okay?" Milo's arms slide around my waist.

I blink a beat too long but cover it with a grin. "Yeah, I'm fine. This looks great, huh?"

"Dopetastic." He pecks me on the lips and then walks back to finish a thick black Zia symbol. "Sun's almost down. Want to pack it in?"

"Yeah, in a few. I'm just going to—"

"Hey, Johanna? Do you have a second?"

I swing around, face-to-face with—"Tim?"

He stuffs his hands deep in his jeans pockets, staring down at his feet. There's something weird about him when he looks up, though—something off. A bit of smugness faded from his pretty boy face.

"What do you want?"

"I need to talk to you," he mumbles. "It'll only take a second."

"If you're here to heckle me, can it wait?" I grab a paintbrush, squeezing it in my fist. "We have, like, ten minutes of daylight left, and I'm kinda on a deadline here. We only have a few days to finish the mural. Not that you care."

"I'm not going to heckle you," he says. "I swear."

The defeated edge to his voice trips me up. I let the brush dangle by my side, red paint dripping off the bristles. "Spit it out, then."

"It's—" He pauses, cheeks pink with Milo and Leah gawking at him. "It's private."

"Oh, please. You have absolutely nothing private to say to me."

I start to turn away and he blurts, "It's about FakerX."

"What?"

"It was me."

I gasp. Which annoys me because it's not like this is even remotely a surprise. But I don't know. I'm speechless.

"I *so* called that," Leah mutters.

"But why?" I finally manage.

"It was only a joke."

"Sick joke," Milo says, walking up behind me.

"It wasn't supposed to go viral. I mean—" He snorts, a hint of the real Tim shining through. "It was pretty funny when it did! And, like, I don't know what to say about those bullshit photocopies around campus—I didn't post that shit. But when you brought one to the hearing, it dawned on my father to check my Photoshop account. Since then, he's been talking with Sanders and Coach Fishkin. They're going to bench me for a game."

"*One* game? You poor thing," I say. Voice sweet, eyes nuclear.

"Hey, I'm their best scorer!"

Hate rolls through me faster than a bowling ball, knocking down any amount of Zen atonement this stupid mural is supposed to have brought me. The spell breaks, and I scream, hurling my paintbrush right at his dumbfuck face. Tim raises an arm to block it, but I get him anyway, bloodred paint streaking his leather jacket.

"What the shit!" Tim barks, fingers rubbing against the leather, only making it worse.

"Don't what-the-shit *me*, you disgusting pig."

I feel Milo's hand wrap around my bicep, holding me back as I lunge forward.

"That picture nearly destroyed me," I say, tears welling up in my eyes. "And you expect me to feel bad that you can't run down a field with a stick for one stupid game? Go to hell! I wish they'd expelled you!"

"God, lighten up," he says, swallowing hard. "I said I was sorry."

"What? When?"

"Yeah, you *so* skipped the S-word," Leah chimes in.

"*Sorry.* Okay?"

I scoff at his ten-cent apology.

Leah rolls her eyes. "And the Academy Award goes to . . ."

"Butt out, freak."

"Watch your fucking mouth!" I roar.

Tim's eyes get huge. A little bit Jack Nicholson *Here's Johnny!*

mixed with a nugget of true remorse. "Look. Are you going to let me finish, or do you have more paint to throw?"

My eyes narrow. "What are you talking about?"

"I'm not *just* sitting out one lacrosse game." He pauses, gesturing toward the mural, which has become almost indecipherable in the twilight. "Sanders wants me to do community service."

"*Here?*" I gasp.

"Look, I'll admit it was shitty. Photoshopping that picture was mostly Brandon's idea, but whatever. I'm not going to narc on my best friend."

Milo cringes. "Your morals go sky-high, man."

"Thanks but no thanks, ass-hat. I'm declining your humbly altruistic offer."

"Sadly, I don't think you can."

I groan, wailing up toward the first star in the night sky.

"Would you stop freaking out?" he says. "I'm not going to sabotage your pathetic masterpiece. Give me a stupid brush, okay?"

Ugh. The utter unholiness of Tim Ellison darkening my peaceful opus. Another one of God's ironic jokes. "This is a nightmare. Right? I'm living an actual fucking nightmare."

Leah chuckles, a smile edging onto her lips. I can just picture Dharma, her psychic, urging me to see the good in Tim. As if there is one fingernail-clipping-sized shred of virtue within his entire dickhole self.

"Fine." I grab a paintbrush, thumbing the soft, clean bristles. "You can help."

"I'm *honored*." He stands up straight, reaching out for the brush.

"Not so fast." On second thought, I slide the brush in my back pocket and point to a dozen trays of dried-out paint and cracked, congealing brushes. "Clean this stuff up. We need to start fresh tomorrow."

Leah laughs her ass off as I toss another couple of dirty brushes on the stack. Tim's face sours, but he doesn't argue.

Inside my head, a stadium full of bullied teens cheer for me.

• • •

Grandpa's standing in the doorway when I open it, hanging Magic's leash back up on the wall.

"Welcome home, Picasso!" He laughs, and I look down at my clothes and hands, smeared with paint.

"It's from Gabby's," I lie. "Her mom had us help out with a new painting."

"I hope you'll be getting a commission for that!"

I stare blankly at him, and he shakes his head. "Never mind. Glad to see you and your friends are having fun in between all that studying."

"Can I go to my room now? I ate at Gabby's."

In the kitchen, we hear water running, the garbage disposal churning. Grandpa sighs, eyes drifting back to me. "Are you ever going to talk to her again?"

"Don't blame *me* for this. I think I'm being pretty damn cordial, if you ask me."

"Hey, now."

My eyes lower. "Sorry."

We stand there for another minute, Magic looking back and forth between the two of us, wondering if he's getting a second walk tonight. Dishes continue to clatter in the kitchen, and I think about the old days, how I'd be helping Gran while Grandpa watched TV. Now, she either cooks alone or he struggles through peeling and chopping vegetables. The two of them silent. Barely speaking to each other under the strain. Forty-five years of marriage, and I've completely broken my grandparents. No guilt there.

"We miss you, JoJo," he says softly.

I hesitate. I should bite my tongue, but—"Yeah, well, it's kind of hard to miss the people who kept this giant secret from me," I say. "*Now* can I go to my room?"

Grandpa lets out a slow, defeated breath as his eyebrows draw in. "Go on, then. I've got turpentine in the shed if you can't wash off that paint. Let me know if you need it."

His gentle voice takes shape around my heart. I'm horrible. He loves me, and I'm making him into my punching bag. I wish it didn't have to be like this. I wish things could have gone differently. *So* frigging differently. But they didn't.

I look at my rough, multicolored hands and frown. "I'll be okay."

35

MY ASS IS NUMB.

All three hundred Chavez students are sandwiched together like baby chicks, crammed onto every patch of grass outside the science building, with our knees banging and shivery, aglow with anticipation. The mural's done. It's bold and glorious and beyond breathtaking. The president of the gun violence prevention group is here for the unveiling, along with Barb, and even someone from the newspaper.

A muffled hush falls over the crowd as Dr. Sanders approaches the podium.

"*Gun violence. Stops. With us,*" he says, pausing like some beret-wearing beatnik between each phrase. Practically every word. "*Besos. Not. Bullets . . . G(un)safe.*" And finally: "*Hashtag Enough.*"

Okay, *Hashtag Enough* sounds about the dumbest, but all the words Barb helped us curate for the mural sound a little bit douchier coming out of Colonel Sanders's ancient, ChapStick-deficient mouth.

"I'm honored to be standing here with all of you today. Such a bright, talented, courageous group of students."

Leah gives the air in front of her a pretend hand job, low enough so Sanders can't see. I don't laugh, though. Not after the way he antagonized me and belittled me and fanned the flames. Now he's up there, eating his own shit pie with whipped cream, talking about the perils of gun violence as if it *means* something to him. As if our voices *matter* to him, and we're going to be the change and the salvation and blah-blah-blah.

I squirm a little in my cross-legged position on the ground as his eyes sweep the crowd, a Jedi master holding the gaze of as many students and faculty as possible. The last person he looks at is me, and my shoulders droop.

"As you all know, none of this would have been possible without the focus and perseverance of one Chavez Academy student." His lips tighten. "Johanna Carlson."

Gabby squeezes my shoulder.

"All of you are here today to show your commitment—as young people, as citizens—by taking part in the fight to reduce gun violence. And it was Miss Carlson's commitment to uniting the student body that has made this pledge possible. It is every Head of School's dream to rear students with such determination and fearlessness."

I start to feel enormous under his magnifying glass. Not only does he sound massively insincere, but he's making me look like such a brownnoser—calling me a beacon of hope, a force to be reckoned with; totally playing into the theory that I only did the mural to bulk up my extracurriculars. Maybe a fifth of the kids don't clap, and I hardly blame them. I'm not the next Banksy, even though Colonel Sanders actually makes that comparison. Cringe.

A few rows over, I wait for Annette to audibly moan or roll her eyes, but she stays quiet. Distracted, almost. In fact, Tim seems to be sitting pretty damn close to her. Tim, who showed up twice to clean paint brushes. What a saint.

"You sound like president material!" Leah says, poking my ribs.

"Shut up," I groan.

Milo's lips brush against my temple. "You're incredible."

If I were really all that incredible, I probably wouldn't want to *Exorcist* puke on the whole school right now. Which I kinda do. The praise is humiliating, but it's not what's making my insides numb. *That* feeling has been building up for weeks.

I ignore it and kiss Milo back. The core of me is calcifying, but I can still control my smile, so I make it bigger. "Thanks."

The Johanna sermon finally ends, and Colonel Sanders reels off a few announcements about midterms and next month's spring break volunteer opportunities. I make a mental note because it's not like my grandparents are whisking me off to Paris anytime soon. After that, before we're excused, Sanders gets the whole school to pose for a picture over by the mural, the dandelion-yellow sun bursting over our heads. The reporter has to stand on the roof of the auditorium in order to fit everyone in. Of course, they put *me* front and center.

Sanders shoves Annette right next to me too. Some cruel, sadistic punishment.

"Hey," I say out of the side of my mouth. "How's it going?"

"Bet you're loving this," Annette mutters.

"Actually?" I shrug. "Not so much."

"Don't like being Sanders's new pet?"

"Not even close. But that's not—" I pause, lost for words as I drag my knuckles along my forehead. Rather than complete the thought, I reach into my pocket for a glossy cinnamon lipstick. "Can I? It'll make your lips pop in the picture."

"Really?" Annette frowns. "I mean, okay. Sure."

"So, you and Tim Ellison?" I ask, making my lips wide and flat for her to mimic.

Her mouth obliges, and she shrugs.

"I still think he's a dick," I add.

"He's not that bad when you get to know him. He's even had some sorta nice things to say about you."

"You're joking."

"Maybe a little. But he said he didn't mind cleaning brushes." I snort.

"It really does look good, Johanna. You must be ecstatic."

I'm not sure what to say, so I press my lips together a couple of times, and she does the same. "There. Looks great."

"So does the mural. I mean it. Everyone thinks so." She bites her cheek, hesitating slightly. "Even if not everybody is *able* to see it, I bet they love it. At least, that's what I think."

Maybe it's a lie, but it makes the lump in my throat burn.

36

To: Newton_Robert@mymail.org
From: Princessthrasher@gmail.com
Subject: Drum roll, please . . .

Dear Dad,
Sorry I've been kinda MIA. Guess what, though?! The
mural is DONE! There's a picture attached. Our
headmaster gave this big speech, and a guy from the
paper covered it, and people are super impressed.
I know I should feel happy because it really does look
cool, and I fought hard to make it happen, but mostly
I'm super tired and feeling kind of weird. Remember
how you were talking about counting sheep? Like, how
thinking about Mom helps you sleep and stuff? I guess
I was hoping the mural would be my sheep or
something. Does that make any sense? I'm not trying

to say I did the mural only for ME. God, I sound completely selfish. Never mind! The mural is great! Yay! Anyway, how are you? How's Houston and your new promotion? Oh, hey, so, remember how you said you'd come visit when the mural was done? Just wondering if that's still a plan.

xox, Jo

To: Princessthrasher@gmail.com
From: Newton_Robert@mymail.org
Subject: Re: Drum roll, please . . .

Good news! I'm cleared for takeoff. See you Sunday? Congrats on finishing the mural, it looks AMAZING. And no, you don't sound selfish. I get it.

Love,

Dad

37

GRAN'S MUFFLED VOICE CALLS out from the kitchen on Sunday morning. Something about carrot cake? Something else about soup? They're heading to church, she says, and they'll be home around noon. I stay quiet, waiting in bed for the sound of the garage door, unfazed by its ominous mechanical growl. Well, maybe half-fazed.

I don't go to church anymore; I can't take any more of God's judgment. Now I don't have to fake being sick, and Gran doesn't have to get her hopes up. We both silently agreed that I'd hit pause. It's been nearly two months of Sundays, and I wonder if I'll ever go back.

The doorbell rings an hour later. I race down the hallway, knees shaking at the sight of my father on my front porch in his trusty bomber jacket and leather boots. His wavy blond hair has grown, brushing his jawline; all his facial hair is gone. It's almost as if a stranger is standing before me. I guess he feels the same way because any kind of comfortable seems to have vanished between us.

"Do you want to head straight to school and see the mural?" I ask, reaching for my keys.

Robert nibbles at his thumbnail. "Let's hang out here for a minute."

I look at the clock, then across the street. "Um, sure. We've got a little time, but it's probably better if you don't stay on the porch."

"Right, right. Okay, sure."

We half hug. A clumsy double-back-pat combo as he skirts around me. Magic is in the living room when we get there, sleeping in front of the fireplace.

"Nice-looking dog."

"That's Magic. We've had him forever."

"Smells good in here."

"Pretty sure that's vegan black-eyed pea gumbo," I tell him. "Want some?"

"Do I have to?" He laughs. "I'm kidding. How 'bout a glass of water?"

I race into the kitchen and quickly tighten the lid over the Dutch oven.

"Everything looks the same," he says, raising his voice over the kitchen tap. When I come back in, he nods around the room. "Your grandparents' stuff. It hasn't changed since Mandy and I visited them in Little Rock, way back when. Same armchair. Same dining room table and old cuckoo clock. Even that needlepoint of Abe Lincoln in the stovepipe hat."

"God, was she doing those back then?" I groan. "She's been an old lady her whole life, hasn't she?"

We joke about their weirdly endearing artistic outlets for a while, but then Robert puts his glass down on the table, pushing it away as he falls limply onto the sofa. "We need to talk."

I ease down beside him. "That sounds bad."

"It's not. Or, I mean, it doesn't have to be."

Heat prickles my face as I watch him exhale.

"I know I've been gone a while. And I *did* get a promotion, but—" He pauses, fingers running through tangled blond hair. "The truth is, I've been scared to come back."

"What?" I flinch. "Why?"

"All of this," he says. "Knowing that I'm the one who told you about Mandy."

"I'm *glad* you did."

"Yeah, but, I hate feeling responsible all over again. I wasn't sure I could face you, knowing what I did to you."

"What *you* did?"

He frowns. "I failed you. In so many ways. I let Kate and Jimmy adopt you when it should have been me and Mandy raising you."

"That's not your fault."

"All I wanted was to protect you. That's a parent's main job, right?"

I think back to Annette's words from the hearing: *A father's right to protect his family.* I'm queasy even thinking it. Queasier still to see tears welling up in Robert's eyes.

"Are you okay?"

"Yeah," he says, but his smile is too strained. "It took me years to accept my role in Mandy's death, and I'm finally okay with it. I know what I did. And I know what I *need* to do."

"What do you mean, *need to do?*"

As soon as the question's out, I regret it. Robert's eyes look so wild and un-fatherly. It makes my stomach clench.

"I have to keep trying," he says. "That's what Reverend Tucker is always telling me. He's great, the way he's helped me get my life back on track. He always knows what to do—like, making me find you."

I blink.

Wait . . . what?

For a minute, it hangs in the air. My brain reeling, the knot in my stomach tightening, plummeting to the ground. Little sounds trickle into my eardrums, mingling with my pounding heart. The drip of our kitchen tap; Robert's breath, heavy and frustrated. My heart, though. It won't shut up in my ears.

"Wait," I say, nearly choking. "It was your pastor? That's who *made* you contact me?"

Robert's face twists almost sheepishly. As if it never occurred to him how this might sound. I look away, retracing his words in my mind, gluing them back together, forward and backward, piece by piece, until only one thing makes sense.

Robert used me.

My own father. *Tricked me.*

I gasp like I'm coming up for air. "This whole time—it's been about *you?* Getting *your* life back on track?"

He blushes. "I mean, no. It sounded way better the way

Reverend Tucker said it. Like, that I'll never truly be able to move on without your forgiveness."

"Forgiveness?" I repeat. The word sounds harsh and dirty, three clunky syllables lurching off my tongue. He wants me to stop resenting him, but maybe I'm just getting started. "Yeah, that sounds *much* better."

"Come on, don't look at me that way. Everyone deserves to be forgiven. I know you want the same thing."

My stomach wrenches. "I do, but—"

"We're the same, you and I. Remember what you said in your email, about the mural not making you feel better? It's the same for me. You wanted the mural to heal you, and I need *you* to heal *me*."

I don't want to cry, but tears sting my eyes anyway. My face reddens, every part of me unraveling. "Stop talking," I whisper.

"Please—"

"Stop," I say again.

But he doesn't. "Maybe it sounds pointless to you, but it's really important that you tell me what I did was *okay*."

"What? How do—"

"Goddamn it, Jo. Come *on!*"

My body lurches, dizzied by the bark of his anger.

It wakes Magic too, his head jolting, growling at the sight of a stranger. I shush him and glare back at Robert, who apparently doesn't have *time* for my childish confusion.

I try to respond, but the room zigzags around me, words skittering into darkness like rats. I can't think. I can't breathe. But that's just it. "*I can't!*" I finally shout.

"What do you mean, you can't?" he shouts back. "Why can't you?"

"Did it ever occur to you that it's not my place to forgive anyone?"

He shakes his head, eyes twitching.

"*I'm* the one who killed her," I say. "We both know it's my fault."

"That's not true," Robert insists. "You were a baby."

"Why do people keep saying that like it changes *anything*?"

"Because it was my gun!" he cries. "I left a loaded gun where my two-year-old could find it. Shit—what if you'd had a play-date over? Can you even imagine?" He shudders, wiping away tears. "I was young and stupid, and I didn't think someone so small would know how to fire it. I just. Didn't. *Think*. And now you don't have a mom and I don't have her, and it's all because of me and that goddamn gun that I told myself I needed." His shoulders rock like a tethered boat as the words come tumbling out of him. The way he forces his eyes shut, squeezing them, I know he's back there again—that day, those memories. "Why did I leave it there? *Why?* She's dead because of *me*, not you. And I would do anything to go back and change that."

Robert sniffles pitifully while I sob these wild, debilitating tears. My head feels thick and fat and throbbing, and I can barely breathe, I'm crying so hard.

"I need you to tell me you don't hate me," he begs. "Because *I* put that gun in your hands, and *I* let you take her life. You have to forgive me. That's the only reason I'm here!"

The only reason.

His words burn like hot wax on my heart. God, I'm such an idiot. I can't stop crying, but now I'm full-on hysterical. Overwrought. Done. I'm just *done*.

"How awful for you," I say, hiccupping through snot and gritted teeth. "Having to listen to me ramble over coffees. Getting to know your own daughter? It must have been torture."

"That's not what I meant."

"Yes, it is."

I wipe my eyes, seeing Robert clearly for the first time. Seeing *us*. Little clues adding up, building me into a fool, breaking me down into nothing. It wasn't about me. It never was. For a minute, I stare at him, wanting my pain to seep into him. But I don't think it's possible. He's not capable.

I force myself off the sofa, my breath growing thinner. Faster. Hotter in my mouth. "My grandparents will be home soon."

"Please, don't push me away."

He reaches for me but I jerk back. "You used me."

"That's not—" He sighs as I start to leave the room. "Please wait."

"Gabby warned me," I mutter, mostly to myself as I walk toward the front door. "I nearly lost my best friend over you because I deluded myself into thinking you actually cared about me. Why didn't I listen to Gran when she told me to stay away from you? She's *always* looked out for me. God, I defended you to all of them!"

Robert pads after me. "I get that you're upset."

"Upset? *Upset*?!" I roar. "You *ruined* my life with your selfish bullshit."

"Joey, you have to calm down."

"Don't you dare call me that." I push his chest and he stumbles. "I'm not your little baby anymore. I'm not your *anything*."

"I never meant to hurt you."

"Yes, you did! You did, and you know it."

He can't even look at me. His eyes sink to the ground.

"Get out of my house," I whimper. "I don't want you here. You're not welcome. Just *go*."

"But—"

"Get out." I grab the door handle, all set to kick his groveling ass to the curb, but when I open the door, Grandpa nearly topples in through it.

"JoJo?"

"Grandpa?"

"*Robert?*"

"Mr. Carlson?"

Oh. Shit.

38

"YOU BASTARD!" GRANDPA GROWLS.

"Jimmy, hang on," Robert says, but it's too late.

Grandpa's fist is already colliding with Robert's cheek, making this awful cracking sound. I can't help screaming. Gran gasps too, lunging to shut the front door before our dirty laundry can be aired out for the neighbors.

"Robert, what in the hell are you doing here?" she shouts, but my father only groans, blood dribbling from his nose. She sighs. "I'll get some ice."

My insides spin, jerking me in every direction. I want to breathe, but it's like I forgot how. Like my lungs are inching down a wood chipper. *Breathe, don't think,* I tell myself, *breathe, don't think*—but everything itches. Throbs. This skintight ache.

Robert uses his shirtsleeve to soak up blood before it can stain our shiny brick floor, and his eyes plead with me. I look at the ground, arms tight around my ribs, one thought banging relentlessly into me: *Your father doesn't love you. He never loved you. He never—*

"Johanna?" Robert says.

"Not one word," Grandpa barks. He pushes me back, ushering my body behind his for safekeeping.

Gran returns with two ice packs, pressing the first against Grandpa's knuckles and tossing the other in Robert's direction. I'm wheezing now, my heart tightening inside my chest. *Breathe, don't think. Breathe, don't think*—but my insides thunder. A flood of water filling up behind a door I can't hold shut for much longer.

"Sweetheart?" Gran's voice sounds far away. Underwater. "Are you okay?"

There's blood spatter on her peach dress, hurt in her eyes. All I can see is that small spray of red. Was there blood on her clothes back then? Did they let her hold her daughter's lifeless body before carting it away?

Something fuzzy erupts in me, fast and sharp. It charges up my chest and down to my stomach; up and down and up and down until black dots flicker in my vision, clawing at all parts of me.

"I'm going to call the police," Gran mutters, turning toward the living room.

"Stop," I scream.

"What?" she says. "What is it?"

"I can't breathe."

"JoJo, honey—"

"I can't breathe! This doesn't feel right. *I* don't feel right. It hurts."

Air punches my lungs, holding me tight. Shorter, tighter, tingling. Making me light-headed, vibrating my skin. I start to pace, going nowhere, shaking my hands frantically like they're dripping wet. Like if I try, I can flick this feeling away.

"She needs fresh air," Robert says, grabbing my hand. He reaches for the doorknob, but Gran grabs my other hand, yanking me back. "Kate, I'm not stealing her. Look at her—she's hyperventilating."

Gran's eyes latch onto me. She's blurry as she frowns, eyebrows knitting together. Finally, she nods, keeping her grip firm as Robert opens the front door, and we all tumble onto the porch.

"Is that better?" he asks softly.

The cold air takes away some of the burn, but I shake my head no to punish him.

"Sweetheart, what's the matter?" Gran asks.

"I don't know."

"Tell me how I can help."

"I said, I don't know!" I extend my shivering arms. "Here. Squeeze my wrists," I order. "There's a pressure point."

I fight dizziness to remember what else Milo said or did.

"I need a pill. Get, get the pills that are in my backpack."

Grandpa limps off to the kitchen and comes back with my bag. Milo gave me a few Xanax, just in case, and Grandpa finds them, pulling a little orange bottle out of the front zipper of my bag.

"Daniel Schmidt?" he reads. "Alprazolam? JoJo, what in God's name . . . ?"

"It's Xanax," Robert says. "For anxiety."

I tear my eyes off my wrists long enough to glare at him. "What are you still doing here?"

"Jo," he pleads, orphan eyes as he sniffs back blood. But then says nothing. Does nothing.

Gran pulls me close to her and the déjà vu-ness of it gives me goose bumps, picturing myself on her lap that day as the cops swarmed our house. Robert backing away, admitting defeat so easily—back then, and today too. Some things never change.

"Get the hell out of here!" I shout.

"But—" His eyebrows pinch. "What about the mural?"

"She asked you to leave," Grandpa booms, angrier than I've ever heard him.

Robert flinches, nose raw and cartoonish, eyes brimming with feigned affection. Definitely feigned, though. I know that now, and I make my expression hard and fierce in response.

"All right," he finally says. With a nod, he turns to leave. Gran and Grandpa watch him stagger down the gravel path, but I can't.

"I'm sorry," I say into my hands. And I'd say it again but I'm bee-stung to my core, the porch spinning around me. "I really need that pill. Will you give it to me?"

Gran snatches the bottle from Grandpa and reads the label again, tucking it in her pocket without unscrewing the cap. She leads my rigid body back into the house.

"Wait—the pill," I shout, but she only shakes her head.

"Honey, you don't need it." She gently pats my back. "I'd rather we work it out together."

The thought of it sends my breath into hyperspeed. She can't do this to me; I can't do this alone. She shows me slow, steady breaths and I try. Mostly I hyperventilate, but I try. Fail. Keep trying. We go into the living room, and she reaches for the TV remote.

"How about a distraction?"

"No, don't."

I can tell I'm frustrating her, and I'm sorry. But my heart is on fire, and this might never, *ever* end and—it's dumb, but, like—I don't want TV to be associated with this belowground feeling. She lets go of the remote and starts giving my neck this cloying, knobby-fingered massage.

"Stop," I pant. "It's not working. Nothing's working."

"Well, why don't you tell me what *will* work?"

"Don't yell at me!"

"She's not," Grandpa says from the doorway. "We aren't sure what to do."

"I don't know either!"

I feel trampled beneath my beating heart. Hyperaware of the sofa cushions against my skin, the hum of overhead lights. Gran keeps breathing, so I try again. Fail. Try. Somehow, one minute ticks by. Two . . . three . . .

Gran's eyes get this soft Bambi quality, and she starts to hum one of her favorite church hymns. One hymn, then another. Dizzy heat erupts through me, then dulls. She keeps humming, and I start to notice my heart slowing. Another minute goes by. Two . . . three . . . I'm nearing the last lap of the race.

I inhale a wave of panic, surf it for a second, and then let it go. "I'm sorry."

"Hush," Gran says. "It's going to be okay."

I nod, trying to believe her, wondering if she means the panic attack or my whole messed-up, fatherless, motherless life. Because it's over. After months of secrets and stories and maybe-I-thought-but-I-guess-I-was-wrong *love*, it's . . . finished. I exhale, and I remind myself that this feels right. Me plus the two of them is how it is supposed to be. We are a family. Not him.

After a while, when I'm finally breathing right, I start to talk. They don't force it—maybe don't want to hear it at all—but I tell them. Everything. My poor grandparents, still in their church clothes, reeking of God and faith and disappointment. Gran's hand goes over her mouth when I admit that Robert and I have been in contact this whole time, even after my promise to cut ties. Coffees, phone calls, late-night texts.

They're quiet at first, contemplating, then Grandpa clears his throat, almost reluctantly. "Did it bring back anything from the accident—learning about your mother?"

A dust storm blows through me. All the nights I've lain awake, picturing my childhood as a movie trailer, wondering what's real or imaginary. Mom's arms around me, golden sunlight streaming through white curtains. Me, sliding off the bed in search of a doll, a ball, a book. Not in the closet, not in the hamper, but what's that catching light under the bed?

Nothing's ever concrete.

I quickly shake my head, ashamed for my amnesia.

But Gran says, "Thank *goodness*," and relief seems to swell within her. "Thank the Lord you don't remember."

"I wish I did."

"You *don't*," she says. Urgently, passionately, which really pushes my rage button.

"I'm not saying I'd be better off if I'd grown up remembering all the gory details, but if you'd given me *something*, maybe I would have listened when you told me to stay away from Robert. You kept on pretending, even after you *knew* I knew. I don't get it."

Gran nods, fumbling with the tissue in her hand. "I know it seems cruel, but it's so much more complicated than you make it sound. This has been hard for us. Amanda's death was a secret for so long, and I . . ."

Grandpa clears his throat, squinting toward the ceiling. "Some people can always find their way back home," he says softly—which means *what* exactly? But I don't interrupt. "No matter how long you've been away, those old familiar roads come back to you. But we couldn't find our way back to that time." He pauses, sad eyes meeting mine. "JoJo, you're young. Got your whole life ahead of you. The thing is, when you get older, things that happened in the past, they get hazy. We came up with that car accident story such a long time ago. Moved to a new town, met new people, and we told that story over and over again. We rooted ourselves in that version until it was a part of us."

I let the bizarre poetry of his words sink in. "Are you saying you forgot?"

"Of course we didn't," Gran snaps, but there's guilt in her sigh. "We simply lost the language to talk about it. The truth was so painful. That first year, especially, was one of the hardest I've ever been through. For weeks after Amanda's death, you'd ask for her, and it broke my heart. But the doctors said there was a good chance you wouldn't remember the trauma. So, we waited to see what you'd say about that day, if anything. And then you asked about her less and less. The nightmares stopped, and you started to seem like your old sweet self again."

"But what about now?" I ask. "I mean, I get that you didn't want to 'go back there' or whatever, but what about me? What about what I've been going through? Couldn't you tell I was hurting?"

"Oh, baby." Her voice breaks. "Believe me when I tell you, it's only *ever* been about protecting you. Maybe we tried too hard, and maybe we did it wrong, but we committed to keeping those memories away, just like the doctors said."

"Repressed memory," Grandpa adds, summoning a long-forgotten word.

"That's right," Gran says. "Repressed memory. You unconsciously blocked the events of her death, and we worked hard to keep it that way."

"But you didn't just repress the memory of her death," I cry. "You repressed *everything*. You erased her. You threw her away."

"Oh, Lord." Gran covers her mouth, choking on tears. "It was selfish, keeping her from you. I see that now. But Amanda was my baby. Losing her was—a mother shouldn't have to bury her own child."

My body rattles as I cry. Because, holy shit, how could I do it? How could I make her bury her own daughter?

"Hey now, don't cry," Grandpa says, patting my knee across the coffee table. "There was a break in the clouds. We got *you*. God gave us a second chance at a family."

He's trying to be nice, but it only makes my heart twist and burn. I ruined their first chance, and I'm ruining this one too. All they want is a family, and I keep finding ways to screw it up.

"I'm so sorry I took her away from you," I whisper. "I'm sorry for all of it."

Gran shakes her head fiercely. "Don't you ever apologize for that. Not ever."

"It's Robert who should be apologizing." Grandpa's fingers graze his bruised knuckles. "Damn that man for coming back."

"We should have known better," Gran says, "but he gave you up so easily. I wish he'd kept away and let you grow up in peace."

So easily. He didn't fight for me, not even then. Maybe it's fact, but it still stings. I lower my gaze, unable to meet their shame-filled eyes any longer. My brain aches, unsure what to say next. I want to keep pushing them. Keep torturing them for hiding this from me . . . but maybe they've been through enough. Maybe we all have.

"Y'know—" Gran pauses, eyes darting down the hall. "We

have some things of Amanda's. Odds and ends, mostly. Books and things. Grandpa will bring them in from the shed."

My heart leaps, dipping just as quickly. "You've had her stuff all this time?"

"Well, we didn't know what to do with it." She laughs defensively. "I threw so much away when we first moved. Couldn't bear the smell of *her* on her clothes. But we held on to some. I guess a part of me thought you wouldn't find it until later."

I almost ask, but *later* clearly means *after we die*, and this conversation is already bleak enough. Instead, I hug her. For the odds and ends. For the truth. For feeling close to her for the first time in months. She squeezes back, smelling of sugar and Earl Grey and everything I love about her stubborn-ass self.

Magic whimpers from the doorway, wanting to be walked.

"I'll take him," Grandpa says, joints creaking as he stands.

I should probably offer, but I'm so worn out. I feel lighter, though, too.

I yawn, and Gran squeezes my knee. "Why don't you have a lie down?"

"I'm not tired," I say, but really, it's that I don't want her to leave.

"I'd better go do some dinner prep," she says.

Knowing Gran, she's going to be guilt-cooking till the end of time, but before she can leave, I grab her hand. Even though my friends will hear all about this later, for now, I want things to be the way they used to with Gran. I want to feel safe, like on sick days when we'd spend all day together. The way I'd curl into her on the couch, tucked into the crook of her arm, watching movies or reading aloud from *Baby Island*—one of her childhood favorites, also one of mine, maybe Mom's, too.

"Wait," I say, voice small. "Can we hang out for a while?"

"Still feeling anxious?"

I nod, and she settles back down, coaxing my head toward her chest. She rocks me for a minute, then pulls back. "Sweetheart, where did you get those pills?"

"What?"

"The little pink ones. From your backpack."

"Oh." I pause, but the lying part of my brain feels broken. "They're from Milo."

"Who's Milo? It said Daniel on the label." Her eyebrows rise as she gasps. "Oh my Lord, are they drug dealers? Is that what this secret has done to you? Turned you into a—"

"Gran, stop it!" I shriek, feeling my cheeks burn. "I swear I'm not a drug addict. I took *one* Xanax, *once*. Daniel is his dad; they're his pills. Milo's my—" The *b*-word freezes on my lips. I'd never had a *b*-word before, and I *never* imagined this conversation stemming from a bottle of prescription pills, but: "He's my boyfriend."

Gran hiccups. I'm afraid to look at her, but when I do, it's kind of sweet. The way her brain goes all Rubik's Cube-y at the thought of it. Blushing, nose pinched. It makes me wonder about Mom, and how Gran reacted to *her* first boyfriend.

"You're going to like him," I add. "He's been there for me a lot."

"And I'm sorry I haven't," she says, then hesitates. "If I could go back . . ."

The way she trails off, I'm not sure how far back she's talking. A few months, to when we lost each other? Or all the way back? I picture them visiting my mother in California—sitting in their hotel room, maybe out for a walk—getting that phone call. A police officer telling her there'd been an accident, that they couldn't reach my father and someone needed to come for the baby. How it must have destroyed her.

"You okay?" Gran asks. When I don't answer, she squeezes me tighter. "I think you should talk to someone."

"What?"

"You know—" She swallows. "A professional."

"You mean a shrink?"

"A therapist, yes. It doesn't mean there's anything *wrong* with you," she adds quickly. "It's something we should have offered you a long time ago."

I bite my lip, thinking of Jenny Ireland. It sounds kind of good, actually.

"If you want," Gran says cautiously, "I'll go with you. When you're ready. So much of this is my fault."

Her fault.

Not that Gran accepting blame justifies anything or feels like vindication. I'm still mad. And hurt and guilty and confused and really, really tired. But hearing her say that? I don't know. It makes it a little more bearable. Makes me wonder if this could be the beginning of something better.

"Just something to consider," she says after a minute.

"I'll think about it," I say quietly.

But my mind is already made up.

39

ROBERT TEXTS ME AROUND 7 a.m. on Monday, asking if I'll meet him outside before school. I get dressed in a daze. Almost forgetting a bra, nearly mismatching my shoes, not sure how to reply. When I do decide to open the front door, he rises tentatively from the porch swing.

"I won't come in," he says. "I'm here to say goodbye."

I glance over my shoulder. Gran's in the kitchen, experimenting with tofu sausage. Maybe she'll kill me, but I grab my purple hoodie and slide through the door anyway, keeping a comfortable distance. His nose is swollen, a shadow of dull purple making a home for itself below his left eye.

"If you still want me to forgive you, that ship has sailed."

He shakes his head. "I never should have said that. It was selfish; you're right. The truth is, I have honestly loved getting to know you. You're this cool seamstress who's obsessed with old music. You're funny. And smart. And beautiful. And I didn't think it would be possible to love you so much." He pauses, eyes moist and severe. "I love you, Jo. I needed you to hear me say that."

I slide the sweatshirt zipper up over my heart. "It's too late."

"Okay." He nods. "Okay. But I—"

The front door swings open, and Gran shoots out like there are fireworks in her pants. She takes in Robert's banged-up face and then raises the cordless phone to her ear. "Thanks for the call, Tina. You were right."

My eyes narrow, shooting across the street toward Steve's house.

Gran ends the call, waving the cordless phone at Robert as if it's full of mace. "This time I *will* call the police."

He hooks his thumb toward the street. "I'm leaving this morning. There's my car. Bags packed. I wanted to say good-bye to my daughter. Please, Kate."

"Not on your life, you son of a—"

"Gran!" I yelp. "It'll only take a second. I won't leave the porch."

Anger concentrates itself in her eyes. She scowls at Robert one last time and then nods, a smile softening for me as she heads back into the house. The door stays open, though.

"Thanks," he says.

I shrug, arms folded.

He stares silently into my eyes like he needs to memorize them.

"Is that all?" I demand. "Because I have to get ready for school."

I should turn and slam the door, but suddenly he's covering his eyes with his hands, tears whooshing out alongside a thousand apologies. "I never should have done this to you," he wails. "Not just the gun—God knows I shouldn't have done that. But coming back here. That first day, when you thought Mandy had been in a car accident? I'm so sorry I didn't go along with it. I should have come to my senses, but instead, I upended your life. I'm sorry, Jo. I know you won't forgive me—and it was stupid to ask—but please know how infinitely sorry I am. I never meant to hurt you."

His arms shoot around me, tight and strong and squeezing the life out of me. It makes me cry, hating how much I need this. To feel like at least *part* of what we had was real. Because we did laugh together, shared stories, played stupid computer games. Those things have to mean something. They *have to.* Because of that, I let him hug me for too long, knowing it might—hoping it won't—be the last time.

When I get the guts to push away, he looks wounded.

"You have to go," I choke. "I'm not ready to forgive you. I don't know if—"

"It's okay," he whispers. "You don't have to. But know that I'm here for you, if you ever need me. I love you, Joey. I never stopped."

With a final, somber smile, he races across the lawn to his car and slams himself inside. My tears create polka-dot stains on the cold wooden porch. I can't move, but I might fall, so I grab onto the porch railing to steady myself. A trail of exhaust wheezes from his tailpipe, and then, that's it. He's gone.

I'm pathetic for watching the empty street, but I let myself do it.

Even after Gran calls me back in, even after she physically has to escort my flimsy body back into the house, the empty street is all I can see. Broken daydreams of Houston, of French toast and late-night chats. Gran leads me to my bedroom, tucking me gently under the covers, wiping my tearstained cheeks. Before she leaves, she kisses my forehead, because there's nothing left to say.

• • •

Gran lets me skip school in favor of sleep, and when I wake up, I almost can't remember why there's a cardboard box on my floor.

But it's the box—as in *the box*—full of odds and ends, as promised. I rub my eyes, peeling back the covers as I slide onto the floor beside it. A layer of orange New Mexico dust clings to the top. I blow it off with a soft puff of air. The tape across the lid has long since lost its stickiness and the flaps open easily. I want everything, but I want to savor it too, so I only grab the rubber-banded stack of CDs. Which almost gives me goose bumps because, I mean, music is the window to the frigging soul, right?

But then my heart sinks.

The first CD is *Oops! . . . I Did It Again*. By Britney Spears. It is a crime, and I want to weep for my mother's musical taste, but I try not to get too judgy. Britney can be fun. She can drop a beat, I guess. Now I'm nervous, though, flicking through the rest of the stack. Sinéad O'Connor, Prince, Faith Hill, Ace of Base, Matchbox Twenty. *These* are the CDs my grandparents chose to box up from her collection? I lay them out like flashcards on my white shag carpet, trying to digest the harsh realization: My mother was mainstream.

I take a deep breath. I can work with this. Prince, I mean. An obvious genius. Ace of Base are . . . I have no idea. But I'm going to find out.

I leave everything on the floor to grab Grandpa's old CD player from the laundry room, plugging it in by my desk. I reach for Sinéad O'Connor first. Her name is familiar, but I can't remember why, and the thought of rocking out to Ace of Base sounds too *woohoo* for the cinderblock feeling inside me.

And then, yeah. As soon as the first few notes waft through my tinny speakers, I recognize it. A breakup song; this oddly specific amount of time she's been missing someone.

I put the song on repeat because I know it's going to be one of those nights and then sink back onto the floor, unearthing my mother's jewelry box, running my fingers over rows of cheap drugstore jewelry and legit antiques, all nestled between cushions of red velvet. Grandpa made the box for her. I know, because it's almost identical to the one he made me on my sixteenth birthday. Small and rectangular, made with love and solid wood and a glossy finish. Smooth and delicate. Did it break his heart, duplicating it? Did he resent me as he sanded the wood and tightened hinges, knowing that I took her away from him?

It only makes me want to cry more when I find my baby album nestled among her things. Pink cloth cover with painted-on hearts; the musty smell of history. There's a baby blanket beside it, and I pull both into my lap, flipping open the first page.

All About Johanna Katherine Carlson

Each page holds a memory I can't place. Me, making faces, crying, dressed as a strawberry or a bumble bee, smiling for a family selfie with my parents on either side. Almost always, I'm holding this yellow polka-dot blanket. My very own lovey, completely foreign to me now.

In the margins, Mom has jotted down occasional notes. Nothing super interesting. Baby stuff like, *First tooth—five months* or *Joey tried sweet potatoes today!* The best part is seeing her handwriting. Clear, bubbly print like mine. My fingers trace every word.

The last entry feels like a particular papercut to the heart. It isn't supposed to be the last one, you can tell. There are still a dozen blank pages. I haven't had my first haircut or learned to use the potty. Haven't turned three. The last photograph is blurry. Me, running straight toward the camera with laughter on my face, and the caption: *Joey won't stay still for pictures anymore!*

And then . . . nothing.

Blank.

Only me and Sinéad in my bedroom, wondering how we went wrong.

The best songs are the ones that read your mind, speak to

your soul, and I imagine her doing exactly this—wallowing and curled up, blasting "Nothing Compares 2 U" at the end of a shitty day. I wonder what her problems were before I stole them from her.

Tears burn behind my eyes. Maybe there's panic hiding back there too, but I distract myself, walking over to my bookshelf, pulling out my old photo albums. The ones with pictures from my first day of kindergarten; Christmas Eve on Canyon Road in a sea of farolitos. That time Leah, Gabby, and I dressed as tacos for Halloween.

I flick through and find my best memories—the ones I would have wanted to share with her—and slide them into the blank pages of my baby book.

40

I WAIT TILL LEAH'S driven all the way into the student parking lot on Tuesday before handing my friends each a little white box wrapped in leftover Christmas ribbon. Gabby rattles hers. Leah actually sniffs it. Hopefully it doesn't seem forced, or like a bribe or whatever. After I pored through Mom's jewelry box, there was too much good shit to keep all of it to myself. Sharing it with them feels like something Mandy would have wanted.

"What is it?" Leah asks.

"Think of it as a pre-spring-break token of my esteem."

Gabby raises an eyebrow.

"You know. Like, a *thank you* thing." I pause to close the heat vent pointed at me. "In the past few months, I've put you guys through so much more than best friends should ever have to go through. I'm constantly freaking out. I don't know how to act. I bite your heads off when all you're trying to do is help.

I—I'm a mess. So, yeah. This is me saying sorry. You didn't sign up for this, and I love you for sticking it out. I don't deserve you guys."

"Sweetie." Leah's eyes glisten. She leans across the gearshift while Gabby reaches forward from the back seat, the two of them ambushing me with hugs. "Teddy Bear Club forever, right?"

"Por vida."

"And don't feel too lucky," Gabby adds. "It's not like we've been perfect best friends either. Me, anyway."

I shake my head. "No, I should have listened to you better."

"It's okay."

She frowns supportively, and my skin crawls—not because of her, but thinking about how wrong I was about Robert. How badly I want to stop aching. That's not what this moment is about, though, and I force my brain to switch gears.

"Open your presents already! We're going to be late for school."

Gabby tears the lid off her box, pulling out two dangly, tornado-looking gold spirals. "Holy shit, Jo."

"Gran bought those earrings for Mom on her eighteenth birthday."

"You can't give these away."

"Oh, please. You borrow my shit constantly." I snicker. "But this is different. Literally, my mom had so much jewelry. I'm keeping most of it, but I want you guys to have something of hers. Leah, that moonstone ring? I know it's your birthstone, but it was my mom's too. June twenty-sixth."

Leah slides the cloudy oval stone over her ring finger. The sun catches it, glinting this fantastic cerulean blue. "It's beautiful, Jo. I'm honored."

"But, seriously." Gabby raises an eyebrow. "Backsies are totally permitted with this stuff. Okay?"

I laugh. "Yeah, okay."

Seeing them both looking all bedazzled like this, though, it turns my smile lopsided. Because my heart, it still hurts.

"Are you okay?" Leah asks.

"Yeah," I say, faltering. "I don't know. I keep thinking I should be. Like—the mural was *supposed to make me feel better.* Asking Robert to leave was *supposed to give me closure.* The box of my mother's things was *supposed to bring me closer to her.* Nothing's working."

Leah squeezes my hand.

Gabby rests her chin on my shoulder.

"Sorry, you guys. I'm being stupid."

"You're not," Leah says.

And Gabby adds, "Maybe there's not going to be any one thing to make it better."

I nod. Not wanting to admit out loud that I will live with this grief forever. That it is going to become a part of me—*is* a part of me already.

We sit in the car a while longer, still and uncertain.

All day at school, we look shiny and dazzling in Mom's jewelry. Me in a heart-shaped locket with the letter *A* engraved on the front. I mean, I'm *so* not a heart-shaped-locket person, but

I love it. One side already had a baby picture of me, and beside it, I've inserted a baby picture that Gran had of Mom—blond and goofy and inquisitive.

Side by side like that, you can't even tell us apart.

41

OVERNIGHT, IT RAINS. JUST enough to make the world look a little greener. A new beginning. After school, I drive to Dr. Cornelia Ireland's office on the west side of town. Which isn't really an office, actually. More like a casita attached to a larger adobe house where, presumably, Jenny Ireland is sitting inside doing homework. I park on the sidewalk and a giant Portuguese water dog comes bounding up to meet me, attacking me with slobber as soon as I open the driver's side door.

"Sammy, stop!" a voice shrieks. The dog backs off, whimpering uncontrollably. A tall, heavyset woman with long, curly, blond hair rushes out of the casita, smiling brightly at me. "Sorry about that. He's a lovebug, really. You must be Johanna."

"Yeah. Hi, Mrs. Ireland. Or, I mean Dr.—sorry, what am I supposed to call you?"

"Connie is fine."

"Okay. Connie."

We shake hands, and I let myself get judgy of this boister-ous, tunic-wearing hippie. She's a bit weathered-looking; older than I expected. Are old people capable of handling normal teenage problems? Not that my problems are teenage. Or nor-mal. Okay, fine, she's probably a genius.

The casita smells of rosemary and has this chilled-out pan-pipe music easing out of a corner stereo. Hieroglyphic prints and diplomas dot the walls. There's a giant suede sofa on one side, two oversize armchairs opposite, and I must be staring at them like it's *Sophie's Choice* because Connie says, "Sit anywhere."

"Is this one of those things where I lie down?"

She smirks. "How tired are you?"

I stare blankly back at her.

"Feel free to lie down. Sit, stand on your head. Anything, so long as you're comfortable." She picks up a yellow legal pad, resting it in her lap as she nestles into one of the armchairs.

I lower myself onto the sofa like I'm recovering from hip surgery.

The room goes quiet.

"So, Johanna. How are you?"

"Fine," I say too quickly.

Because, I mean, where do I start? Therapy isn't how we Carlsons *do* things. And I'm glad that I'm here—maybe even grateful—but it's also weird and forced, and how does she expect me to just *open up*? Plus, there's no way Connie could have other clients as screwed up as I am, the thought of which only makes me more tongue-tied.

"Sorry," I mutter.

Rather than saying, *There's nothing to be sorry for*, like I think she might, Connie merely smiles and lets another minute pass. "Anything in particular you want to talk about?"

"Oh. Um." I shift on the couch, tucking my legs up under me, picturing myself blurting out that I shot my mother. But I can't. Not yet. I pull a pillow into my lap and shrug. "I don't know."

She shrugs too. "That's okay."

A wall clock ticks in the background, and my heart pounds three times faster than the second hand. Connie looks at me, smiling, until I can't take anymore. I clear my throat.

"What do people usually say?"

"Everyone's different."

I nod, bottling too much air in my chest.

"Y'know—" She puts down her pen. "I have an idea. Before we get into too much of a conversation. How are you on breathing?"

"Breathing?" I say.

"Yeah, the in-out-in stuff. I ask because you sound like a donkey in labor right now. Assuming that's not normal for you."

"I obviously know how to *breathe*."

"Obviously," she says. "You're alive, aren't you?"

I shrug.

"I think breath could really help you calm down and keep the panic at bay."

"How do you know I have panic attacks?"

"Psychic," she says, jazz hands-ing around her graying temples. "That or your grandmother told me when she booked the appointment. Let's try it, though, huh? If you're like, *To hell with this breathing shit*, we'll go back to awkward silence."

My eyes bulge. Partly because she's swearing, but also—
"Gran told you about the panic attacks?"

Connie nods.

"Did she also tell you about what I did?" I ask quietly. "To my mother?"

"She told me about what you've been through. You make it sound as if you orchestrated something."

Hot tears burn the corners of my eyes. I look at the ceiling to dry them.

"Hey," she says. "I'm not trying to push. Not at our first session, anyway."

We both get quiet for a minute. My eyes stay upward, but I can feel her looking. Drilling a hole into me. Willing me to open up, emote, share, even if she claims she's not *trying* to. I move my knees around, pulling them into my chest, hugging them tight. *Stay in, tears. Go away, you dicks.*

In response, Connie kicks off her Birkenstocks. "As I said, you look like a girl who could do with breathing lessons. You ready to get schooled?"

I look back at her. "Schooled at breathing?"

She smiles, folding her legs into one of those yoga pretzel-looking poses. It isn't nearly as therapy-ish as I thought it would be, but twice as new age. At least she's not hypnotizing me or making me horseback ride my problems away (there was an article).

So, I give it to her. My breath.

I guess we'll take it from there.

42

MY FIRST *ASSIGNMENT* OR whatever from Connie is to take my grandparents to see the mural. Something about the three of us healing together. They'd heard about it, obviously. Had seen the newspaper article and been given secondhand praise from Pastor Thompson. But I'm a nervous wreck taking them right up to the thing.

"You did all this?" Grandpa marvels.

Gran's old Southern face is harder to read. Brow furrowed, but eyes bright. I want to tug on the hem of her skirt like when I was little, asking her a thousand times if she likes it. Especially the girl I painted, all curled-up and crying beside a broken heart. Or Milo's Zia symbol with the Mexican sugar skull at its center. *Do you like it, Gran? Do you, do you, do you, do you?* If she tells me it's perfect—that *I'm* perfect—will my heart unlock and spill open?

"A bunch of us worked on it," I say, smiling at a few kids

walking past. As of 3:30 p.m., it is finally spring break, so people are giddily streaming to their cars, ready to peace out for nine glorious days. "Our teacher supervisor was Mr. Donnelly, and he's great. He backed me up from the beginning. The art teacher helped too. My whole art class, actually. Plus a few friends. And Milo, who I was telling you about? And there was this totally brilliant artist overseeing the whole thing. She helped us find our voices and draw initial sketches, and then taught us how to grid it all out on paper before starting on the wall itself. We tried to keep the message positive—no actual guns painted anywhere. See?"

It's nerves that are making me talk a mile a minute, so I bite my lips together and try to let the moment happen. There really is a lot to take in. One of my favorite parts is this trickle of bullets transforming into peace signs. The whole thing is bright, brimming with hope and soft edges. I mean, not to brag, but—

"I used to be a gun owner," Grandpa says, filling the silence.

"Wait, *what*?" I blink. My brain's not there yet. "You have a gun?"

"Had," he corrects, keeping his eyes on the mural. "For hunting."

I wait for more, but that seems to be the whole story. Grandpa: a wellspring of information. But I'm not ready to drop it, so I turn to Gran.

"Did you know about this?"

She shoots me a quizzical smile. "Well, of course I did. Grandpa shot a lot of game back in Arkansas. Deer, mostly. And before you give me that sourpuss look, there is nothing wrong with hunting if you are trained and licensed and your guns are properly locked and stored. I was always impressed by the level of care and safety Grandpa went to."

Grandpa coughs. "The fact is, hunting didn't feel right anymore. After that day, that was it. We were taking you in, and we didn't want firearms in the house. Not even locked in the shed."

"Grandpa sold it to one of those—what do they call it?"

"A buyback program."

She nods. "A buyback program. Where I suppose they sawed it into pieces."

My brain is completely exploding right now.

"I'm not quite sure what happened to Robert's gun," Gran muses.

"Evidence," Grandpa says, rocking back on his heels as he nods.

"That's right, evidence."

Evidence. The word hovers around us, dissipating like smoke until we're standing in silence again. My grandparents are back to serene smiles and appreciation, but my insides are screwed tight and airless. A gun. My grandfather was a hunter, and he gave up his favorite hobby. I took their daughter from them. I uprooted their lives. I changed all three of us down to the very core of our being, in a single second.

"Should we take a picture?"

I blink back to reality, swallowing a lump in my throat. Grandpa's already dutifully unzipping his coat, reaching for the phone in his breast pocket. Gran's lightly coaxing my dazed body toward the mural.

"Make sure you get her standing next to it."

I tousle my hair, smiling self-consciously.

"Do you want to be in the picture, Katie?"

"No, just *take* the picture."

He takes three zillion, all of them in portrait mode when clearly the mural is landscape, but whatever.

I want to freeze time—or at least the sheer pride on their faces—but Gran's feet start to ache, and dinner isn't going to cook itself. We head toward the parking lot, Gran fiddling with her turquoise bracelet.

"Grandpa and I wanted to talk to you about spring break," she says, kind of weird and hesitant. "We'd like to take you to Little Rock."

My face crinkles. "Where you guys used to live?"

"Yes," Grandpa says. "And where your mother is buried."

My insides freeze. "Are you serious?"

Clearly they are because they almost never joke, so why start now.

"You haven't been to Amanda's grave since the funeral," Gran adds, like I don't already know that. "We *thought* we were saving you the heartache. Anyway, we'd like to make it up to you. I can't miss my fundraiser meeting, so we'll leave on Monday."

"What do you think?" Grandpa asks.

A year ago, I would have screamed *yes* at the top of my lungs.

Three months ago, even. Now, I swallow, trying not to look petrified, because I can see how much this means to them. How much of a peace offering it is.

So I hug them. I thank them. I say yes.

And I don't let myself cry until they're back in their car, driving toward home.

43

THE NIGHT BEFORE WE leave, Milo comes over for dinner.

I know. It is terrifying for all of us.

"Nice tie." I smirk, putting a napkin in my lap.

"Why, thank you," he replies evenly.

No joke, he's never looked more ridiculous. Blue gingham button-down, striped tie, pressed khakis. Frigging *khakis*. I mean, did he mug a golf pro on his way over? There's even mousse in his hair. Frigging *mousse*. Still sexy, but in a Max-from-*Rushmore* kind of way, which Gran and Grandpa seem to approve of.

"You're from Nevada?" Grandpa asks after saying grace.

"Yes, sir. Las Vegas."

Gran raises an eyebrow, as if Milo is currently spinning a roulette wheel rather than eating asparagus. I roll my eyes.

"It's not all casinos," he adds with a laugh. "There are parks and stuff."

"And what do your parents do?"

"Gran," I moan.

She opens her mouth in protest but then closes it, nodding politely. "Sorry to pry, Milo."

"No, it's cool. My mom's a pastry chef. She works at that bakery, down on Water Street?"

"I've never been." Gran's cheeks pinch with embarrassment.

"I'll bring you something. Next time I come over."

Gran's eyes light up. "Well, tell her not to go to any trouble."

"No trouble." He wipes his mouth, shoulders stiffening. "My dad manages a chain of office supply stores."

"Can't go wrong with office supplies," muses Grandpa.

I gulp down water.

"You have a beautiful home, Mrs. Carlson. That needlepoint over there—is that Martin Van Buren?"

I swear, my grandmother blushes. "Why, yes, it is. People don't tend to recognize anyone apart from Lincoln."

"No, ma'am. Your Van Buren is on point. I wrote a paper on him last year. Did you know the word *OK* actually comes from Van Buren's nickname? People called him Old Kinderhook because of where he was from in New York, and when he was running for president, the Democratic Party would be all like, 'Vote for OK' and stuff. Anyway, random factoid for you."

Grandpa nods, mouth turned down in contemplative fascination.

We eat our vegetarian pizza casserole with the lentils instead of tofu, which isn't actually horrible, and I knock knees with

Milo under the table. He tugs at the collar of his shirt. In a cruel kind of way, it melts my heart a little to see him sweat. Maybe Gran's too, because she offers him the biggest slice of cheesecake for dessert, and extra strawberries too.

"You good?" he asks me after dinner.

There's obviously zero chance of us making out, so we sit at the kitchen counter, fingers laced while the news blares for my hearing-impaired grandparents in the living room.

"I'm okay. Tired."

"Any word from your dad?"

I wince.

"Sorry. I figured you were already thinking about him."

"I *was* thinking about your gorgeous lips," I murmur. "But not anymore."

"Oof. Y'done fucked up, Milo."

"You're right, though." I sigh. "I was thinking about him earlier, while I packed. I wonder how long it's been since he visited Mom's grave. It'll be weird to be there without him. In a way."

"Yeah."

"Yeah."

"You're glad you're going, though?"

"I think so. It's going to be fucking weird. But, yeah, I think so."

He licks his lips and I shiver, leaning in to kiss his earlobe, his chin, his—I pull back. "Have you talked to *your* dad?"

"Wow, who's the mood killer now?" he says breathlessly.

I snort.

"You sure you want to talk about this?"

"I asked, didn't I."

Milo shrugs and pulls back a bit.

"What aren't you telling me?"

"It looks like my dad's finally starting to come around."

"About paying for your summer program?" I shriek, smacking his palm for a high five. "Milo, that's amazing! Why didn't you want to tell me?"

"The dad part?" He winces. "After everything you've been through, I didn't want to rub it in."

My heart sinks, but I tug my lips into a grin because Milo deserves this. "Don't be ridiculous. You can tell me anything. Even if you're not bitching and moaning. Even if you're happy."

"Thanks."

"Are you going to visit him?"

"That's part of the agreement," he says. "I have to spend a week with him on either end of the program."

I raise a *hubba-hubba* eyebrow. "How does he feel about extra visitors?"

"I think I can add that clause to the contract." He smiles. "Your grandparents would let you come to Vegas with me?"

"Oh." I shake my head. "Not a fucking chance."

"Great, I'll buy you a ticket!" He kisses me again, eyes flicking toward the living room first. "So, how long are you abandoning me for?"

"Only three days."

"I'm going to miss you."

"I'll miss you more."

"You all packed?"

"Yep."

"Did you remember your toothbrush?"

"Yep." I giggle.

"And your phone charger?"

I nod, leaning in to kiss him again.

It starts out as a you're-so-silly peck on the lips, but Milo slides his hands around my waist, urging me closer to him. My eyes drift shut, allowing my body to relax, letting myself think about absolutely nothing. Blissful, blank-brained perfection. Only tingling forearms and legs and in-between legs. It's risky, kissing like this with my grandparents in the next room, but I don't want to stop. I want to tell Connie Ireland she's fired, because I've found a better form of therapy and his name is Milo Schmidt. But then Milo moans, and we hear Gran cough in the next room.

"Shit!" He giggles, pulling away.

"Busted!" I whisper, and I don't even care that my cheeks are turning red.

We laugh silently, fingers laced, snorting back lust and embarrassment until the TV flickers off and Grandpa yawns overdramatically. Our flight to Little Rock is early tomorrow. We all need our rest. Milo bids a polite farewell to my grandparents, and I walk him to the front door. The smell of his hair, his broad shoulders as he hugs me. I wish I could pack this gorgeous boy in my carry-on bag.

"Text me when you land?" Milo says, kissing the top of my head.

"Yup."

"And when you get to the hotel?" he adds. "In fact, text me from the car in the morning, and from the airport in Albuquerque."

"Jeez." I laugh, pushing him out the door. "Yes, I'll text you from everywhere. From the bathroom. From the newsstand. Before I put my phone in airplane mode on the runway. In fact, why don't I hand the phone to the security guy and have him text you while I'm walking through the X-ray machine?"

"Perfect." He waves over his shoulder and jogs down the porch steps.

I close the front door, leaning against it.

Right away, my phone buzzes.

Milo: I love you.
Me: I love you too.

44

IT'S STILL DARK WHEN we pile into the car. Grandpa reverses onto the street, and I peer through the back window to see which neighbors are up at 6 a.m. Half the block is still quiet, the other half grinding coffee, news flickering on their TVs. We drive south on I-25, and the sky grows into a bright, exploded-goldfish color as the sun rises over the Sandia Mountains.

"Shall I put on the radio?" Gran asks. "Or should we sit with our thoughts?"

"Radio is fine," I mumble.

She nudges her glasses down the bridge of her nose, squinting and pecking at the dials until a mild country song drifts quietly through the speakers. My thoughts drown it out almost immediately, remembering back to the last time I was on an airplane. Nine years ago, I think. Disneyland, for my seventh birthday. The peak of my mom-questions phase. When I began to realize how badly I needed her. God, what kind of superficial freak was I that a photo op with Cinderella could subdue all that wonder?

"Can we turn up the heat?" I ask, a shiver stinging my spine.

I bite my thumbnail, counting piñon bushes sprinkled like Dalmatian spots on the mountains. Panic begins to nibble at my limbs, burning toward my heart like the lit end of a cigarette. Suddenly, all I can imagine is the airless main cabin of the plane we're about to board, the shake of my knees as I walk toward my mother's grave.

I can't do this, I can't do it, I can't.

I blink hard and stare through the windshield. Blue skies and clouds claw their way through the orange, turning dawn into day. I take a deep breath. Connie told me to inhale slowly when I feel panic coming on, careful not to breathe too fast or exhale too soon. Inhale. One . . . two . . . three . . . four . . . Exhale. But my lungs only pace inside my chest. I reach for Gran.

She squeezes my hand as we dip past the casino. "Getting restless?"

"Yes," I say sharply.

Her eyes dart to mine in the rearview mirror, then over to Grandpa. "Pull over."

"No," I beg. "Don't stop. I don't want to miss the flight."

After a bit of silent deliberation between the two of them, we keep driving.

"Do you know what song I used to sing when Amanda was a baby?" Gran asks, still holding my hand. Her fingers slide up my wrist, squeezing the pressure point I taught her. "'All the Pretty Little Horses.' Do you remember that one?"

I shake my head, trying to replace a wave of panic with a wave of calm. Panic for calm, panic for calm. Gran's voice fills the car. Trees and mountains whiz by, and she sings. Sweet, soft, Southern.

The ice-cream headache in my heart begins to melt.

• • •

Claustrophobia sets in when we get on the plane, as predicted. Me, sandwiched between my grandparents. Fiddling with the air vents, angling all three of them at my bursting temples. Gran strokes my forearm, but it feels like a rake against my skin.

How can she not hate me? For taking her baby, their rifle, their Little Rock life. Forcing them to relocate to some dusty Southwestern town. They haven't visited their own daughter's grave in thirteen years, for Christ's sake. Will her headstone be covered in moss by now?

"It's an hour flight to Dallas, then two hours from Dallas to Little Rock." Grandpa says, grabbing the in-flight magazine out of the seatback pouch.

I look at the cover and wonder if he's ever even heard of Cardi B.

"Pull the shade down," Gran says. "They require that for takeoff now."

Grandpa frowns. "What?"

"The shade. Pull—" She huffs, leaning over me to do it herself. "Gum?" she says to me.

I shake my head, eyelids fluttering. Fluttering more. Maybe

it's better that I couldn't sleep last night, that I saved my exhaustion for this cramped, airless flight. I yawn, and Grandpa shrugs his shoulder a bit, offering it as a pillow. His flannel shirt is soft and smells of cedar.

If they do hate me, they cover it up pretty well.

• • •

We drive from the airport toward the hotel in a mausoleum-like silence. Our rental car has this vague smoky smell— cigarettes from the previous renter, probably—but all I can think about is gun smoke. Is it similar to this? Thin and musty and vaguely sour.

Did smoke come out of the gun when I fired it?

Did my mother die instantly, or did she see me first?

Tree branches sway like dangly earrings as we pass them. Not piñons like I'm used to, but big furry ones, tall and leafless. Buds of spring on their brittle fingers.

"Are we going straight to the cemetery?" I ask.

Grandpa scratches his ear.

"Please, can we go to the hotel?" I add quickly.

"Yes," Gran says, and I hear the relief in her exhale.

This must be torture for them too.

• • •

Our rooms are adjoining, but we don't unbolt the connecting door. I lie on the bed with my arms folded in an X across my chest.

Is that how she was buried?

Did they put her in her favorite dress?

Questions knock around inside me, but I'll never ask them out loud. Even if Gran does have the answers.

• • •

None of us push for hitting the cemetery right away. We nap for a little, then spend the afternoon walking along the river before heading back to the hotel for dinner.

"We'll go tomorrow morning," Gran decides. "That will be better."

I fish an ice cube out of my Sprite. "Okay."

The hotel restaurant still has last month's St. Paddy's Day decorations up, forgotten cardboard clovers and doilies. We're the only ones eating, and yet they put us at the biggest table, the three of us crowded around one side in a half moon. We check our phones while we wait for the food to come.

Me: Greetings from the Natural State. We're saving the cemetery for tomorrow.

Gabby: Good luck.

Leah: Try to relax tonight.

Gabby: Watch something funny.

Leah: There's a Purse Museum.

Leah: I googled it. Might be fun.

Gabby: A purse museum, Leah?

Leah: Hello, purses = fashion!

Leah: Whatever. I'm just trying to distract her.

Gabby: 🙄

I giggle.

Me: Thanks, guys.
Leah: I'm sending you white light for tomorrow.
Gabby: Me too. (Even though white light is bullshit.)
Me: Gracias. Buenas noches. 😴.

The waiter puts a cranberry walnut salad that I barely remember ordering down on the table in front of me. The little goat-cheese rounds remind me of marshmallows, and I wish Leah and Gabby were here with me. They would have brought marshmallows for taffy. We would have watched movies all night and snuck into the hotel gym to reenact that OK Go video with the treadmills. I'd still have the same knot in my stomach, but I would be laughing too.

In the elevator back up to our rooms, there's a toddler having a major meltdown. Kicking her legs, screaming no at top volume. I imagine it's me, wriggling out of my mom's arms. Surely I had tantrums like this. Maybe Gran's thinking the same thing, because she smiles at the mother. One of those *aren't-kids-a-glorious-handful* looks that the lady smiles politely at before whisper-barking at her kid.

"Are you going straight to sleep?" Gran asks when the elevator reaches our floor.

"I might watch TV for a while."

"Make sure you bolt the door from the inside," she tells me. "And if you need ice, call Grandpa. Don't get it yourself. And don't stay up too late."

I smile. "Okay, Gran."

I hug them both good night, double-checking the bolt after locking myself in my room. It feels super weird, staying in my own hotel room with my own miniature toiletries. Is this what being a grown-up is like? Because it's boring. I flip on the TV and change into a pink unicorn onesie, then dial Milo's number.

"Hey, stranger."

Just hearing his voice makes me grin. "There are forty-seven channels on my TV."

"Oh *really*?"

"Yeah." I flip through at super speed, past the news and law dramas and cartoons, until I see a guy in an apron stuffing a bunch of cheddar and onions into a blender. "Infomercials. Perfect. Man, I so need a Magic Bullet. I think they're making nacho cheese sauce."

"Don't buy one before your birthday," he singsongs. "Shit, I don't even know when your birthday is."

"November seventh. Yours?"

"September twenty-first."

"That makes you a . . . ?"

"Virgo," he says. "We're very sensitive."

"One of your best qualities. I'm strong-willed and passionate."

"Wait, seriously?" He feigns a gasp. "That comes as a *huge* surprise."

I roll onto my stomach and stretch my legs on the soft, white sheets. Adulting feels kind of cool, actually, on a queen-size bed surrounded by fluffy pillows. I imagine him here with me, the two of us nuzzled up together. But, like, not with my grandparents on the other side of the wall. I can hear Grandpa snoring already.

"Where are you?" I ask, watching cheddar crumble.

"Home. Mom's paying bills. It's cold tonight so I'm being manly and trying to light the fire. This shit is difficult."

"Are you using kindling?"

"That's the little stick things?"

"Oh, man." I giggle. "You would so die on a deserted island. Not to toot my own horn, but I'm pretty next-level at lighting fires. Grandpa taught me how."

"Nice of him to pass the *torch*," he says gleefully.

"Ouch." I wince, biting back laughter. "Never tell a joke again."

He agrees, and we get quiet for a minute. I listen to him strike matches and swear a lot. The Magic Bullet guy finishes the nachos and starts in on a piña colada smoothie. I crawl up to the top of the bed, pulling the covers up with a yawn.

"I give up," Milo grumbles. "Tell me everything. Did you go to the cemetery?"

"Tomorrow. I guess I should have known it would be weird, but it is *so* weird. I'm honestly dreading it."

"Don't worry," he says. "That's what your grandparents are there for."

"What if I lose it? What if *they* lose it? I don't think I could handle watching my grandpa cry."

"Men cry. Take my word for it. If the dude cries, give him a hug."

"Do you ever cry?" I ask.

"Hey, I am one seriously evolved male specimen."

"What does that mean? You cry *a lot*?"

"Yeah." He laughs. "A shit-ton. But don't tell anybody. I'm not *that* evolved."

"Your secret is safe," I tell him.

Seconds pass and my lip begins to tremble, tears welling up in my eyes. I swallow back the lump in my throat and will my voice not to sound fragile. "I should probably go."

"Don't," he whispers. "Talk to me all night. I want us to fall asleep listening to the sound of each other's voices."

"What about the fire?"

"Fuck the fire. You're more important. I'll crank the thermostat."

"Okay." My stomach does that queasy clench thing again, and I bury my head in the pillow, exhaling a travel day's worth of pent-up energy. "Tell me something. Anything."

"Hmm," he says slowly. "Oh! Have you looked in your backpack yet?"

"What?"

"Your *backpack*," he says, his voice playful. "In the front zipper pocket."

"Wait." I cringe. "Are you talking about my *school* bag?"

"Yeah?"

I pause, waiting for him to get it. And then, he says, "*Oooooh*. You didn't bring it."

"I'm sorry!" I yelp. Then gasp. "Oh shit, what did you put in there? Tell me you didn't get me a kitten or something."

"What?" He snorts with laughter. "Did you *want* a suffocated kitten?"

"No! I'm just trying to gauge how bad I should feel for leaving my Fjällräven at home."

"Wait, *that's* how you say that word? You sound so sexy right now. Say it again."

I clear my throat, lowering my voice. "*Fee-y'all-rrrare-ven.*"

"Damn," he murmurs.

"But seriously. What the fuck is rotting in my backpack right now?"

"Well," he croaks. "I kind of, um, wrote you a song."

"Really?" I squeal into the phone, because, *are you serious right now???*

"Don't freak out too much. It's still rough."

"Milo," I say, my voice breaking. "Will you sing it to me?"

"I'm not really a singer. That was my friend, Andrew, back home. But I guess I could. Promise not to laugh?"

"Of course," I whisper.

He clears his throat. I hear a door click shut. I picture him settling down on his bed, putting the phone on speaker, pulling his guitar into his lap. My whole body tenses. Excitement, bliss, dizziness—a royal wedding's worth of confetti feelings.

And then, holy shit.

My boyfriend sings me to sleep with a song that will go down in history.

45

BEFORE TODAY, I'VE NEVER been to a cemetery for, like, *legit* cemetery reasons. Once, on Halloween, in our Ghostbusters coveralls and back-strapped DustBusters, Leah convinced us to have a séance for this stranger named Agnes Carlita Reyes-Dimas because she liked the rose carvings on her headstone. Agnes's spirit was never successfully summoned, but I can't help thinking about her now, as a thousand headstones watch me from within the walls of the Little Rock cemetery. How close had we been that Halloween night? Minutes, seconds away from reaching Agnes on the other side?

I bite my lip and think about turning back—grabbing a bunch of vanilla-scented candles from the drugstore and setting them up around my mom's grave. But we're already here, my grandparents walking a few steps ahead. Gran somehow managed to remove Robert's blood from her peach-colored dress; Grandpa's in a navy two-piece suit. Is this what they looked like at the funeral? All buttoned-up and ironed. Was Grandpa one of those pallbearer guys? Was my father? A peppermint chill crawls up my spine as I try to picture myself in the midst of it—pigtailed and sucking my thumb, Kenny the Kangaroo dragging at my feet.

I grip a bouquet of white carnations because they're what Gran said is appropriate. Carnations don't feel appropriate. They feel generic. Hallmark, rather than a handwritten note.

Walking along cracks in the path makes my soul wheeze. Part of me yearns for a Xanax, or a frying pan to whack over my head, but it's better that I don't. My mother deserves my full attention.

"JoJo?"

I tear my eyes off a grave covered in calla lilies. My grandparents are twenty steps ahead, stopped in front of a simple, gray headstone. Heavy, dazed frowns burden their lips.

"We're here," Grandpa says. "It's this one."

I nod, hanging back at first, observing their stoic silhouettes. Hunched shoulders, heads lowered in prayer. Something like jealousy pinches the base of my spine. I envy their memories. Gran turns, maybe sensing my eyes on her back. Her own eyes glisten. With a silk handkerchief, she dabs the corners of her eyes, then motions for me.

"Come on over, sweetheart," she says, voice strained. "Take a minute to yourself."

"What about these?" I ask, raising the flowers.

She pats the top of the headstone and then disappears behind me. The whole rest of the world seems to vanish.

"Hi, Mom," I say awkwardly. *So* awkwardly as I cradle my elbows.

Instead of looming over a weathered slab of stone, I sit beside it, crossing my legs and reaching for a tuft of brittle grass. Below her name and twenty-five years on earth, it says: *Loving mother, devoted daughter, and faithful friend.*

"I bet you were a great friend," I mumble, trying not to feel too weird talking out loud to a piece of stone. "My best friends are Leah Fromowitz and Gabby Sinclair. We've been this, like, ridiculous threesome since kindergarten—Teddy Bear Club, marshmallow taffy crew. Gabby's the brains, the sensible one. Leah's all heart. I'm the weird one, I guess. The one who makes too many jokes and wears funky clothes—like this. I actually made this dress. For you, for today."

I lean back, smoothing out the black rayon and running my hands along a gold zipper sliding at an angle from chest to hem. Mo' Tizzy is draped over the dress, keeping me warm.

"It's a bit more formal than I'm used to making. My style's usually edgier. I love skirts you can spin in. One-shoulder tops are probably the easiest, and they look rad. I made the coolest mod dress with big lace pockets for Christmas. Pleats are hard, but I'm getting better."

I sigh, glancing over my shoulder. "Gran and Grandpa brought me here. I still can't believe it. Y'know, they didn't even tell me about you?" I pause, tossing a big clump of grass onto my Docs. "*Dad* tracked me down. He blurted the whole thing out one afternoon. Like, *Hey, you shot and killed your mom. Want a latte?*"

A breeze picks up, and I imagine her voice. Light and soft as daisies. I imagine her asking about him, about our reunion.

"It was nice at first, getting to know him. He says he loves me, but I don't know. It's hard to love someone who abandoned you."

I sniff. Gearing up, getting the nerve. The mound of grass slides off my foot as I sink closer to the ground. Fetal position, fingers tracing over her name as my lower lip quivers.

"I don't remember any of it. I've tried to relive that day and how I could *do* something like that. But I can't."

I wait for a response, but her voice in my mind goes still.

"Are you mad at me?"

Yes, she whispers. And it kills me.

But this is my fantasy, my imagination. Even beyond that, I can feel the truth in my soul. A mother's love. My mother loved me. So, instead of yes, she says, *No, sweet girl. I could never be mad at you.*

Hot tears saturate my eyes. I try to hold them in, blinking up at wisps of cotton-candy clouds as they brush across the sky. Somewhere inside me, a knot unties and floats up toward them.

"I saw the baby book you made for me. Gran kept it. I got to see your handwriting and learn what was important to you about me. I wish you'd had the chance to fill a hundred more pages."

I shake my head. "I mean, no, that's not what I wish. I wish you were still here. You have no idea how much I miss you."

Water drizzles from my eyes, sideways down my temples as my body curls around her headstone.

"I miss you so much," I whisper again. "I used to think your death was just an accident. I mean, an *actual* accident. Now that I know it was my fault, it's like I can't breathe anymore. There's not a single second that goes by that I don't hate myself. I think about how I could have found a gun under the bed. And then picked it up. How could I *do* that? How did I *not know* what it was?

"Did you wake up and see me? Or try to stop me? You must have been so scared," I sob. "I love you so much, and I'm so sorry that I hurt you. I'm *so sorry*."

I'm crying too hard to keep talking. Rough but quiet, out of respect for the dead. I want her to tell me she was fast asleep, that she didn't feel a thing, didn't wake up or see that it was *her own daughter* pulling the trigger.

A palm presses against my shoulder blade, and I gasp.

"Mom?"

"No, sweetheart. It's your grandma."

I look up, smearing salty tears onto the sleeve of my sweater. Gran helps me sit up and picks stray grass from my hair.

"We don't have to leave," she says softly. "You take all the time in the world that you need. I wasn't sure if you were having a panic attack. If you needed me."

It takes me a minute to control my breath. So long that Gran starts walking away.

"Don't go," I call after her. "I do need you."

Her smile is faint. She kneels beside me so I can rest my head on her lap, and it feels good, the way she combs her fingers through my hair. With Gran here, I won't talk out loud anymore, but I imagine saying all the things I still need to say. A swell of apologies and regrets.

Forever the two of us linger, Gran humming and stroking my hair. Her voice gentle as the breeze. I stare at my mother's grave through tears, and a warm calm begins to wash over me. As if I can feel myself floating up into the sky, able to look down on the whole cemetery. From up there, everything looks peaceful. Like I really might be able to move on. My mother's death will always be a part of me, but she doesn't want me to carry that weight forever.

I lift my head, drying my eyes with Gran's handkerchief.

"You ready to go?" she asks.

Before I say anything, I wait for the familiar wave of guilt to roll through me and turn toxic . . . but it doesn't. I feel okay. I am settled. With a deep breath, I rise to my feet and help Gran up too.

"I'm ready."

AUTHOR'S NOTE

In December of 2014, when most of my time was spent nursing a newborn and playing dolls with my four-year-old, I read the headline that an Idaho toddler had accidentally shot and killed his mother. Veronica Rutledge, twenty-nine, was shopping at Walmart when her two-year-old son found a 9 mm handgun in her purse and fired one bullet that went straight into her head.

It was an awful, shocking, tragic story, though nowhere near the first of its kind. Still, it stuck with me. Maybe because everything relating to kids feels so raw and magnified when you become a parent. You can't help but think of your own kids and picture it happening to them. Maybe that's why, after the news cycle moved on, I couldn't. I couldn't stop thinking about the mother, described as a kind, loving, outdoorsy person. Couldn't stop picturing the blurred image of her son, whose name was omitted from news reports. How excruciating for the father to have to explain it. For that child to have to grow up knowing that he took his own mother's life. What a horrible cross to bear.

I think about my own kids and how they basically forget everything. That epic meltdown my daughter had about an umbrella when she was three? No memory of it. My son's black eye from bumping into the bed frame or our three-week trip to South Africa? Not a clue. They were too young. They forgot. For better or worse, *kids forget*. So, I let myself wonder. What if some of these kids have no idea what they did? What if nobody told them and they were allowed to forget?

I wondered so much that I started researching and looking for proof. But, there was none. Because, the thing is, these unnamed, blurry-pictured kids are minors. Their parents are regular people. Before this happened to them they weren't in the news, and they weren't in the news after. And I'm glad, because these families deserve their privacy and their anonymity.

So, instead, I wrote this book. I must have read a hundred stories of children who accidentally shot a parent, a sibling, a friend, or themselves. As of 2018, in a survey by the *Journal of Urban Health*, 4.6 million children were living in homes with loaded, unlocked guns. When I wrote the first draft of this book in 2016, guns were the third-leading cause of death among children. As I write this author's note in 2020, they are the second. This is our reality. Guns are everywhere.

Johanna's story is a what-if. One version, one sliver of *maybe*, because I really do hope it is a possibility. Maybe it isn't realistic to imagine that some of these kids grow up in igno-rance—and not the blissful kind, because they have still lost a loved one, may still have holes in their hearts and minds—but wouldn't it be nice if they had the chance to grow up free from guilt?

For all the children who *do* know, I think about you a lot. I hope you are healing and that you have found a way to move on. I am so sorry for what you went through. I wish you peace and closure, and I wish that preventable accidents involving gun violence may one day come to an end.

ACKNOWLEDGMENTS

Lauren Galit, you sold my book! You are truly the world's greatest agent. Ever since our first email exchange when I wrote, "Fingers crossed that you like my book!" and you replied, "Uncross and let's talk," you have given me a sense of self-worth that I never dreamed possible. I am forever indebted to you and the incomparable Caitlen Rubino-Bradway. Thank you for believing in me, encouraging me, and for replying to every email, no matter how small.

The hugest of thank-yous to my brilliant editor, Mary Kate Castellani. You *got* this book from the moment you read it. Your keen eye and kindness have made this process a true joy. And to the incredible Bloomsbury team, heaps of gratitude to Cindy Loh, Claire Stetzer, Anna Bernard, Lily Yengle, Courtney Griffin, Erica Barmash, Valentina Rice, Jasmine Miranda, Faye Bi, Erica Loberg, Phoebe Dyer, Beth Eller, Danielle Ceccolini, Donna Mark, Diane Aronson, Christa Désir, and

Bhuvaneshwari Ramaswamy, along with everyone else, as well as cover illustrator Adams Carvalho, for your creativity, hard work, and all-around awesomeness in bringing this book to life.

To my husband, Andy. You may be a "doctor," but you are also an exceptional reader, adviser, and father. Thanks for giving me so much time to write, so many laughs, so much love, and the two best kids on earth. Trix, thank you for your fantastic comments and feedback. Harvey, if you could read, I know you would have put in your remarkable two cents too. I love you both more than anything and wish the world for you.

To my sister, India—from our occasionally matching outfits to our aching fits of laughter—BC, BU, because. I am lucky and honored to have you in my corner. To my oldest friend, Julia Ain-Krupa, thank you for listening to me cry. To Amy Hondo, for being my bestie since L&T. To Nellie Harari, for helping me breathe. To my fellow writers in the PSCWW, thank you for sharing your talent and improving mine. To my early readers—Veronica Vega at Salt & Sage Books, Janira Bremner, Carrie Esposito, and Lindsay Schlegal—I am grateful for your eyes and insights.

Thank you to the writing community. I am indebted to the support of the Roaring 20s group and calmed by the wisdom of authors like Brigid Kemmerer, Amanda Maciel, Wendy McLeod MacKnight, and Phil Stamper. And to my hypothetical legal team, Erin Smith Dennis and Ben Zemen, if I ever actually need a lawyer, I'm calling one of you.

To my parents, Claudia and Jon, you have always supported

and championed me tirelessly (and I mean *tirelessly*—you must be exhausted). Thank you for passing on the writing gene, and for reading my work with an unbiased eye (JK—you are completely biased!). And to my UK family, thank you for cheering me on from across the pond, lo these many years.

So many amazing friends have shared in my excitement over selling/publishing this book! Thank you to everyone in the 505 (including the town itself, and the now-defunct Baja for their amazing Frito pie), Bard (and Bard-extensions), Brooklyn Mamas, MSS, BPCS, BND, GG/S&S, and BoA. You are the people who bring me out of my shell, and, for that, I am eternally grateful.

To the countless organizations supporting commonsense gun laws, thank you for your statistics, your perseverance, and your dedication to protecting the safety of our families and communities. And to Miranda Viscoli, copresident of New Mexicans to Prevent Gun Violence—from education and murals to turning guns into gardening tools—thank you for fighting the good fight.

Lastly—and more than anything—I would like to offer my heartfelt sympathy and support to all victims of gun violence.